THE NEMO MURDERS

C. P. Holsinger

Foremost Press
Cedarburg, Wisconsin

Also by C. P. Holsinger

All the Bishop's Men
The Vein to the Heart

Published by Foremost Press
www.foremostpress.com

ISBN-10: 1-939870-17-8
ISBN-13: 978-1-939870-17-9

THE NEMO MURDERS

This book is dedicated to the nineteen firefighters who lost their lives fighting the Yarnell Hill fire, and to all the police officers and firefighters who risk their lives daily for our safety.

It is a curious feature of our existence that we come from a planet that is very good at promoting life but even better at extinguishing it.

Bill Bryson,
A Short History of Nearly Everything

CHAPTER 1

The Body

The dim fluorescent lights overhead barely illuminated the few cars parked along the walls as he made his way past the police cars and up the cement slope of the parking garage floor. The blue and red pulses from the police cruisers' flashing lights bounced off of the car windows and the gray walls as he ducked under the yellow police tape. Passing in and out of the shadows, his eyes soon came upon a small vehicle, the size of a golf cart. The rotating orange light on its white top told him this was the security cart he was looking for.

A uniformed police officer was standing next to it. When he saw the gold badge hanging from the tall man's belt, he knew this was the detective he had been waiting for. He immediately pointed to a pair of legs barely sticking out between two cars about twenty feet farther up the ramp.

The gray uniform of the man sitting in the front seat told the detective this was the security guard who had allegedly discovered the body. As he approached the victim, the guard reached down to the dashboard of his cart and flipped a toggle switch activating the vehicle's headlights. The body became clearer as the lights illuminated the lifeless form of a female lying on her back on the hard cement floor. One shoe was missing, and her once beautiful long blonde hair haphazardly lay soaked in the crimson pool that encircled her head. Her eyes were wide open and emitted an eerie look of shock.

Taking care not to compromise the scene, he walked carefully around the body. The blood pool ran slightly downward, as gravity had pulled it along the slope of the parking garage floor. Bending down, he began to reach to feel her carotid artery, but he stopped when he realized he had no gloves. Then he saw the massive gash across her throat. The cut was deep and spanned her neck, almost ear to ear. He could see both arteries were severed. It was a wonder her head was still attached, he thought. There would be no need for paramedics. This one would be for the coroner. At least she didn't suffer much, he thought.

When the nine-one-one call came in to the Phoenix Police Department stating that the body of a well-known television news personality and part-time anchor, Marti Montgomery, had been found, apparently murdered, Detective Lieutenant Nick Greer was the first one called to the scene. He was the lead detective of the elite Phoenix Special Investigation Unit, a small, specially chosen squad, whose duties were to tackle special, mostly high-profile cases. The murder of a noted television personality would no doubt fit that description.

The detective's first thought was this could be the result of a stalker. He had seen this reporter on the evening news many times. She was an attractive young woman, and he knew the high profile business she was in attracted both admiring fans and the obsessed. He also knew the statistics. Only two percent of stalking victims ended up murdered. Though he doubted the sight before him was the result of a stalker's phobia, it was not to be ruled out this early.

The detective turned and walked over to the security cart. He recognized the police officer, Sergeant Thomas. They had worked together before on other cases. "Hey, Chris."

"Lieutenant Greer," the officer answered. "They got you working Saturdays, too?"

The detective smiled. "Perps have no respect for our time." He looked to the man in the cart, then to the officer. "He found the body, I guess?"

"Yeah, his name is Paul Munder," Thomas responded. "He's a little shook up."

The guard had been silent, as if he was waiting for the stranger to speak. "I'm Lieutenant Nick Greer, Phoenix PD."

"Paul Munder," the guard answered. "Security." As if his gray uniform wasn't enough, he pointed to the plastic identification tag dangling from his shirt pocket.

"You found the body?"

"Uhh, yeah."

Even in the dim light, the detective could see the man wasn't far from losing his dinner. "Can you fill me in a little? Do you have any idea what happened here?"

He looked at the body and then looked away as he answered, "It looks like she got her throat cut."

Nick looked at the white-faced man and said, "Besides the obvious, why was she out here alone at this time of night? I thought you guys were supposed to be watching, protecting. Don't you usually escort the employees, especially the females, and especially at night?"

"Yes, sir, we do. Well, most of the time, that is. I usually drive them or walk them to their cars, especially the ladies. They have assigned parking over there." He pointed to an area about thirty yards away where several cars were lined up, all facing in toward the gray cement wall. "I wait until they get into their cars and get their engines started, and I'm sure they're okay before I leave."

"I assume one of those cars belongs to the victim?" Nick asked.

"Uh, yes, sir. The white Dodge Charger over there." Munder pointed to the group of cars again. Even in the dim light Nick could make out the license plate: MART1.

"Obviously, she never made it. I assume you didn't go with her tonight. Can you explain to me why?" The detective's question was pointed.

"It's not my fault, Lieutenant," Munder answered. Though his tone was defensive, the detective could sense compassion in his tone. "I was supposed to. The desk called and said she was on her way." He pointed to a hand-held radio sitting on the dashboard in front of him. "But just after they called, I heard a car alarm go off. I radioed back and told them I was responding to an alarm, and to tell her to wait until I got back. I said I'd be back to pick her up in a few minutes. I jumped in this thing"—he pointed to the cart—"and I drove it up to check it out. When I got back, she wasn't anywhere to be seen."

"How long were you gone?"

"Uh, about ten minutes, I guess. Maybe a little bit longer. The car was all the way on the top level, seven decks up. After I checked it out, I wrote down the plate number and then I came back down to get her. But, like I said, she wasn't there." He pointed to her car. "I looked over there and saw her car was still there, so I waited a bit. I figured she got caught up in something, or she was talking to somebody and she'd be along shortly." He looked at the detective as if he were seeking his approval. Nick's face was expressionless.

"I waited for a few minutes, and then I radioed back. The lady at the desk said she'd left a while ago, so I went to look for her, and, well, . . ." He stared at the blood pooled around her head. Even in the shadows, the detective could see the man's face was as white as a sheet. Suddenly, he darted out of the cart like an arrow being propelled from a bow and sprinted to the edge of the garage.

Nick and Officer Thomas watched as the man bent over the yellow railing. Thomas shrugged and said, "I gotta go and finish securing this place if you don't need me here, Lieutenant."

"Go. Do your thing. I got it here."

Sue Kim had followed behind the detective as he traveled up the ramp. As she joined him, she peered down at the body. "Wow! Is it really her?"

"Yeah, it looks like it," Nick answered.

She heard the sound of coughing, turned, and saw the guard who was still bent over the railing and heaving. "I sure wouldn't want to be walking below him."

A small smile appeared under Nick's mustache and etched the corners of his mouth. "Neither would I. Not without an umbrella, anyway."

When the guard had finally finished heaving, he slowly returned to his cart. As he sat down, Nick asked, "Are you okay?"

He shook his head. "Sorry about that. I'm not used to—"

"It's okay; you're not the first." Nick reached into his pocket and pulled out a pack of chewing gum and handed a stick to the guard. "Here, perhaps this will help."

"Thanks," Munder said as he took the offering.

The detective was reminded of the first murder scene he had come upon. He had been on the force only three weeks when he and his partner were called to investigate a commotion outside of a downtown tenement. As they were checking out the alley behind the building, they found a man hanging from a light pole. His hands and feet had been duct-taped to the pole, and his stomach had been sliced open; a victim of a gang killing. The unexpected sight of innards hanging out and dripping blood to the ground brought up everything the new officer had consumed that day. When he'd returned to the scene, he was embarrassed, but Bruce Mannion, his sergeant at that time, had said, "Don't worry about it. It happens to all of us. You'll get used to it."

His attention returned to the task at hand. "Did you see or hear anyone?" he asked the guard. "A car leaving or perhaps someone on foot? Someone running, maybe?"

Munder shook his head. "No, sir, no one on foot, that is. Vehicles are coming and going here a lot. I might have heard a car, or maybe a truck, but I didn't think anything of it."

"Did it sound like it was in a hurry? Were the tires squealing?" Nick questioned.

"Huh-uh." Munder shook his head. "Nothing out of the ordinary. Nothing I can think of, anyway."

Nick and Sue Kim had been only three blocks away at the US Airways Arena watching the Phoenix Suns basketball game when the vibration of Nick's cell phone had caught his attention in the noisy crowd. The text message was from Deputy Chief Bruce Mannion. It read: *Body at KTPA parking garage. Know you're at the game but need you to go. Second level. Security guard found body—name is Munder. See Sergeant Thomas. I'll call coroner. BTW, the vic is Marti Montgomery.*

Nick had immediately recognized the name. He knew Marti Montgomery was a young, up-and-coming reporter. She was regularly seen on almost every Channel Four newscast as an on-the-scene reporter. She periodically substituted for one or the other evening or nightly news anchors.

Nick had lifted his cell phone so Sue Kim could see the text message. Then he'd handed her his car keys and said above the noise of the crowd, "It's only three blocks away. I'll hoof it over. I can get a ride home in one of the black and whites."

She'd shook her head. "I'll go with you. The Suns are getting their asses kicked anyway."

Another black and white cruiser came onto the scene and stopped about fifty feet from them. Two uniformed policemen exited the car and walked over to the lieutenant. Nick held up his gold shield and said, "Please, Officers, please stand back. We don't want to contaminate the scene." The detective knew there were five basic contaminants to a crime scene, and the worst one of them all was other cops. "Just finish getting this place sealed off. No one out—no one in, unless they have a right to be here," he ordered.

The coroner's van pulled up just as Nick spoke. Several more black and whites had arrived with their lights flashing red and blue. Each assumed their posts around the entrances to the parking garage. Sue Kim turned and headed toward the coroner's vehicle and soon returned with a forensic kit. She set it on the ground, opened it, retrieved a pair of gloves and pulled them on. Then she slipped a pair of Tyveks over her shoes and said, "I guess I'd better get to work."

You don't have to do that," Nick said. "A crime team should be here any minute." But it was too late, she was already bent over the body and taking pictures with her cell phone.

Sue Kim worked in the Phoenix crime lab and also processed crime scenes when needed. She was well respected at her trade, but her first love was her music. Though born in Okinawa, this naturalized citizen was proud to be an American. Her father, a software engineer, had come to the United States with his wife and only daughter and settled in San Diego, California, when Sue Kim was only two years old. She held two degrees, one in forensic science and one in music, both from Stanford University. Shortly after graduation, she had moved to Arizona and joined the Phoenix Symphony.

She had met Nick Greer during her tenure as an assistant in the Maricopa County morgue. They had gotten off to a rocky start and had navigated some bumps, more like boulders one might say, along their relationship highway. But now they were engaged to be married.

Nick Greer was a Phoenix native, and a two-sport athlete in high school. Although he loved baseball, it was basketball that consumed him. Being well over six feet tall didn't hurt. He was an All-State forward, and was scouted by several colleges. He chose his home, Arizona State University, and the full-ride scholarship they offered. Scouted by several professional teams, he thought he would make basketball a career until, late in his senior year, he blew out his knee so bad that any aspirations of becoming a professional athlete were squashed. But Nick didn't mind so much. He had majored in criminology, and the more he learned, the more he wanted to become a cop.

He graduated with honors and continued on and obtained a master's degree. Upon graduation, he was courted by the FBI. Though a position with such an agency would no doubt take him to many interesting places, he chose to protect the people in the city he grew up in. Phoenix had been good to him, and he felt an obligation to it.

A white SUV rolled up the ramp and came to a stop next to the coroner's van. Nick read the black lettering on the side: City of Phoenix Crime Scene Unit. The doors opened and a man and a woman got out. They opened the back door of their vehicle, grabbed their forensic equipment, and headed toward the body. The female saw Sue

Kim, still bent down examining the wounds, and yelled, "Hey! Get away from there. This is a crime scene. What the hell do you think you're doing?"

Sue Kim looked up and said, "Hi, Tina! I just thought I'd get a head start."

"Oh, I didn't know it was you," Tina responded. "What are you doing here?" Then she saw Nick and smiled. "Oh, I see. Hi, Nick."

"Hi, Tina," Nick responded. "We were at the game when we were called."

"I thought you and Sonny were only working special cases. What brings you to this scene?"

"I guess it's because of who the victim is."

"Who is it?"

"They didn't tell you?"

"Nope. The call just said a DB on level two."

Just then they all heard a loud, "Holy shit!!" It came from Tina's partner as he was snapping pictures and recognized the victim's face. "Tina, take a look at this! Do you know who this is?"

Tina looked at the victim's face and said, "Uh, looks familiar, but I don't know who she is."

"It's Marti Montgomery! You know, the Channel Four reporter. Everybody knows who she is," he responded.

Tina shrugged her shoulders and looked at Sue Kim. "Uh, I watch Channel Twelve."

Nick saw the security guard look up and smile slightly. "If you're feeling better, I'll need a statement, so stick around." The guard nodded and rested his head on the steering wheel of his cart.

"Hey, Gumby, need any help?" came a familiar voice from behind Nick. He knew it was the voice of Sonny Madison.

Nick Greer and Sonny Madison were best friends and had been partners until the department split them up due to budget cuts. Sometimes they would work together on special cases. Though Sonny's personality and Nick's were opposite, they made an excellent pair when it came to solving crimes. Nick was mostly a "by the book" cop who followed rules and procedures and respected authority, while Sonny was the "in-your-face type" who spoke his mind no matter whether you emptied ashtrays or you carried the rank of police chief, or even mayor. But it was his uncanny ability to navigate the information highway that was his claim to fame. Everyone knew if Sonny couldn't find it, it wasn't going to be found.

Nick hated to be called Gumby. By the time he was in junior high school, he was already six feet tall. He was also very thin, and someone, he didn't remember who, had called him Gumby. It stuck with him for a while, but it finally went away. Sonny Madison was the only one who called him that now and the only one who could get away with it.

He turned and saw his friend standing there with a wide grin on his face. "I thought you weren't coming back for another week," Nick said.

The last case Nick and Sonny had worked on had resulted in Sonny being seriously wounded, to the extent he almost died. He had been recovering at home for the past six weeks.

"April got tired of me being around, and I got a call from Bruce. What's up? Is it really her?"

"Yep." Nick nodded. "It's Marti Montgomery, all right."

"Wow!" Sonny exclaimed as he walked over to the body. "Look at all the blood!"

Sonny heard a familiar voice say, "Hello, Sergeant Sonny. Welcome back."

"Hello, little one," he said to Sue Kim. "What are you doing here?"

"She was with me when the call came in," Nick answered. "We were at the game."

"They lost," Sonny stated.

"So, what else is new?"

"Any witnesses?" Sonny asked.

"There doesn't seem to be. The security guard over there found her." He pointed to Munder who was still sitting in the security cart with his head still resting on the steering wheel.

"Why the hell would she be out here alone? That cute young thing probably had a whole line of stalkers. Did you ever see her on the news? Wheeew! What a cutie."

Nick pointed to Munder. "Sonny, I talked with him a little. Do you want to get his statement? Maybe you'll come up with something I didn't."

Sonny nodded and went over to the security cart, stepped up, and sat down beside the driver. He was still hugging the steering wheel and didn't notice he had company. Sonny pulled his badge from his belt and shoved it under the steering wheel. "Hey, coach, wake up. We gotta talk."

The guard turned his head and looked at his visitor, leaned back, took a deep breath, and said, "Yeah, what do you wanna know? I already talked to the other guy."

"Yeah, I know. Now you get to talk to this guy. Tell me exactly what happened. And don't be afraid to start at the beginning; that's usually best."

The lieutenant's eyes surveyed the area as the CSI team and Sue Kim worked unceasingly processing the scene, and Sonny questioned the security guard. Yellow tent cards with black numbers were being placed in several spots along the floor. Flashes went off one by one as photos were taken. Samples were deposited into various-sized vials and clear plastic bags and processed for transport. The team worked together like a finely tuned machine. Nothing would be missed. Sue Kim would see to that.

By now, a news team and other employees from the television station had arrived on the scene. Shocked people looked on. Some were crying, and cameras were rolling. Reporters were trying their best to work their way around the yellow police tape, and the additional uniformed police officers who had arrived were barely successful in holding them back.

Sue Kim walked over to Nick and showed him the victim's purse. "This was under one of the cars." With gloved hands she opened it and saw the wallet was still in it. "It doesn't look like robbery," she commented.

"It was probably a stalker. We'll check the cameras."

"I'm not so sure," she answered.

"Why not?"

"Did you see the way her throat was cut? It almost went from ear to ear, and it was deep. I'll know more after the ME gets finished, but it looks like it cut clean through and severed both carotids. She bled out profusely. I'd say whoever did this was angry and meant to kill her. You're the cop. Does that sound like a stalker to you?"

Just then Sonny returned. "The security guard wasn't much help. It seems he was topside chasing a car alarm. He found a broken window, but no sign of entry. We'll need to send someone from the team up there to check it out."

"I'll get someone up there," said Sue Kim as she went back to the crime team.

"Sonny, see if you can get the tapes from the cameras." Nick pointed to one of the several cameras that seemed to cover the entire parking garage. "They should show something."

"I doubt it," Sonny responded. "According to the security guard, the video surveillance system has been out of order for a couple of days. Something about a mainboard got fried."

Sergeant Thomas returned. "Excuse me, Detectives, but there's a man who says he's the general manager of the station. He's demanding to see her."

"Tell him to hold on. We'll talk to him when we're finished here."

"Uh, he's not demanding to see you. He wants to see the body. He tried to force his way through the perimeter, but we were able to restrain him. He's very insistent. He's yelling and becoming belligerent. He has the reporters and the rest of the crowd pretty riled up. Some of them are yelling and screaming, too."

Sonny said, "Chris, tell him to calm down and call off his reporters. They all need to back off so the CSI team can do their work. If he doesn't comply, cuff him and throw his ass in the back of one of the cruisers. That should look good to his employees. Who knows, maybe he'll be the next star on his own ten o'clock news."

Nick looked at Sonny and smiled. "Well, partner, welcome back to the ongoing soap opera, the bold and the homicidal, or something like that."

"Yeah," Sonny answered. "Like sands through the hourglass, so goes the sixth commandment."

CHAPTER 2

The Suit

The crime scene crew was still busy processing the scene when Nick said to Sonny, "I don't think we can do much more here. Let them do their thing. Let's see what the station manager has to say."

Though a camera was still filming and two reporters with microphones in their hands were trying to push their way to the front of the small crowd that had formed, there was an eerie feeling in the air as the two detectives approached the yellow police tape that separated them from the onlookers. Officer Thomas was standing by one of the cruisers with his arms folded across his chest, waiting for them. "Where's the suit?" Sonny asked.

Thomas pointed to the cruiser next to him. "He's in the back. He refused to cooperate, so I did what you said." He pointed to a man in the back seat who was beating his handcuffed hands against the window of the cruiser. Sonny shook his head and walked over to the vehicle.

As soon as Sonny opened the door of the cruiser, the man started yelling, "How dare you treat me like a common criminal. Let me out of here now! Do you know who I am?"

Sonny leaned over and looked the man in the face. He dangled his gold shield and said, "See this? This is who I am, and I don't care if you're Warren fucking Buffett. You're interfering with a police investigation. If you don't calm down, your mug shot will be on your and your competitors' newscasts tonight after we escort your ass to the slammer, that is." Sonny grinned as he looked at the man sitting in the seat. "Ahhh, I can see it now." He raised his arms and made half circles with his hands. "There you are sitting in a holding cell wearing that expensive three-piece suit. Oh, yeah, and you're surrounded by pimps, drug dealers, and probably a gangbanger or two. Whoopee! You're gonna love it"—he shrugged—"or not!"

The man looked like he was going to speak, but he suddenly sat back in the seat, dropped his hands into his lap, lowered his head, and became silent. Sonny could see the fear on the man's face and added, "Think about that for a while," as he slammed the door. He waited a couple of minutes before he opened the door again and said, "Okay, now, are we on the same page here?"

The man looked up and said, "Please accept my apologies, Officer. I won't give you any more trouble, I promise."

"First of all, it's Detective, or Sergeant; and, second of all,"—the detective's eyes widened as he stared into the eyes of his adversary—"you'd better not!"

Sergeant Thomas was standing beside the car and had heard the entire conversation. Sonny told him, "Get him out of there and unhook him."

The man stood and held out his hands as Officer Thomas removed the handcuffs. Jacoby rubbed his wrists and said loudly, "I am Harlan Jacoby. I run this TV station. Why are you treating me like this?"

Sonny looked at Sergeant Thomas, who raised the handcuffs, held them in front of Jacoby's face and shook them. Jacoby understood the warning and nodded.

Sonny said, "Okay now! Mr. Jacoby, we need to talk. Can we go somewhere private?"

He nodded. "My office. It's upstairs."

A camera was aiming in their direction as Nick and Sonny followed Jacoby into an elevator. Jacoby pushed a button and the doors shut. They were silent as they rode to the top floor. Jacoby led them into a plush conference room. The detectives waited until he sat before they took seats across the table from him.

Nick began, "I'm Lieutenant Greer, and I think you've met my partner, Sergeant Madison. First of all, we want you to know we are both sorry for your loss of your employee." Sonny nodded.

Jacoby answered, "She was more than just an employee. She's family." He swallowed and said with a shaky voice, "She's my niece. That's why I wanted to see her."

The detectives looked at each other, then back at Jacoby. "Again, sir, we're sorry for your loss," Nick answered. "But they're still processing the scene, and we cannot allow you or anyone else in there."

He exhaled. The concern on his face appeared legitimate. "I understand. I'm sorry. I guess I lost control. Please, when can I see her?"

"After the medical examiner sees her. Maybe Monday."

"My God! What am I going to tell my sister in Tulsa? She didn't want her to come here in the first place." As his eyes began to well up, he reached under his glasses, wiped them with his fingers, and said, "I'm sorry, Detectives. Please tell me how I can help."

Sonny spoke, "First of all, your security guy, uh—"

"Paul Munder."

"Yeah. He said the video surveillance system is out of order. Is that correct?"

"Yes, it's been down since Thursday."

"What happened to it?"

Jacoby shrugged. "I don't know exactly. I guess the system somehow shorted out and fried the mainboard. They ordered another one, but it won't be here until Monday afternoon, or maybe Tuesday. I ordered extra security, but the guy who was supposed to be here tonight called off, so I'm told."

"Why?" Sonny questioned.

"Why what? I order—"

The detective interrupted, "Why did he call off? He must have given a reason."

"Paul said something about car trouble."

"What security company do you use?" Nick asked.

"Secure-Max, out of Tempe. They're on contract with us," the manager answered.

"I would think they would've sent someone to replace him."

"They said they were shorthanded. Paul Munder, our regular night guy, said he could handle it. He's been here a long time. He's pretty good."

"Obviously not good enough," Sonny commented. "Does he work for Secure-Max?"

"No. Paul is an employee of the station. He has worked for us for several years."

Nick spoke, "Tell me, Mr. Jacoby, do you know anyone who might want to hurt your niece?"

Jacoby shook his head. Again, tears began to form in his eyes. "No one I can think of. She was a very likeable person."

"I know this is a competitive business," Nick added. "Could there be a jealous employee who might want to take advantage of the broken security system? It just seems too opportunistic." One thing

Lieutenant Nick Greer didn't believe in when it came to crime was coincidences.

Jacoby took a deep breath, leaned back in his chair, then exhaled. "Lieutenant, you are correct about this being a competitive business. Jealousy and backstabbing are common in our profession. Our field reporters want to be anchors, and our anchors want to keep their jobs. Some of the field reporters think they're better than the anchors and they should have their jobs, and sometimes the anchors are worried they might be right."

"But they seem so friendly on the tube; like a family," Sonny commented.

"Most of the teams get along well. It's the underlings who have the problems. They all want to be in the limelight. They want to be celebrities. Now, don't get me wrong. Most of them get along. Some are as sweet as candy, but this industry can corrupt the nicest people. In this business you not only have to be good, but you have to be tough or you can get stepped on and squashed like a bug. You're only as good as your last report or last night's ratings."

"What about your niece?" Nick asked. "How was she perceived by her peers? How did she treat them? And what about her relationship with you? From what you tell us, that in itself could cause jealousy. A lot of people would call it nepotism."

"First of all, no one knew we were family. I made sure of that. Martha—Marti, that is—worked her way up. She earned her spots. I made it perfectly clear to her on her first day here that since she was my niece, she would have to be better and work harder than anyone else. She did. I was proud of her. I may run the station, but others handle personnel placement."

"But you are the boss. I would assume the buck stops and all that stuff," Sonny added.

"Yes, I have the final say, but I base my decisions on what I am told and what I know about the person and their value to this station. When it was suggested to me that Marti become a permanent anchor, I made no comments one way or the other."

"Anchor? Permanent?" Sonny asked. "Uh, who was she replacing?"

"Katy."

"Katy McKenna?"

"Yes. Katy McKenna."

"Wow! She's been around a long time. She's pretty popular," Sonny responded. "Actually, I'd say she's a Phoenix icon!"

"Yes, Detective, you're right. Katy McKenna is a Phoenix icon. She's been an anchor for over twenty years. That's what made it so hard."

"Why was she being replaced?" Nick asked.

"It was a very difficult decision, but she's lost her touch. She doesn't deliver the news like she used to. Her enthusiasm is gone, and she's been stumbling a lot lately. We tried to work with her, but she wouldn't participate. Like I said, it was a hard decision. Let me tell you, I was somewhat afraid to let her go. She has a huge following, you know, and if she went to another station we might lose viewers. But we've received a deluge of emails and letters lately and our ratings have dropped, so I spoke with our parent company. They agreed that we would not renew Katy's contract. We were going to replace her with Marti. I told her yesterday afternoon, but it hadn't been announced yet. I figured I'd decide over the weekend whether to announce it or to just bring in Marti. Mark Alvarez covered for Katy last night. We had a special crew scheduled to come in tomorrow to shoot the new intro for Monday's newscast."

"How did she take it?" Nick questioned.

"Uh, she wasn't what I would call happy, but she didn't seem surprised. Like I said, her contract was up for renewal, so I told her we wouldn't be renewing it. She has sixty days left on it. I told her we were going to continue to pay her until it ran out."

"That could be a motive for murder, if I ever saw one," Sonny said.

Jacoby shook his head. "I don't think so. I've known Katy for fifteen years. She's not the type. She said she wasn't surprised, got up, and left my office. Truthfully, I think she was tired. I think she was ready to call it quits, but she wanted to do it on her own terms. Besides, Marti had nothing to do with it. It was my decision, and, with or without Marti, I was going to let Katy go. If she wanted to take it out on somebody, it most likely would have been me."

"We'll talk with her anyway," said Nick. Jacoby nodded. Nick continued, "Mr. Jacoby, we'll need to see all of your personnel files, and we want to talk with everyone who might possibly know something, anything. We'll start with everyone here tonight. No one goes home until either Detective Madison or I say so."

Sonny had gotten up from the table and was talking to someone on his cell phone. "Uh-huh. Got it. Hold on a sec." He looked at Jacoby. "How many people are here tonight? Employees, visitors, if any? How many people total?"

"No visitors. I'd guess, maybe around twenty employees."

"Yeah, I guess we could use the help," Sonny said into the phone. "There's about twenty, or maybe more. . . . Okay." He disconnected the call and said to Nick, "Bruce is on his way, and he's sending a couple investigators to help out. He said that Sergeant Thomas is pretty savvy. We can use him to get started."

Nick looked at the station manager. "We'll need some private rooms to interview your crew. The more rooms, the quicker we can get this done. We can do it at our station, but it would be quicker and easier for all of you if we did it right here."

"This conference room is yours, as is my office. I'll get a couple more rooms for you," Jacoby said.

"First, can you get me a list of everyone here tonight? I'll need their title and their duties, too. Also, number them one, two, or three according to the amount of contact you think they would've had with the victim—one being the most contact. Everyone, even whoever cleans the toilets. If they were in this building within the last six hours, I want to talk with them."

Sonny added, "Also get us names, addresses, and phone numbers of anyone who was here and has gone home during that time period." The station manager nodded and left the room.

Nick said to Sonny, "Good catch! You still got the touch."

"Uhhh, yeah!" Sonny chided. "I'll go get Sergeant Thomas, and we'll get started."

CHAPTER 3

The Assistant

Deputy Chief Bruce Mannion came onto the scene just as Nick and Sonny were about to commence the interviews. Mannion was the Chief of Detectives for the Phoenix Police Department. His pet project, a special investigation unit, had just gotten off of the ground a couple of months earlier. Lieutenant Nick Greer and Sergeant Sonny Madison were the two he had handpicked to begin the operation. Their first case had been to find a serial killer who was terrorizing the city and cutting off the ring fingers of the victims. They were successful in solving the case, but Sonny was seriously wounded in the process, and today was his first day back.

"Okay, what do we have?" Mannion asked.

"Like you said in your text, it's Marti Montgomery all right," Nick answered. "Her throat was cut ear to ear. She was so young."

"Yeah, what a waste." Mannion shook his head. "What can I do to help?" He looked at Sonny. "By the way, welcome back, Sergeant."

"Yeah, Chief. Thanks."

The station manager had provided the two detectives with the information they had requested, and he had numbered them as directed. Sonny looked at the ones with a number one on them—three. He kept one, handed one to Nick, and one to the deputy chief. "Let's start with these. The station manager is setting up rooms for interviews. Chief, why don't you take the conference room?"

"Got it," said Mannion.

Nick's first person to be interviewed was a young lady about twenty-four, whose name was Megan Findlay. According to the paperwork, her current position was assistant to Marti Montgomery.

They met in Harlan Jacoby's office. There was a brown leather sofa and two matching chairs in the center of the office, and Nick decided this would be less intimidating for her than if he sat behind the desk. He greeted her as she came in. "Ms. Findlay, I'm Lieutenant Greer. Please have a seat and be comfortable."

She nodded as she sat across from him.

Nick began, “First of all, I’m sorry for your loss. I understand you were Ms. Montgomery’s assistant. Is that correct?”

She nodded. Her dishwater-blonde hair was pulled back in a ponytail, and her long bangs touched her black eyebrows, bringing attention to red eyes that showed evidence of crying.

“How long have you been Ms. Montgomery’s assistant?”

“I’ve been her part-time assistant for almost a year now.” She dabbed her eyes with a tissue as she spoke.

“Part-time?”

“Yes. My time is split between a couple of the field reporters, but mostly with Marti—excuse me—Ms. Montgomery.”

“What did you do before that?”

“After graduation from college, I interned here for a while. Then I became an assistant to Ms. McKenna, then to Ms. Montgomery.”

“Were you close to Ms. Montgomery?’ Nick questioned.

“I don’t know. I guess it depends on how you interpret close. I helped her with projects, and I set her schedule. I handled her fan mail, and I did whatever she needed me to do.”

“Tell me, what was she like? How was she to work with?”

“Oh, she had her moments. Not as much as some of the women in her position, but, all in all, not so bad,” she answered.

“Moments? Can you elaborate?” Nick asked.

“Oh, I really don’t know how to explain it. She was okay. She treated me well, but sometimes she acted like a diva. I guess that goes with the job. She certainly wanted the evening anchor position. There was no doubt about that. The whole station knew it, and rumor had it she was getting it.”

“Rumor? What rumor? Where did it come from?”

“Oh heavens, it was all over the station. Katy was out and Marti was in. It was only a matter of time,” she answered with a sense of affirmation in her voice.

“Do you know anyone who would want to harm her?” Nick questioned.

She looked down, took a breath, and shook her head. When she looked back, Nick thought he saw a trace of cloudiness in her eyes, but she seemed to retain her composure. “No, sir, not that I can think of.”

“I understand this is a very competitive business, is it not?”

"Oh, yeah," she affirmed.

"I'll bet there's a lot of jealousy."

"I'd agree with that statement."

"So what about Ms. Montgomery?"

"Oh, some people were jealous of her, I guess, but I don't think anyone here would harm her, if that's what you're getting at."

"How about her mail? You said you handled her mail. Does that mean you read it?"

"I didn't read her personal stuff, but I read her fan mail."

"Tell me about her fan mail."

"Oh, she got a bunch of it, mostly from guys. She is, was, an attractive woman, you know."

Nick nodded and cupped his chin with his hand as he thought for a moment. "How about stalkers? Is there any chance someone was stalking her?"

She shook her head. "I don't think so. Some of the letters asked her to go out on a date, but there was nothing I ever saw or heard to make me think she was being stalked. I think if she was, she would've said something to me."

"Can I see the letters?"

"Uh, they kinda got shredded, except for her personal mail. She kept that. There wasn't a lot of it."

"Is that normal? The shredding, I mean." Nick questioned.

"It depends on the person. Some of them keep them; some don't. Marti preferred I shred them."

"Was there anyone she might have been really close to? How about her love life? Do you know if there was anyone special?"

Megan paused for a moment and looked away. "I don't think so. She worked long hours. She was very dedicated. She once told me she didn't have time for a love life. I remember she said, 'My career is my only love.' "

Nick sensed there was something she wasn't saying, so he leaned forward and said, "But there's more, isn't there, Ms. Findlay?"

"Uhh . . . like what?"

"You tell me." He leaned back in his chair to give her space.

"Well, there was a rumor."

"A rumor? What kind of rumor?"

"Yeah. Her and Bill."

"Bill who?"

"Bill Scanlon."

"And who is Bill Scanlon?" Nick questioned.

"He's one of our cameramen. She requested him every time she went out in the field."

"I see. Were the rumors true? Were they lovers?" Nick asked.

"No. Not at all." She shook her head.

"You seem pretty certain. How do you know for sure?"

"First of all, he's married. And, second, he's not her type."

"So why the rumors? Do you know where they came from?"

"I really don't know who started them, but ever since they covered the Yarnell Hill fire together, there have been stories floating around the station."

The detective leaned forward like an old gossip looking for the next tidbit. It worked. She leaned toward him like she was telling the latest neighborhood secret over a cup of tea. "The story is they had adjoining rooms, and only one bed was slept in the whole time. I don't know where it came from or who started it, but I'm sure they were just friends. Like I said, he's not her type."

"What is her type?" Nick asked.

She shrugged and looked away. Then she looked back and said, "Like I said, he's married. He's also a lot older."

Nick's instinct told him there was something she was hiding, but he wasn't going to be able to drag it out of her tonight, so he dropped the subject. He looked at the list of interviewees, but he didn't see Scanlon's name anywhere on it. "Have you seen him tonight? Is he here?"

"No, sir, I haven't seen him all day. I believe he's covering the flooding up north. He'll probably be there all weekend."

"Ms. Findlay, thank you for your help. Here's my card. If you think of anything, even something that seems petty, please call me." He turned it over and scribbled his cell phone number on it. "Here's my personal cell phone number, okay?"

She nodded as she stood and took the card. She turned to leave, but suddenly stopped, turned back around and looked into his eyes. Large tears rolled down her cheeks as she said, "Detective, promise me you'll find the person who did this to Marti."

"We'll do our best," Nick assured her. She left the office.

After all the interviews were completed, Nick, Sonny, and Bruce Mannion were sitting at the conference table comparing notes. Mannion looked at the clock on the wall, and then glanced at his watch. “It’s almost midnight, gentlemen. Let’s call it a night. The crime scene unit is finished. Nick, your little fiancée is waiting down in the lobby. Why don’t you take her home? I’ll see you both on Monday.”

CHAPTER 4

The Dropped Anchor

Katy McKenna was waiting for the detectives when Nick rang the doorbell of her north Scottsdale home. His earlier phone call this Sunday morning had secured an eleven o'clock appointment. She answered the door and greeted her visitors with a smile. "Come on in, Detectives."

They stepped into a large foyer. Both sides of the white walls were adorned with pictures and plaques. There were several awards with Katy's name on them. Nick was the first to speak, "Ms. McKenna, I'm Lieutenant Greer, and this is my partner, Sergeant Madison. Thank you for seeing us this morning."

"It's no problem, Detectives. Let's go out to the patio where we can talk."

Sonny noticed the home displayed a lot of antiques as she ushered them through a nicely furnished living room and through a set of French doors that led to a large covered patio. Both detectives were awed by what they saw as they stepped out onto the Mexican-tiled patio floor.

The home was located on one of the higher elevations in north Scottsdale. Just below the patio was a large grassy plateau with a beautifully designed swimming pool in the center. On one end of the pool was a rock waterfall; on the other end was an oval-shaped, in-ground spa. But it was what was beyond the sparkling pool that caught them both. The patio offered a panoramic view of the city of Phoenix. They sat on plush concealed motion chairs that were arranged in a semicircle and perfectly placed for conversation without sacrificing the scenic view. Four ceiling fans whirred above, sending a comforting breeze down upon them.

"You sure do have a beautiful view here, Ms. McKenna," Sonny remarked.

"Thank you," Katy responded. "You should see it at night when the city is all lit up. That's why I bought this place. After the newscasts, it is a great place to sit down and relax." She looked out at the cityscape and said, "Sometimes I just sit here, sip on a glass of wine, and look out over the city and try to pick out places I reported on." She looked at the detectives. "Can I get you gentlemen anything to drink? Tea? Lemonade? There's coffee." She pointed to an oval glass table that held a silver coffeepot along with bone china cups.

"No, thank you, ma'am," Nick answered. "We're fine. We don't expect to take up much of your time anyway." He looked at Sonny who nodded in agreement.

Katy McKenna went right to the point. "So, I assume you're here to talk about Marti Montgomery." She shook her head. "How tragic!"

Nick responded, "Yes, we are. First of all, please know we are both sorry for your loss. I've seen your newscasts. I assume you were friends."

She nodded, but there appeared to be no emotion in her demeanor. "Thank you. She was a nice girl."

Nick continued, "How well did you know Ms. Montgomery?"

She shrugged and answered, "She was a field reporter, mostly. Sometimes she sat in for me if I was on vacation, or ill, or on assignment. I didn't know her outside of the station though, but she seemed like a nice girl even though she had a lot to learn."

"Do you know anyone who might want to harm her?"

McKenna shook her head. "I don't think so."

"What about a stalker? She was an attractive young lady, you know."

"We all get fans who have become fascinated by us or with what we do. It's the price of fame, I guess. God knows, I've had my share over my career. Most of them are harmless. We get used to it after a while. It's just a part of the job."

"But what about Ms. Montgomery? Did you know or hear about anyone who may have been following her too closely? Perhaps a heavier than average amount of phone calls, letters, or email?"

Again, she shook her head. "You'd have to ask her . . . uh, I'm sorry, I mean, maybe ask Megan, her assistant. If anyone would know, it would be her."

"We did. She said she didn't know of any problems. But I understand there was a rumor about her and one of your cameramen, uh, Bill Scanlon. Do you know anything about that?"

"You know, that Megan is a little busybody. That's one of the reasons I got rid of her."

"I see, but do you know anything about the rumor?" Nick stuck to the subject.

"I heard it."

"And?" Nick questioned.

"And what?" The newscaster was beginning to become defensive.

"Did you believe it to be true?"

"Lieutenant, the news business is based on rumors. You hear something, and if it seems newsworthy you check it out. Sometimes it leads to a story, sometimes it doesn't. I know Bill Scanlon. I don't believe it. He's married, and besides, he's in his forties, Marti is in her twenties." She gazed out at the city and was silent for a moment. Finally, still looking away, she said, "He wouldn't be involved with anyone like her."

"Uh, anyone like her? What do you mean by that?" Nick questioned.

"Nothing. I didn't mean anything by that. Nothing at all."

Nick sensed something as he continued, "Ms. McKenna, how did you feel about Ms. Montgomery on a personal basis?"

"She was okay, I guess."

"Why am I getting the feeling you didn't care for her very much?"

"Like I said earlier, she was young and she had a lot to learn."

Sonny knew it was time to pick up the pace. "Ms. McKenna, we understand there were some changes being made at the station." Again she looked out at the vast city as if his words had never made it to her ears, but Sonny kept pushing. "We understand Marti Montgomery was replacing you as the anchor on the evening news. Isn't that correct?"

She pursed her lips, turned and glared at Sonny. Both detectives knew a nerve had been struck. "Where did you hear that?"

"Is it not true?" Sonny prodded.

She again looked out at the city below. When she looked back to Sonny, she had regained her composure. "I had decided to take some time off."

"Uh, time off?" Sonny asked. "What do you mean by time off? How much? Why?"

Again, she looked out and away from the detectives. Finally she said, "Harlan and I disagreed on the direction our newscast should go. He said he wanted someone younger to anchor. I think he just wanted to give his niece the job."

Nick couldn't hide the surprise in his voice. "You knew she was his niece?"

"Of course I did. The whole station knew it." Her response was a mixture of matter of fact and sarcasm.

Nick remembered his discussion with the station manager the previous night and how Harlan Jacoby was so sure their relationship had top secret stamped all over it.

"So it would be safe to assume there was some jealousy there at the station?" Sonny questioned.

"What do you think? It's a very competitive business," she answered.

Sonny continued, "I imagine you must have been pretty upset. I mean, you were being replaced by a younger woman, and it looks like a little nepotism may be a contributing factor. And, to be honest"—he looked into her eyes—"you don't seem at all distraught over her death."

"Detective, I can see where you're going with this. Before you ask, no, I'm not a murderer. I didn't kill Marti Montgomery! Her death has hit me hard. We all handle our emotions differently. I grieve in my own way, privately."

"So, you are grieving, but in your own way?"

Though Sonny's tone seemed to mock her, she didn't allow it to shake her. She asked, "What do you think, Detective?"

"What I think is I would like to know where were you last night between, say, seven and nine o'clock?"

She looked at her accuser and replied, "Right here. Sipping on a glass of Chardonnay, alone, watching the city lights." She stood up, looked back and forth between the two detectives, and said, "Now, Detectives, if there is nothing else."

Nick said, as he and Sonny both stood up, "Thank you, Ms. McKenna. We appreciate your time. We'll see ourselves out."

As the detectives began their ride back to Phoenix, Nick said, "Wow! What a cutthroat business!" He thought about what he had just said. "Uh, there certainly was no pun intended."

Sonny said, "I'll say. You know, the liturgist in our church used to be a TV anchor somewhere way north of here, I don't know, uh, Idaho or Montana, or someplace like that. I guess he's related to Missy Fensl, the Channel Six anchor; cousins, I think he said. Anyway, he once told April that when he first came here, he called his cousin and asked her if she could open a door or two for him. If I understood correctly, she never even returned his phone call. I guess that's the way the industry works."

Nick shook his head. "Who'da thunk it?"

Sonny said, "You got anything else pressing? I promised April I'd go with her to our nephew's birthday party this afternoon."

"No, go ahead. I'm gonna drop in on our absent security guard and see what he has to say. Then I'll probably call it a day."

"I can go along if you want," Sonny said.

"No, go be with family. I'll see you tomorrow."

CHAPTER 5

The Guard

After the first ring of the bell, the door opened and a man appeared. Lieutenant Greer displayed his gold shield and said, "Are you Leo Cardinale?"

"Yes, I am he," the man nodded as he answered.

"I'm Lieutenant Greer, PPD. May I come in?"

"Is there a problem, Lieutenant?"

"I'm just checking out something, and I have some questions. May I come in, please?"

"Sure, come on in."

Nick entered, and his host motioned toward the living room.

The room was small and sparsely furnished with two soft gray chairs separated by a TV tray table. A flat screen television sat on a stand against the wall across from them. He seemed welcoming as he smiled, pointed to one of the chairs, and said, "Please, have a seat."

There weren't any pictures on the walls nor was there a sofa or love seat in the room. Either the man had just moved in, Nick thought, or he was not concerned about decor. He sat down and his host asked, "What can I do for you, Lieutenant?"

"Mr. Cardinale, I'm investigating the death of Marti Montgomery. I assume you've heard about it."

"Yes, sir. I saw it on the news. Terrible thing. I kinda feel a bit responsible. I was supposed to be there to help with security last night. Perhaps if I had been there."

"Yes, sir, that's why I'm here. I understand you were scheduled to work at the KTPA parking garage last evening, but you called off. May I ask why you called off?"

"Yeah, some asshole slashed two tires on my truck!"

"Really? Wow! What time did that happen?"

"I'd say sometime between noon and three-fifteen. Everything was okay when I got back from getting it washed; that was around noon. I was leaving for the work site when I saw both tires were flat; like I said, three-fifteen. I was supposed to be there at four. If I ever get my hands on the bastard who did it, he'll never do it again. It cost me over five hundred dollars and a night's pay."

"Do you have any idea who might have done it?" the detective questioned. "Is someone pissed off at you, or something?"

He shook his head. "No clue. There aren't even any gangs in my neighborhood; at least none that I'm aware of. Hey, you're a cop. Are there any gangs in this area?"

"I'm not on the gang squad," Nick answered. "But they usually don't slash tires. They'd take the whole truck. Did you make a police report?"

"No, I didn't think about that."

Nick continued questioning, "Are you married? Perhaps someone got mad at your wife?"

"I'm not married anymore. I live alone."

"A girlfriend, maybe? An ex-girlfriend?"

He shook his head. "Nope."

"How about a girlfriend's ex? A girlfriend's boyfriend, or husband maybe? Is there anyone you can think of?" Nick smiled. "Speaking from personal experience, I know ex-wives can be pretty vindictive."

"Detective, if I had any idea who sliced my tires, you'd be here to arrest me, not ask me who could've done it. Those tires were less than a month old. I really have no idea who did it." His answer seemed sincere to the detective.

"I saw a pickup in your driveway. I assume that's the vehicle?"

"Yeah. I've only had it a few months."

"It's a nice-looking truck. You don't park it in your garage?" When Nick had pulled up to the house, he'd seen a shiny white pickup parked in the driveway.

"Come with me, Lieutenant," Cardinale said as he got up from his chair. "I want to show you something."

Nick followed him through the kitchen to a door that Cardinale opened, then reached to a switch on the wall. Nick heard the sound of a garage door opening. As the light rushed its way in, he saw a car under a gray cover. Leo removed the cover, and Nick was impressed by what it revealed: a shiny, candy-apple red Ford Mustang Shelby.

Though it was a two-car garage, between the Mustang and tools, the detective could see there was no room for the pickup. "Wow, that's a nice-looking car. What year is it?"

"Nineteen sixty-seven. I'm almost finished restoring her," Cardinale said proudly. "I'm just waiting for a couple of parts, and she'll be ready for the road."

Nick looked at his host and said, "Sir, the cameras in the parking garage were out of commission. Were you aware of that?"

"Yeah, that's why they wanted a second security guard. I called into dispatch. Didn't they send someone else out?"

"No," Nick answered. "According to the station manager they said they didn't have anyone to send out."

"You know, that makes sense now that I think about it. We're pretty well spread out, personnel-wise. They're looking to hire a couple more people. You know, if it was only one tire, I could've changed it. I'd have been a little late, but I would have still been there." He hung his head and said, "Maybe it wouldn't have happened. It's too bad. She was really a cutie."

"Had you ever met her?" Nick asked.

"Nope. I never had the pleasure, but I've seen her on TV."

"Thank you, Mr. Cardinale," Nick said as he handed him his card. "If anything comes to mind that may help, please give me a call."

Nick turned and left through the open garage door. As he walked across the driveway and got into his Taurus, the detective noticed the little rubber bits sticking out of two of the tires, both on the right side of the truck. The tires were brand new.

CHAPTER 6

The Spa

Sergeant Sonny Madison was already sitting at his desk and was typing away on his computer when Lieutenant Nick Greer walked into the room that housed the Special Investigations Unit. "Hey, Gumby. Happy Monday!"

"Well, you're in bright and early." He looked at his watch: 8:05. "You must be anxious to get back to work."

Sonny nodded. "I got in about a half hour ago. I thought I might get a start on the Montgomery case. It's been all over the news, but you already know that, I'm sure."

"Oh, yeah," Nick stated as he sat down at his desk. "They seem to be interviewing the second cousins of everyone who ever met her."

"Yeah, even our guy Jacoby was on television. Did you see him?"

"How could I miss him? He was on every newscast. So, are you having any luck? You got the case solved yet?"

Sonny laughed. "I started running backgrounds on all of the station employees. That's gonna take a while."

Nick heard the ringing of his cell phone. He retrieved it from his belt. The display read: Restricted Number. "Nick Greer," he answered.

"Lieutenant, this is Harlan Jacoby."

"Yes, Mr. Jacoby, how can I help you?" Nick responded as he put the phone on speaker and motioned to Sonny to listen.

"I wanted to let you know that we haven't been able to reach Bill Scanlon. We've tried everywhere; his home and his cell phone. All we've been able get is his voicemail. We've left several messages. It's unlike him not to return his messages."

"That's the camera guy, right?"

"Yes. I'm thinking about sending someone over to his home."

"Where was he last seen or heard from?"

"He was with a crew covering the flood up north, but one of our reporters said the moment he was informed of Marti's death, he left the location. He hasn't been seen or heard from since. His equipment is still up there."

"Do you have his address?" Nick asked.

"Twenty-seven sixty-two Desert Crest Drive."

"We'll check it out," Nick responded. "We need to talk to him anyway."

"Will you let me know? I'm really worried about him. He's a good employee, but he was close to Marti."

"I'll let you know." Nick disconnected the phone and said to his partner, "Let's go for a ride. You got your keys?"

Sonny shook his head. "Some things never change. Who drove while I was gone?"

"Uh, they sent me a chauffeur." Nick grinned.

"Yeah, right," Sonny reached to his desk and picked up his keys.

Though Nick outranked his partner, he never used it to his advantage. But when they went anywhere on police business, almost always it was Sonny who would drive.

It was shortly after nine a.m. when the two detectives pulled off of the 101 freeway, turned north, and then made a right onto Desert Crest Drive. The tile-roofed, stucco-on-frame home of William and Shannon Scanlon sat at the end of a quiet cul-de-sac. They got out of the car and followed the sidewalk to the front door. Sonny pushed the doorbell. The chime brought the sound of a dog barking from inside the house. After several unanswered rings, they decided to leave. Nick reached for his business card with the intention of putting it in the door when he heard Sonny say, "Hey, Nick, the side gate is open. Maybe he's in the back yard."

Nick nodded and followed his partner along the front of the house and through the open wooden gate. They followed a sidewalk to the rear yard, and as they turned left onto a patio, they saw the naked back and shoulders of a man sitting in a hot tub. As they approached him, Sonny was the first to see the red hue of the water. He looked at his partner and pointed to the water.

Nick looked at the tinted water, and then he lifted the man's head and saw the huge gash across his throat. Just like Marti Montgomery, it was cut all the way across his throat. He shook his head and looked at Sonny. "It looks like we've got another one. He's pretty stiff. He's been here for a while."

Sonny looked at the wound. "Wow! Ear to ear, almost. Looks like it got both carotids, just like our little reporter lady."

Just then, they both heard a scratching sound at the patio door and instinctively drew their weapons. They heard a grinding sound as Nick slid the large unlocked glass door open and saw the buff-colored cocker spaniel that had been scratching to get out. "I got him," Sonny said as he grabbed the dog and held onto it.

Nick went through the house from room to room but found nothing. When he returned, Sonny was sitting on the floor, holding onto the dog with one hand and his cell phone in the other. "I called it in."

Nick nodded. "Leave the dog in here. I'll snoop around outside and see what I can find. Maybe I'll get lucky."

Being careful not to compromise the crime scene, Nick stood on the edge of the patio and let his eyes frisk the rear yard, starting on the south side on to the north side and back again. The pool was ice blue, and the block walls were lined with oleanders and yellow and violet lantana, giving it a comfortable, homey look. It reminded him of the refreshing pool the family had enjoyed when he, Cassie, and the kids all lived together. His mind wandered back as he remembered the fun he had teaching each of the girls to swim and how proud each one was when they were able to shed their swimmies. He thought when he and Sue Kim got married, perhaps he would sell his townhouse and buy a house with a pool.

Nick's thoughts were interrupted, and he was back on the job again as he heard Sonny say, "The wagon's on its way along with a CSI team."

Sonny looked out at the yard. "It seems so nice and peaceful." He looked back at the victim. "Certainly no place to die such a violent death."

Then they checked the sidewalk that ran from the patio to the front. "It looks like the perp came through the gate," Sonny commented. "He must have surprised the victim from behind."

Nick nodded. "The poor guy never had a chance." He shook his head. "The inside of the house looks untouched, so we probably can rule out robbery. I don't think that dog would scare away a burglar. We'll have the gate checked for prints."

"Where's the wife?" Sonny asked. "He's married. Her name is Shannon."

Nick shrugged. "It's Monday morning. Maybe she's at work."

Nick noticed something glimmering from the sun's rays, and he bent down to look at it. "Hey, Sonny, take a look at this."

Sonny's eyes saw what his partner was referring to. A razor knife was lying on the ground between the sidewalk and the house. Sonny bent down and examined it, being careful not to touch it. "It looks like there's blood on it. What do you think? It looks like we found the murder weapon."

Nick retrieved his Android from his belt and aimed it at the razor knife. Sonny laid a dollar bill next to the knife to show the size, and Nick snapped a picture. Just then they heard the sound of a siren blaring as a vehicle pulled up in front of the house. The detectives walked out through the still-open gate to the front of the Scanlon home. A police cruiser had arrived, and as the two uniformed officers got out, a crime scene van pulled up behind them.

Both detectives approached the vehicles. Sonny told the uniformed officers to get the street cordoned off, and Nick met the crime scene team as they got out of their SUV. There were three of them: two men and a woman. He showed them his badge and said, "The body is in the back. Be sure to dust the gate. It was already open when we got here, so we didn't touch it. Maybe you'll find some useful prints. The body is in the hot tub. The motor was off, so see if you can find prints on the switch. Either it's on a timer or somebody turned it off." The CSI nodded. "Also, don't forget to check any place the perp may have touched if he leaned down to flip the switch."

"Uh, this is not our first rodeo, Lieutenant," the CSI said politely.

Nick nodded and said, "One of you come with me." The female CSI followed Nick past the open gate and onto the sidewalk. He pointed to the razor knife still lying on the ground. "We didn't touch it, so get some pictures and process it. It could be the murder weapon." One of the CSIs came through the open gate while the other took a small brush and began dusting the gate and latch for prints. One headed for the body while the other placed a yellow plastic tent-shaped marker next to the knife, along with a ruler. He took two pictures, picked up the knife, bagged it, and tagged it for processing. They all began working the scene looking for anything that could possibly help find the perpetrator.

"We need to find the wife," Nick said.

Sonny nodded, picked up his Android and dialed. Shortly, he disconnected the call and said, "You remember the Walgreens we saw a couple of blocks from here?" Nick nodded. "It appears she works there. She's the assistant manager."

"Let's head over there," Nick answered.

The two detectives walked back up the sidewalk and saw two more police cruisers had joined their counterparts. Two officers were in the process of unrolling yellow police tape and cordoning off the area. Two others were laying out street flares and waving off anyone who attempted to enter the cul-de-sac. A small crowd was beginning to form. One of the uniformed officers came over to the detectives and said, "There's a woman insisting on coming in. She says she lives here. I checked her ID and it checks out—a Mrs. Shannon Scanlon at this address." He pointed to a woman being restrained by two policemen.

"We'll handle it," Nick stated as he and Sonny walked over to the woman. She was about five-foot-ten and wore a blue Walgreens' smock. Both detectives pulled their badges from their belts and held them up for her to see. Nick asked, "Are you Mrs. Scanlon?"

"Y-yes," she stammered. "What's happening here? Where's my husband?"

"Uhm, ma'am, I'm sorry to tell you, but there is a body in the hot tub on your patio. It appears to be your husband."

She looked at the two detectives and tried to go to the house. They both restrained her. "I want to see my husband. It's my house! You have no right!"

Nick looked into her face and said, "Ma'am, you can't go in there right now. This whole house is a crime scene." The look in her eyes was one of terror, but there were no tears. "Once the crime scene crew is finished, the body will be taken downtown to the county morgue. You can see it there. In the meantime, let's go somewhere and talk."

"I'm not going anywhere," she screamed, and again she tried to force her way past the two detectives. She shoved Sonny hard and almost knocked him over. Nick tried to grab her. He was caught by surprise as she took a swing at him and caught him on the right cheek.

Two uniformed officers came over to them. One asked, "Do you need any help, Lieutenant?"

Nick grabbed Mrs. Scanlon and turned her around and said to the officers, "Cuff her. Take her in. Hold her until we get there."

Shannon Scanlon struggled, but the officers overpowered her. They put her, screaming and kicking, in the back of their cruiser. As they pulled away, the coroner's wagon came on the scene.

Sonny looked at his partner. "Uh, it looks like she's got quite a temper."

"Ya think?" Nick held his hand to his cheek. As he pulled it away, he saw blood on his fingers.

"Let's head for Walgreens. Let's see what we can find."

Sonny grinned as he said, "Uh, there's a first aid kit in the car. Hey, we're going to Walgreens. I'll bet they have a physician's assistant on duty."

"Funny, Madison. Funny!"

CHAPTER 7

The Store

The two detectives went directly to the Walgreens where Shannon Scanlon worked. Nick walked up to the front cashier, showed his badge and said, "We would like to see the manager on duty, please."

She pointed to a man talking to a customer in the middle of one of the aisles. "That's our store manager over there."

Nick walked over to him, while Sonny went down another aisle. Nick waited until the customer walked away before he flashed his badge and said, "I'm Lieutenant Greer, Phoenix PD. I would like to speak with you about one of your associates."

"Sure. I'm Bob Price. I'm the store manager. How can I help you?"

The detective stated more than asked, "I understand Shannon Scanlon is an employee here. Is that correct?"

"Yes. She's one of our assistants. She's not here now. She works nights, mostly."

"Did she work last night?" Nick questioned.

"Yes, she did."

"What time did she get here and what time did she leave?"

"Her shift is from midnight to eight in the morning," he answered.

"Was she here the whole night? Did she leave at all?"

"Oh, no." Price shook his head. "It's company policy that there must be a manager on duty at all times."

"What about breaks or lunch?"

"Like I said, there has to be a manager present at all times. She works nights so she would be the only manager here. She wouldn't be allowed to leave the store. No way. We have a break room in the back. She'd either have to bring her lunch or buy something here, a sandwich or something. What's this all about anyway?"

"We're just checking to see where she was all night. Do your managers punch a time card or something?"

"No one punches a time card anymore. We swipe our name badges, but it amounts to the same thing. It's all on computer."

"Either way, you have a way to show what time she arrived and what time she left, correct?"

"Yes."

"I'd like to see it."

"Sure. Follow me."

The detective followed the manager to the back of the store where he pushed a code into a keypad and opened a door. He went to a computer and punched in some numbers. Soon the detective heard the sound of a printer coming to life. The manager looked at the paper and said, "She clocked in at eleven-forty-two last night. She was still here when I got in this morning a little after nine-thirty. She signed out then. See?" He handed the detective a time sheet. The name at the top read Scanlon, Shannon, and had her employee number behind it. She had clocked out at 09:39. Price added, "She stayed late this morning because I was late. My car wouldn't start."

The detective nodded. "I'll keep this if you don't mind." He folded the paper and put it in his pocket.

Just then there was a knock on the door. Nick looked through the window and could see it was Sonny, so he opened the door. Sonny came in and handed something to Nick. It was a razor knife, exactly like the one they had found on the ground at the Scanlon home.

"Mr. Price, this is my partner, Sergeant Madison." He and Sonny shook hands.

Nick looked at the packaged knife and asked, "Do you sell many of these?"

"Sporadic. Why?" Price asked.

"I'd like to see a record of all sales of these knives and anything like them within the last week; no, how about a month? Are you able to provide that?"

"I think I can," Price responded. "I'll scan the UPC code and see what the computer has to say."

Nick and Sonny stood as the manager punched some numbers into the computer. There was a wraparound counter attached to three sides of the wall that supported three computers, a printer, and several plastic bins. Price sat down and began typing. Soon the detectives heard the sound of the printer. The manager retrieved a single sheet of paper, looked at it, and handed it to Nick. "This should be what you're looking for. Now, please, can you tell me what's going on? Is Shannon in some kind of trouble?"

Nick said, "William Scanlon was found dead this morning. We have his wife in custody for questioning."

Price's eyes widened. "Wow!" He sat back down when he heard Nick's words.

"I assume the employees get a discount. Is there a way to find out if she purchased one of these?" Nick asked.

"If she used a credit or debit card, or if she used her discount, yes." Price answered. "Let me see." Nick handed him the list. Price looked at it. "There's no way to tell. There are three cash sales on the item, but none are recorded as an employee sale and her number isn't on any of them."

Sonny had been unusually quiet but finally spoke, "What can you tell us about her? How long has she been here? How well do you know her?"

"She's been at this store for about a year. She transferred from one of our Glendale stores. She works hard. She's honest. She's always on time, good with customers, and she's never given me a bit of trouble."

"Were you close? Would she confide in you if she had a problem?"

"Uh, not really. She works nights. I barely see her. When we talk it's mostly about store stuff."

"How about marital problems? Did she ever say anything about having any marital problems?" Sonny prodded.

"Not that I know of."

"Do you know anything about her husband? Have you ever met him?"

"Her husband works, excuse me, worked for one of the TV stations, but I never met him." He looked up at the ceiling, and then his eyes dropped down to the detectives. "There was one time though when I overheard a conversation between her and one of our cashiers." He paused.

"Go ahead," Nick said.

"Well, I was changing a price at the end of one of the aisles. Shannon was working the day shift at that time. I remember we were prepping for inventory. Shannon and one of our clerks were working together on the east wall. I heard the girl ask Shannon what she would do if she caught her husband with another woman. She said something about cutting his throat."

"Who said?" Nick asked.

"Shannon."

"Who was the cashier, and how can we contact her?" Sonny asked.

Price picked up the phone, dialed two numbers, and said over the intercom, "Tiffany, to the office, please."

A few seconds later, a young lady who appeared to be in her mid-twenties came into the office. Price said, "Tiffany, these are policemen, and they need to ask you some questions." The frightened look on her face caused him to say, "There's nothing to worry about. You're not in any trouble. They just want to ask you about a conversation you had, that's all."

She nodded, and Nick asked, "Tiffany, I understand you had a conversation with Shannon Scanlon about cheating. Do you remember that?"

She shook her head. "Cheating? I don't remember. What do you mean?"

"Did you ever ask her what she would do if she found her husband with another woman?"

"Oh, that kind of cheating. Yeah, I remember. That was a couple of months ago. We were facing the cosmetics wall, and somehow the conversation got around to cheating husbands. I told her if I ever found my husband cheating, I'd cut his nuts off." She giggled. "Sorry." Her face turned red with embarrassment as she realized what she had just said.

"It's okay." Nick smiled. "Keep going."

"Shannon laughed and said a gelded husband was useless, that I may as well just cut his throat while I was at it and get it over with. We both laughed. I thought it was kind of funny."

The detectives looked at each other. Sonny held up the razor knife and asked, "Did you ever see her with one of these?"

She nodded. "They're all over the place. We all have them. We cut boxes open all the time. What's going on here? Is Shannon in some sort of trouble?"

"We don't know yet. We're just checking some stuff out."

"Her husband was found dead this morning," Price stated.

Her eyes widened and her mouth flew open. When she composed herself, she asked, "Do you think Shannon did it?"

"We don't know yet, ma'am," Nick responded. "We're just checking out all angles. Thank you for your time." She looked at her boss, who nodded permission for her to leave.

"I think that's all we have," Nick said to the manager. "Thank you for your time, Mr. Price."

Almost as an afterthought, Nick asked Price, "Is there anyone still here from last night?"

"No, they've all gone home."

"We'll need a list of all those who worked with her last night. Names, addresses, and phone numbers, and when they'll be here next."

Tiffany was almost out the door, but turned as she heard their conversation. "Excuse me, but I saw Helen Chambers going back to the pharmacy just as you called me in here. She works the night shift. She might still be here."

The manager reached for the phone and paged Helen Chambers. A couple of minutes later she entered through the office door. "Helen, you love us so much you come in on your morning off."

The gray-haired lady who looked to be in her sixties smiled. "Yeah, either that or I had to pick up my husband's prescription. Take your pick."

The manager laughed and said, "These are two policemen from the Phoenix Police Department. They have a couple of questions you may be able to answer better than I."

She looked at Sonny, then at Nick, and nodded. "Go ahead."

"Shannon Scanlon worked here last night. Is that correct?"

"Yes."

"Was she here the whole night?"

"Oh, yes. She was the manager in charge."

"Did she leave the store at all?"

"Uh, she went outside for a smoke break a few times. We aren't allowed to smoke in the store." She looked at Price, who nodded.

Nick looked at the manager, who responded, "Yeah, that's okay. Some people take their breaks in the break room and some go outside. Smokers go outside for sure. There's a bench for them and a place for cigarette butts. Most all of the stores have them."

Nick looked back to Helen. "Did she go out last night?"

"Oh, yeah. I was the front cashier. She went out there three or four times, like always."

"Do you know what times or how long she was out there?" Nick asked.

"I don't remember exactly."

"How long was she gone each time?"

"Oh, only about ten minutes. Long enough to have a cigarette, I guess . . . except . . ."

"Except what?" Nick questioned.

"Well, once last night, she went out, and I don't remember seeing her come back in until about a half hour later. I asked her if everything was all right. She said she had gone out to her car to get something. I don't remember seeing her come back and go out again, but she must have."

"Did she have anything with her when she returned?"

"I didn't notice anything."

"Helen, did you have a good view of the door from where you were?" Nick asked.

"I see most people as they come in or go out, unless I'm busy ringing."

"Were you busy last night?"

"Up until a little after midnight. After that we were dead."

"What time was it when she went out and seemed to be gone a while?"

"Uh, around two, I think."

"How did she look when she came back? I mean, did there seem to be anything unusual about her? Did she look nervous or was her clothing rumpled?"

She shook her head. "Not that I noticed."

"Thank you, ma'am. We appreciate your help." She turned and left.

Nick said to the manager, "Thank you for your help, Mr. Price."

"Uhm," Price said, "I have a store to run. Should I get her schedule covered?"

Sonny looked at the man and shook his head. He almost threw the razor knife onto the counter. "For Christ's sake, her husband just died. What do you think?"

The detectives turned and began to leave the store when Sonny said to Nick, "Come with me."

Nick followed him to the other side of the store. A lady in her mid-thirties, dressed in medical garb, was waiting for them. "I'm PA Michaels. Let me take a look at that cheek, Lieutenant."

Nick looked at Sonny, who shrugged. "Hey, it's a pretty good cut. It might get infected."

The physician's assistant cleaned the wound and, as she covered it with a butterfly bandage, asked, "How did this happen? Did you have a tussle with a bad guy?"

Sonny grinned. "Uh, you might say that."

* * *

They were silent as they got into Sonny's Malibu. Finally, Sonny spoke, "Well, what do you think? Maybe she found out her hubby was pointing more than a camera at that cute little thing, and she took them both out?"

"Well, if her husband was banging the reporter, we have motive," Nick answered. "She lives close enough to her work. She could have easily slipped out, sliced his throat, and gone back within a half hour or less, so that presents opportunity. Let's see what the ME says about the time of death. If it is around two a.m., we'll book her."

"Yeah. I agree. And it would be premeditated. She's looking at murder one!" Sonny stated.

"Let's head back and see what she has to say."

CHAPTER 8

The Wife

Shannon Scanlon was sitting alone at a small table as Lieutenant Nick Greer entered the interview room. "What am I doing in here?" she yelled. "I want to see my husband! You can't hold me. I didn't do anything." Her hostile eyes pierced his. "You let me out of here right now!"

"Ma'am, you can see your husband's body when the medical examiner says you can. In the meantime, you are not going anywhere. You're being charged with assaulting a police officer—two counts!" He pointed to the butterfly bandage spanning the cut on his cheek.

"You didn't have the right not to let me see my husband. It's my house. You infringed upon my rights as an American citizen. I know my rights!"

"Ma'am, apparently you only think you do. You were impeding a murder investigation. That in itself is a felony offense. Now, do you want to talk with me now, or should I put you in a cell where you can think about it for a while?"

She lifted her handcuffed wrists and said, "Take these things off! They hurt."

Nick thought for a moment as he reflected on the temper she had displayed earlier. "Mrs. Scanlon, if I remove the handcuffs, are you going to settle down?"

She nodded. Nick walked around the table, removed the handcuffs, and tossed them onto the table. She rubbed her wrists and said, "Why are you treating me like a common criminal? My husband is dead. I need to tend to him. I need to call our son." She put both hands up to her face and covered her mouth. Her eyes widened as she exclaimed, "Oh, God! What will I say to him?"

"Where is he?"

"In Tucson. He's a freshman at the U of A."

"We'll get ahold of the school and get a chaplain out to see him. Will that help?"

"No. It needs to come from me. I am his mother. I don't want no stranger—"

"When was the last time you saw your husband?" Nick interrupted.

"Uh, last night. Before I left for work. He was at home. He was pretty broken up about the little newsgirl who was killed. I tried to talk to him, but he said he wanted to be alone. He told me not to answer the phone. He said it would just be a bunch of reporters asking questions, and he didn't want to deal with them."

"Was he close to Ms. Montgomery?"

"He was a mobile cameraman so he worked with several of the reporters. He liked them all, but he was impressed with her. He said she had the special talent to make it big."

Just then the interview room door opened, and Sonny walked in. He handed Nick a note and sat at the end of the table, between Nick and the suspect.

Nick looked at the paper and asked her, "Where were you last night between one and three a.m.?"

"I was at work. I'm the night manager at Walgreens. Why?"

"You were there all night?"

"Yes, of course. I'm the only manager on duty."

"Did you leave the store at any time?"

"Of course not. I told you I was the only manager on duty. There has to be a manager in the store at all times."

"I imagine you take breaks."

"Yes."

"Do you go outside during your breaks?"

"Of course. I'm a smoker. We aren't allowed to smoke in the store or in the break room, so I go outside during my break. It's okay. We all do it." She looked at the detective. "We're allowed to go outside and take a break. We just have to be where someone can get us if we're needed, that's all."

"Mrs. Scanlon, we understand you were seen leaving the store around two a.m. Is that correct?"

"Uh, yeah, that sounds about right."

"How long were you gone?"

"About ten minutes, I guess. Just long enough to smoke a cigarette."

"I'm confused about something. You were seen leaving at two, but you weren't seen returning until a half hour later. Can you explain that?"

"That's bullshit. I'm a smoker. I went outside to have a cigarette. I came right back in. I wasn't gone no half hour. Who told you that? Helen? That old woman has no idea what goes on. Her husband has dementia, and I think she does, too."

"Then why were you seen coming in the door a half hour later?" Nick asked.

She shook her head like she was puzzled, and then said, "Oh, yeah, I remember. I left my cell phone in the car. I went out to the parking lot to get it." She stood up as she spoke. "Now, I'm leaving."

Nick pointed to the handcuffs, still sitting in the center of the table. "Sit down, Mrs. Scanlon. You may leave if and when I say you can."

"I don't like the way you're treating me. I'm a citizen. I have rights, you know!"

"Yes, and one of those rights is to a speedy trial. We'll do our best to see that you get one."

Shannon stared at the detective as she sat back in the chair. Nick continued questioning. "How were you and your husband getting along?"

She looked down as she answered. "Fine. We got along fine. We had no problems."

Her failure to make eye contact and her body language told the detective she was either hiding something or lying, so he continued to press her. "Has your husband ever cheated on you?"

"No!" she answered sharply. "Why would you even ask such a thing?"

Sonny spoke, "Tell me, Mrs. Scanlon, if you found out he was having an affair, what would you do?"

"I don't know. This is stupid. Why would you even ask me such a thing? My husband and I got along fine! We had a good marriage."

"You didn't answer my question, Mrs. Scanlon. I'll ask you again. What would you do if you found out your husband was cheating on you?"

Her eyes widened. "I told you, I don't know!"

"Would you, say, cut his testicles off?" Sonny questioned.

"Huh?" She looked puzzled. "Every woman says she'll do that."

"Isn't it true you had a discussion with one of your associates about cheating husbands? And when she said she would castrate hers, didn't you say"—Sonny removed a notebook from his pocket and looked at it, then he looked into the eyes of his suspect—"a gelded husband is useless. You may as well just cut his throat while you're at it?"

Her face reddened. "That was a joke." She looked at Sonny, then at Nick, then back at Sonny. "What happened to Bill? How did my husband die?"

Nick looked at Sonny and back to the suspect. "Are you telling me you don't know?"

"Know what? All I know is he's dead. And I don't even know that for sure because you won't let me see him."

Suddenly her eyes widened. "Are you telling me his throat was cut? Like the girl?" Her mouth was partly open as her eyes darted back and forth between the two detectives.

Nick nodded. "Marti Montgomery was killed the same way. Her throat was cut, just like your husband's. Now, tell me, where were you Friday night around eight o'clock?"

The shock of what she had heard was still evident in her face and in her voice as she slumped in her chair. "At home. I was at home getting ready for work."

"Can anyone substantiate that?"

"Of course not. It's only Bill and I, and he was on assignment up north. Hey, wait a minute. Do you think I . . . ?" Suddenly she seemed to realize the true nature of their questions. She folded her arms as she stared at Nick and stated, "I want a lawyer!"

"I'm sure you do," Sonny said as he and his partner stood and left her in the room alone.

* * *

ADA Shelley Kisler and Deputy Chief Bruce Mannion had been watching through the two-way mirror and listening to the entire conversation. Shelley spoke first, "I don't know if she did it."

"You gotta be kidding," Nick responded.

"I was good with it until I saw the look on her face when you told her the manner of death. Either she's one hell of an actress, or she didn't know his throat was cut."

The deputy chief said, "Look, we have motive, we have means, and we have opportunity."

Sonny looked at Nick, then back at Shelley. "I'm sorry, Shelley, but I agree. Her husband was messing around, she can't really account for her time, and they sell the murder weapon at her store. She did exactly what she told her friend she would do, but she took out his lover, too. I think she's good for it."

Just then, Nick's cell phone rang. It was a text message from Sue Kim. It read: *TOD between 2–3 a.m.*

Nick showed the message to Shelley, who nodded and said, "Okay, book her. Murder one!"

CHAPTER 9

Bad News

The news stations were all over the story. Last night's regular television programming had been interrupted several times with "breaking news" bulletins and updates. Later, both the evening and nightly news broadcasts aired interviews with friends and co-workers of both victims. A collage of pictures of Marti Montgomery from childhood through her latest photo shoot was shown on Channel Four. Pictures of Bill Scanlon were also displayed, along with the booking photo of Shannon Scanlon. They tried to interview some of the Walgreens' employees, but Bob Price was able to keep them out, though a shot of the Walgreens' sign was shown on one of the newscasts. The reporter even showed which Walgreens it was by airing a camera shot of the black-on-white street signs on the corner.

As the afternoon sun snuck its way through the slats of the partially opened miniblinds and painted small stripes of light on the wall of the SIU, Nick and Sonny were finishing their reports. They would be sent off to Assistant District Attorney Shelley Kisler. It all would be in her hands soon, but both detectives would be present at the arraignment.

The rollers on Nick's chair squeaked as he pushed back from his desk and said to his partner, "Yesterday wasn't bad for your first day back."

"Yeah, they should all go that smooth. Two murders solved with one perp."

Nick's phone rang. He picked it up from his desk and answered, "SIU, Lieutenant Greer."

"Lieutenant, this is Paul Polanovich from the lab. I wanted to let you know we have the results from the alleged murder weapon on the Scanlon case."

"Yes, Paul, go ahead." Nick's senses told him by the way Polanovich emphasized the word alleged that this would not be the news he wanted to hear.

"It's not the murder weapon."

Nick grimaced when he heard the words. "What do you mean, it's not the murder weapon? We found it near the scene. It had blood on it. Are you telling me it wasn't the victim's blood on the knife?"

"Oh, it was the victim's blood all right, but it was there for at least a week, maybe longer. It's not fresh. And the only prints on it were his. There weren't any epidermal traces either. If it was used to slit his throat, especially as deep as the wound was, there would have been traces of skin, even if it was wiped off. We did find traces of insulation. Was there electrical wiring of some type near where you found the knife? My guess is he was doing something with wiring and cut himself. He probably dropped the knife and never picked it up."

Nick reached to his desk and picked up his cell phone and looked at the picture he had taken. There were a couple of traces of white on the ground. It could have been wire insulation. He shook his head. "Thanks, Paul." Nick disconnected the call.

"What's wrong, Gumby?" Sonny asked. "You look like someone just beat you with a three-pointer at the buzzer."

"The razor knife we found at the Scanlon place?"

"Yeah, what about it?"

"It's not the murder weapon. It had Scanlon's blood on it and his prints, but it was old. The lab says it wasn't the murder weapon."

"Okay," Sonny said. "It's no big deal. We have enough on her without it."

"Yeah, but I'd sure like to have the murder weapon."

"I guess we can search the house," Sonny said. "We'll probably be looking for that proverbial needle in a haystack, but, who knows, maybe we'll get lucky. We can check the dumpster behind her work, too, and don't forget her car."

"Call the Walgreens' manager and find out when they empty the container. I'll call the lab and send a team out there posthaste."

Nick was on the phone with the lab when Sonny came over to him. "Forget the dumpster divers. They picked up the trash this morning."

"Never mind," Nick said into the phone and disconnected the call. "Shit!"

"We'll have to go over the house," Sonny stated. "Tomorrow will work. I'm tired and I gotta pick up April. Her car is in the shop. I'll have Scanlon's place put on patrol. Then I'm going home."

"Yeah, me, too." Nick responded. "Tomorrow will work."

CHAPTER 10

Good News

Nick Greer had just turned into the entrance of his townhouse complex when his cell phone rang through his car speakers. The caller ID read: Cassie. He hesitated to answer it. Nick knew when his ex-wife called, it usually meant some sort of trouble, and almost always that trouble was directed at him. After a couple more rings he gave in and pushed the phone button on his steering wheel. "What do you want, Cassie?"

"Well, that's some way to greet the mother of your children! Are you in a bad mood or something?"

"I wasn't."

"I just called to give you some good news."

"That would be a change of course. What is this supposedly good news?"

"You don't have to drive up here this weekend."

Cassie had moved to Prescott a few months after their separation and had taken their three daughters with her. She moved in with her parents. She used the excuse that it was safer and there was less crime, but Nick knew the truth. He knew her mother had influenced her and being that far away would make it difficult for him to see his daughters. He had them every other weekend, spring break, and certain holidays. Cassie knew the added distance would be a strain on him, especially if he was on an important case. But Nick was bound and determined to make it work, and so far he had. Sometimes he would stay at a hotel in Prescott, and sometimes he would pick his girls up and bring them to Phoenix. This weekend he planned on driving to Prescott Friday afternoon and bringing them to Phoenix.

Several times Cassie had called at the last minute to tell him not to come because she forgot to tell him about plans, band camp, a church retreat, or something else. He figured she was doing it again, but he would go up there anyway and savor what time he had with his daughters.

"What is it this time? Why can't I see my kids? What did you forget to tell me this time, Cassie?"

"Why, nothing, Nick. I'm shocked you would say such a thing." He was about to comment, but she didn't give him a chance. "I'm coming to Phoenix for the weekend. I thought I'd bring the girls for you. They're anxious to see you and your little girlfriend."

Nick parked his car and sat there for a moment. She wants something, he thought. He knew his ex-wife hated Sue Kim. She had, more than once, tried to break them up. "Sue Kim is my fiancée, not my little girlfriend."

"Okay. Whatever!"

"When are you coming?"

"I'll drop them off at your townhouse Friday afternoon. I assume you'll be there."

"One of us will be there," he stated.

"You be there! I don't want to be alone with that woman. She might assault me again! You be there, or I'm not getting out of the car!"

The last time Cassie and Sue Kim had seen each other, it ended up with Cassie on the floor with a bloody lip. Nick smiled as he remembered it as if it were yesterday. Sue Kim, barely above five feet tall, had decked Cassie, who was much taller and at least fifty pounds heavier. A real David and Goliath moment, he thought. "Okay. Why are you coming to Phoenix?"

"I'm just going to see a friend, that's all."

"Anybody I know?"

"Maybe, maybe not." She disconnected the phone.

Nick killed the engine, got out of his car, and went into his townhouse. Sue Kim was waiting for him as he came through the door. She kissed him and said, "How was your day, baby?"

"Uh, normal stuff."

Sue Kim went to the refrigerator, pulled out a cold bottle of beer, twisted off the cap, and handed the bottle to Nick. "I just got home a little while ago. I ordered a pizza."

"Okay."

"I have some good news for you."

He took a long drink and said, "I could use some good news."

"You don't have to go to Prescott this weekend."

"I thought you said news. I already know. How did you know so soon? Cassie just called me a couple of minutes ago, and I know she sure as hell wouldn't call you."

"Kelly sent me a text. She said her mother is bringing them. The girls want me to take them to the mall."

"Uh, what about me? I'm their father, you know."

"You can come along, I guess. You can bring your debit card, and you can carry our bags." She giggled. "You can be our caddy-daddy!"

He looked into her eyes. "They love you, you know."

"They're good girls. I love them, Nick." He could see the sincerity in her eyes. "When we get married, I'll be saying 'I do' to the whole package: you, Kelly, Kasey, and Kaitlin."

"I know," he said as reached out and took her in his arms. Their kiss was long and they held each other tightly. Passion began to rise between them. Nick glanced toward the bedroom.

Suddenly the doorbell rang. "Uh, that must be the pizza guy," Sue Kim said. She looked down at the bulge in Nick's pants and giggled. "Perhaps I should get the door."

CHAPTER 11

The Search

The two detectives spent most of the morning searching through the Scanlon residence. They went over every inch, turning up chairs and sofa cushions, checking every pocket in every piece of clothing in every closet, and sifting through every drawer. After thoroughly checking the car in the garage, Nick saw a stepladder hanging on the wall. He pulled it down and moved it to the center of the garage where he climbed it and pushed back the square scuttle-hole cover in the ceiling. He coughed as he stuck his head up into the dark, dusty attic and carefully shined a bright flashlight over every inch of the insulated surface. He found nothing. The only items they removed from the home were two razor knives and an X-Acto knife that they found hanging on a pegboard in the Scanlon garage. When they returned to the SIU, Nick would send them to the lab, but he was sure they would produce nothing.

As Sonny pulled his car away from the house, Nick commented, "What a waste. I don't even know why we did that."

"No stone left unturned," Sonny answered. "Maybe she dumped the knife in the dumpster or in the store trash. Heck, she could have thrown it anywhere and we'll never find it. The crime lab didn't find anything in her car either, you know."

"Yeah, I know."

They were quiet as they drove back to the station. As they entered the elevator, Sonny remarked, "Uh, you're unusually silent."

Nick looked at his partner. "Sonny, what if she didn't?"

"Didn't what?"

"What if she didn't do it? What if she didn't kill her husband?"

"You sound like you have doubts."

Nick shrugged. "No, I'm just wondering, what if?"

"Then we'd be back to square one, I guess."

The rest of the day was spent going over the interviews and trying to make some sense out of the two killings. As Nick read the file over and over, he kept wondering if he was missing something.

That evening, Sue Kim was sitting on the living room sofa as Nick came into his townhouse. The stereo was playing in the background, and she was typing something on her laptop. He tossed his keys on the kitchen table, walked over to her, bent down and gave her a kiss. "How's my favorite fiancée?"

"Oh, I'm glad to hear I'm your favorite. Exactly how many fiancées do you have?"

"Uhhh, I'm pretty sure there's just one."

"That's right." She giggled. "How was your day?"

"Nothing special. We spent most of it finding nothing at the Scanlon house and the rest of it getting our stuff together for Shelley. The arraignment is tomorrow. This one looks like a slam dunk, except we don't have a murder weapon." He lifted his head and whiffed the air. "What's for dinner? Something smells good."

"Spaghetti. I was just waiting for you." She reached to the coffee table, picked up the remote, aimed it at the stereo and shut it off. They both went into the kitchen. Sue Kim had a salad prepared and set it on the table. She loaded two plates with pasta, ladled marinara sauce on each of them, and placed them on the table. Nick poured two glasses of wine, and they sat down.

"Yeah, I heard about the murder weapon," she said. "Is that going to be a problem?"

He shook his head. "It shouldn't be. It's so small and easy to get rid of. We have a good case, but a murder weapon always helps."

"Shelley is a good prosecutor," Sue Kim stated.

Shelley Kisler was an assistant district attorney. She, Nick, and Sonny had worked many cases together. She was good and had a respectful conviction rate.

"Yeah," Nick responded. "She doesn't like to lose. I think this one, like I said, should be a slam dunk. We got her on murder one, two counts. Jealous wife takes out her husband and his lover. Case closed! If she's smart she'll plea, and Shelley will probably spare the needle."

Nick looked at Sue Kim and said, "Boy, this sauce is good. A family recipe?"

"Uh, sort of." She giggled as she pointed to the kitchen counter. Nick smiled when he saw the Ragu label on the jar sitting next to the sink.

"So, you say Marti Montgomery was having an affair with her cameraman, and his wife found out about it and slit both of their throats in a jealous rage?" she stated more than asked.

"Yep. That's what we think."

"Are you sure?"

"Uh, yeah. We have motive, opportunity, and means. She works just a few minutes from her home, and she can't account for her whereabouts when either one of them were killed. She claims she was at home the night Montgomery was killed. The only one who could have verified that would have been her husband. I'm sure she knows the terrain at the TV station, and he probably told her the cameras were out of service, so she figured it was her chance to strike. Both Sonny and I witnessed her temper, and she's as strong as an ox." He pointed to the cut below his right eye. "She did it. I'm sure."

"Okay, I understand what you're saying, but are you really, really sure?"

"Uh, yeah." Nick squinted as he looked at her and said, "I don't think I like that look on your face. Is this the time when you tell me you know something I don't?"

"I had lunch with Carole today."

"You have lunch with her almost every Wednesday. What's that got to do with anything?"

"You know she's gay."

Carole Schmidt was Sue Kim's best friend. They had been friends since college, and they both played in the Phoenix Symphony. Nick was aware that Carole was a lesbian. "Uh, yeah; and your point?"

"So was your reporter lady."

Nick dropped his fork. With a surprised look on his face, he said, "Huh? No way!"

She continued to roll pasta onto her fork as if she had said nothing. "How do you know for sure?" he asked.

She finally looked at him. "Marti Montgomery and Carole had dated a couple of times. Your sweet little lady reporter was a confirmed lesbian. I hate to put a wrinkle in your slam-dunk case, but Carole is positive there's no way she was screwing her cameraman."

He thought for a moment as his mind processed the information it had just received. He looked at Sue Kim like an attorney would look at a jury during the final summation. "Okay, but that doesn't mean the wife didn't do it. If she thought he was cheating, she could have still done it."

He noticed a slight gleam in her eyes as she said, "Yeah, I guess. Maybe you're right. You're the big bad cop. I'm just a little CSI girl." She shrugged. "I just thought you should know, that's all."

Nick shook his head as he said, "You know, I love you, but sometimes you really piss me off."

"Hey, I'm always willing to be helpful." She giggled as she picked up her empty plate and put it in the dishwasher.

CHAPTER 12

Nemo

Lieutenant Nick Greer and Sergeant Sonny Madison walked into the outer office of Deputy Chief Bruce Mannion. During their drive into the station that morning, both detectives received a text from their boss: *Got something for you. My office. ASAP.*

Tricia greeted them as they walked in, and she nodded toward her boss's office. "The chief is waiting for you. Go on in."

"Good morning, Detectives. Have a seat," Mannion said as Nick and Sonny entered.

They both sat. Nick said, "You wanted to see us, Bruce?"

"Well, how did it go at the Scanlon place? Did you find anything?"

The lieutenant shook his head. "Nothing. Nothing at all. The place was clean. I take that back; we found a couple of razor knives, but I'm betting the lab will find them clean. You don't kill someone and hang the murder weapon on a pegboard to be found, especially something as small and as easy to get rid of as a razor knife. I think she dumped it somewhere, and we'll never find it."

"Well, what I have for you isn't going to help the case much either," Mannion said, as he shook his head and with gloved hands held up a manila envelope. He laid it in the center of his desk, retrieved a pencil from his desk drawer, and with the eraser end he removed two pieces of paper and turned them for both detectives to see. One was a clipping of yesterday morning's *Arizona Republic* newspaper's headline. It read:

Killer of Newscaster Caught

The other paper was an array of cut-out letters glued to a piece of lined, yellow tablet paper. It read:

SHE DID NOT DO IT. I DID.
NEMO

"I wanted you two to see this before I sent it out for prints, though I doubt there will be any on it. He probably wore gloves. A couple of uniforms found it on their windshield when they came back from a code seven yesterday." He turned the envelope for them to see. Glued to the front were more cut-out letters forming the words:

PHOENIX POLICE CHIEF ONLY.

"They took it directly to the chief. Once he opened it, he bagged it and gave it to me. What do you guys make of it?"

The two detectives looked at each other, then looked back to their boss. Sonny was the first to speak. "Nemo? Who the hell is Nemo? What do you think it means anyway? Maybe it's some idiot trying to screw up our case, or maybe some friend of Shannon Scanlon."

"And maybe it's the real killer," the chief responded. "It's probably a nickname or maybe a code of some kind. If he was careful enough to paste the letters, I doubt he would be dumb enough to use his real name."

"Maybe it's a code," Nick said. "*Finding Nemo* was a cartoon movie about a lost fish. My kids have it on DVD. Maybe he's saying 'You can't find me.' Maybe it's his way of taunting us. Or hers."

"Or maybe it's an acronym?" Sonny added.

"An acronym for what?" Nick asked.

Sonny shrugged. "I don't know. It was just a thought."

"You may be right, Sergeant, but I just thought of something else," Mannion said. "Did either of you ever read the book *Twenty Thousand Leagues Under The Sea*?"

Both detectives nodded. "Yeah," Nick answered. "The Jules Verne book. I read it as a kid. Wasn't Nemo the captain of Nautilus submarine?"

Mannion responded, "Yeah, perhaps this is his twisted way of stating he's in charge."

"Or her," Nick added.

"Captain Nemo was a male," the chief responded. "Nemo is a male name."

Sonny said, "You know, in Latin, Nemo means nobody or no one!"

Mannion and Greer looked at each other in surprise, then they both looked back at Sonny, who continued, "In Homer's *Odyssey*, Ulysses blinds the Cyclops, the Cyclops asks him: 'Who are you?' To which

Ulysses replies: 'Nemo.' When the Cyclops was later asked by his father, Neptune: 'Who did this to you?', he answers, 'Nobody did it.' "

The two men were still staring at Sonny. He looked back and forth between them. "What? My high school literature teacher was a Homer nut."

Mannion said, "See what you can do with it. See if anyone at the TV station went by Nemo. Maybe it's a nickname or something, you know, like Gumby." He grinned at Nick as he continued, "In the meantime, I'll send this to the lab. Who knows? Maybe we'll get lucky."

As the two detectives walked down the hall to the SIU, Nick said, "Homer? Sonny Madison studied Homer?"

"Hey, I'm not just good looking, you know. I got an intellectual side, too, Mr. Master's Degree!" Sonny grinned.

"You 'have' an intellectual side," Nick corrected his partner's grammar.

Sonny nodded. "I'm glad you agree."

They went into the Special Investigations Unit and each detective took a seat as his own desk. Sonny fired up his computer and said, "So, what do you think about Nemo? Do you think it's for real, or did someone fall out of the cuckoo's nest?"

"Maybe," answered Nick. "We'll see what the lab tells us. We'll have to check it out no matter what."

"Yeah, I know."

"There's more, Sonny."

"More what?"

Nick sighed. "You know Carole, Sue Kim's friend?"

"The lesbo?"

"She dated the first victim."

"What?"

Nick commenced to tell Sonny about last night's enlightening conversation with Sue Kim.

"No shit!" Sonny exclaimed. "Wow, that's a shocker. I don't want to be there when you tell our favorite assistant district attorney."

Nick let out a deep breath as he reached out, picked up the phone on his desk and dialed ADA Shelley Kisler's office.

"Shelley Kisler," came the answer from the other end.

"Hey, it's Nick."

"Did you find something?"

"You got a minute? We need to talk."

"Sure. What's up?"

"I'm on my way. I'll tell you when I get there."

* * *

Nick went into Shelley's office and sat in front of her desk. She read the look on his face and said, "What's wrong, Nick? You look like you just got beat by a three-pointer at the buzzer."

"What's with you and Sonny and all the basketball analogies?"

"Uh, 'tis the season." Shelley smiled. She looked at the file in front of her. "I'm going over the Scanlon file now."

"I assume you heard the razor knife we found wasn't the murder weapon used on Scanlon," Nick stated.

"Is that what you're worried about?" She almost laughed. "That's no biggie. You should have more faith in me than that. I can make a case without it. It would have helped, though. So I take it you guys didn't find anything at the Scanlon place?"

"We were there most of yesterday—nothing. I take that back. We did find a couple of razor knives and sent them to the lab, but I doubt they'll help us any."

"She probably dumped it somewhere. It's small, easy to get rid of. No problem. A first-year law student could sell that to a jury. Besides, we have a big-time motive. Shannon Scanlon found out her husband was having an affair. His mistress was much younger and a beautiful woman at that. I've seen her on TV. Hey, if I liked women in that way, I'd do her myself."

The detective looked at her as she smiled and continued, "Shannon Scanlon couldn't compete, so she took out her competition. Her husband either figured it out, or he was so distraught over his girlfriend's death that she took him out, too. Who knows, maybe she planned on taking them both out. Either way, it's a slam dunk, to use another basketball analogy."

"Yeah, well, before you start slam dunking, take a look at this." Nick had taken pictures of the Nemo envelope and letter with his cell phone. He handed it to her.

The ADA scanned through the pictures and said, "Do you think this is legit? You know there are a lot of nutcakes out there. You'll probably get more. With all the publicity this case has garnered, it's bound to shake the crazy tree."

"I don't know if it's legit or not," Nick answered. "I was certain we had the killer. I was sure she was good for it until this came, and then there's also what Sue Kim told me last night."

"Uhh, what did our young CSI tell you, pray tell?"

"Well, it kinda has to do with the motive."

The ADA leaned forward. Though her eyes said, don't you dare screw up my case, what rolled off of her tongue was, "Go ahead, Lieutenant."

"Well, we all figured the two victims were having an affair, right?"

Shelley leaned back in her chair, crossed her arms, squinted, and looked out over her black-rimmed glasses at her visitor. "Yes?"

"Well, I now think it's kind of doubtful our second victim was having an affair. Or if he was, it wasn't with Marti Montgomery."

The ADA's eyes grew bigger as she responded, "Uh, and you say this because?" Shelley leaned farther back in her chair like she was hoping to be too far away to hear what the detective was going to say next.

"Remember what you said earlier? If Marti Montgomery were gay—"

"Nick Greer! You know I'm not gay. You know I was just kidding—"

"She was!"

"Was what?"

"Gay!"

"Huh?"

"Yeah, Marti Montgomery was a lesbian."

Shelley looked at Nick. Her voice shook as she asked, "Are you sure? How the hell do you know, anyway?"

Nick let out a breath. "Sue Kim has a lesbian friend. She and Montgomery had gone out together a couple of times, I guess. She swears the girl only liked women."

"So, the rumors around the TV station were wrong." Shelley thought for a moment. "But still, what if the wife heard the rumors and thought they were true so she aced them both. I still think I can sell that to a jury as long as you think she did it and as long as nothing else gets in the way."

Just then Nick's cell phone rang. It was a text from Sue Kim. Nick looked like a balloon that had just lost all of its air as he let out a breath, pursed his lips, shook his head, looked at the ADA and said, "Uhh, it looks like you may have spoken too soon. There appears to be one more little problem."

The ADA uncrossed her arms, leaned forward, and stared at the detective in silence as she awaited the rest of his words. Nick didn't speak. He laid his Android on the desk and slid it across to Shelley. She took it and read the text from Sue Kim. She looked at the lieutenant and back to the cell phone and read the text again: *Sorry to spoil UR day, but the killer was right handed.*

Shelley looked puzzled and shook her head as she pushed the phone back to the detective and said, "Uh, soooo?"

He pointed to the cut on his right cheek. "Uh, it kinda looks like she's a leftie."

The ADA looked at the detective. He could see the disappointment on her face as she let out a loud breath and said, "Great!" She rubbed her forehead. "Goddamn it!"

"Shelley, maybe she's ambidextrous."

The ADA shook her head. "Look, I know her defense counsel. She's good. She's better than good. When she gets wind of this, and you know we'll have to include it in discovery, she'll eat it up and spit it back in my face. Now, I have my doubts it would even make it to trial, but even if it did, she'd beat the words 'circumstantial evidence' so hard into the jurors' minds, we wouldn't have a snowball's chance. Shit, there's enough doubt to at least hang a jury, if not cause a full acquittal." Her blonde hair fell down over her glasses as she said, "I'm sorry, Nick, but I'm going to need more evidence. Maybe you can find out who this Nemo character is. Until then, release her. I can refile if you find more evidence." She closed the file folder.

Nick shook his head and let out a breath. "I thought this one was too easy."

* * *

Sonny was sitting at his desk, leaning back in his chair with his hands locked behind his head, when Nick came back into the SIU. "Well, how did it go with Shelley?"

"Not good. She wants Scanlon released."

Sonny unlocked his fingers from behind his head and sat straight up in his chair. With eyes as big as golf balls he said, "What? You're kidding, right?"

"There's no murder weapon, and this Nemo thing didn't help—"

Sonny interrupted, "Nemo is probably some fucking cuckoo and the murder weapon is no biggie. We have motive and opportunity."

Sonny stood and walked over to his partner's desk. "So what if the reporter was a lesbo? If Shannon Scanlon didn't know it and she thought her husband was banging her, we still have motive. And don't forget, she works within minutes of her house, and there are conflicting accounts for her whereabouts at the time of both murders—Hello, that's opportunity!" Sonny's voice had gotten louder. He was almost yelling. "And what about what she said to her co-worker about slitting a cheating husband's throat? She's good for it, Nick." He continued, "Hey, and what about her temper? You've got proof of her rage right there." He pointed to Nick's cheek. "What's wrong with Shelley anyway? Is she so worried about her conviction record that she doesn't see a slam dunk when it's right in front of her?"

Nick handed his cell phone to Sonny. "Uhm, you need to read this."

Sonny's face turned white as he read Sue Kim's text. He looked up at Nick who was pointing to his right cheek. His face changed to red as he saw ADA Shelley Kisler standing in the doorway.

"Well, Sergeant Madison, I'm sorry to hear you have such little faith in me." Her angry red face contrasted with her blonde shoulder-length hair. "Katelynn Hensen is her attorney. Do you think for one minute she won't use all this shit to her advantage? I know you think she did it. So do I, but if we take this to trial with what we have, we'll lose and she'll go free!"

Shelley looked directly at Nick. "I just came to tell you in person that I talked with my boss. He agrees. Release her and get me something to recharge her with." She nodded toward Sonny and continued in an angry tone, "And tell your asshole partner over there to go fuck himself! Maybe you should find some duct tape and put it over his big mouth!" She turned and stormed out of the room.

"Uh, Shelley . . . I didn't mean . . ." It was too late. She had left, and she either didn't hear Sonny or she ignored him.

Sonny looked repentant as he said to Nick, "You know, I really didn't mean; about Shelley, I mean . . ."

"Yeah," Nick responded. "I know it, but she doesn't."

"I'll go talk with her," Sonny said. "I'll apologize." He began to stand up.

"If I were you, I'd wait a while until she cools down."

"I'll send her flowers."

"Don't send roses," Nick warned.

"Why not?"

"I wouldn't send her anything with thorns just in case she shoves them up your ass!"

Sonny nodded. "Point well taken." He looked at his partner and shook his head. "You know, I thought it was too easy. Do you want to tell the chief, or should I?"

"Go ahead and start the paperwork to release her. I'll tell Bruce."

As Nick turned to leave for their boss's office, he heard Sonny say, "Goddamn it! I didn't want to go back there!"

Nick stopped and turned. "Back where?"

"Square fucking one!"

* * *

Deputy Chief Bruce Mannion took it all in stride as Nick told him step by step what had transpired. He asked his detective, "What do you think? Did she do it?"

"I thought so, but I guess if I were on a jury, I couldn't vote to convict her. There's just too much reasonable doubt."

"Well then, you know what to do."

The look on Mannion's face was intense as he continued, "But first, tell your partner to fix it with ADA Kisler. We want her on our side. Tell Sonny to buy her candy, or flowers, or kiss her ass. Whatever he has to do to fix it! Tell him that's a goddamn order!"

When Nick returned to the SIU, he was surprised to see that Sonny was not at his desk. His computer was shut down. It looked like he had left for the day. Nick knew his partner was feeling bad about what he had said about Shelley. He thought about calling him, but he decided to let it rest. He knew Sonny would handle it in his own way, when the time was right.

CHAPTER 13

The Judge

The news of Shannon Scanlon's release was all over the media. Several times during the day, they interrupted their regular programming with updates. They aired interviews with Shannon Scanlon and with Katelynn Hensen, who was not a bit camera-shy. Shelley had once said Katelynn Hensen never met a camera she didn't like. The second thing she seemed to enjoy was making the police and the prosecuting attorneys look like idiots, and she didn't hold anything back in this case. Of course, she knew neither the police nor the DA's office could comment publicly on the case. She used that to her advantage as she held a press conference and spun the whole story her client's way. By the time she was finished, she had painted the police department as incompetent and the prosecutors as inadequate.

Sue Kim was at symphony practice and Nick was alone in his townhouse. He had had all he could take, so he reached for the remote and found The Phoenix Suns basketball game. He sat on the living room sofa and began going over all of his notes again, looking for some sort of angle to rearrest Shannon Scanlon. He found nothing. Suddenly, his cell phone rang. It was a text from Sonny:

(Sonny) *Talked with Shelley. We're ok.*

(Nick) *You apologized? Really?*

(Sonny) *All is well.*

What Nick didn't know was that Sonny remembered what Shelley had said about duct tape, so he had gone out to his car, opened the trunk, and retrieved a roll of duct tape.

Sonny had walked into Shelley's office and sat in front of her desk. He was perfectly silent. She'd said, without looking up, "What do you want, Sergeant? I'm busy!"

Sonny was still silent. Shelley hadn't looked up until she heard what sounded like a muffled clearing of her guest's throat. Although the ADA was still angry, she couldn't help but laugh when she had finally looked up and saw Sergeant Sonny Madison sitting there in front of her with gray duct tape over his mouth. On the tape was written in black marker: "I didn't mean it."

"I know," she had said. "I know."

* * *

Nick had been studying the paperwork and notes for so long it was becoming like a crumpled-up road map in his mind. He was about to go over them once again when his cell phone rang. The display read: Chief Mannion.

He wondered what his boss would want at this time of the evening. He answered, "Lieutenant Greer."

"Nick, where are you?" came an immediate and frantic answer from the other end.

"I'm at home, watching the game and going over the case. What's up?"

"We have another one. You and Sonny need to come. I'm already here. I'll text you both the address." There was a momentary silence. "Nick, it's Rich Cavallo."

"Uh, like in Judge Richard Cavallo?

"Exactly!"

"What? What happened?"

"I'll see you here." Mannion disconnected the call.

Nick immediately dialed Sonny.

"What's up, your Gumbyness? I just got a text from the chief. It's just an address."

"Meet me there right away. We have another one. This time it's Judge Cavallo."

"Whaa—?" The call was disconnected.

CHAPTER 14

The Scene

The entrance to the Harbor House condominium complex was in the process of being cordoned off as Lieutenant Nick Greer arrived on the scene. Police cars were parked throughout the complex and along the street. The plethora of blue and red lights pulsing from the roofs of the cruisers mixed with the flashing wigwags in their grills could have challenged any light show. Uniformed police officers were stringing yellow police tape across both entrances and exits.

The lieutenant followed the walkway until he came to a pair of elevators. Both elevators had been disabled, and the doors were wide open. A uniformed officer was standing guard in front of them. When he saw Nick coming, he pointed to the one on the right. Nick looked inside and immediately recognized the face of Judge Richard Cavallo who was lying on the elevator floor. His snow-white hair contrasted against the crimson liquid that surrounded his head. The blood pool was still liquid around the edges, and fresh blood splatters had barely stopped leaving their gravitational trails along the walls of the small cavern, telling the detective this had just happened. Bruce Mannion was squatted down next to the body when he looked up and saw his detective. He pointed to the neck of the victim. The deep gash across his entire throat confirmed what the detective had already feared.

A moment later Sergeant Sonny Madison arrived on the scene. He peered into the elevator and saw the body lying on the floor and the gash in the victim's throat. He shook his head. "You gotta be shittin' me!"

Nick was about to speak when the crime scene crew arrived. Since the space in which the body lay was so small, Nick and Sonny didn't go in. Let the CSIs do their thing, they both thought.

Bruce Mannion got up, left the elevator, and joined his detectives. It was apparent to both detectives their boss was overcome with sadness as he said, "You know, I've known Rich for over twenty years. He was a good friend." He lowered and shook his head. "I can't believe he's dead."

"He was a good judge," Sonny commented.

Nick's eyes were scanning the entire area. He looked up and down the walkway and out into the parking lot.

"If you're looking for cameras, there aren't any," Mannion stated.

"You'd think a nice place like this would have cameras all over the place."

Mannion responded, "I live here, Nick. I'm on the third floor. I'm on the HOA board. We've been talking about putting them in, but we haven't gotten it done yet. They don't want to spend the money."

Nick asked, "Who found the body?"

"The lady over there." He pointed to one of the uniformed policemen standing at the end of the walkway. He was talking to an elderly lady sitting on a folding lawn chair. "Her name is Marian Krebbs. She's a resident here."

"I'll go over and talk with her," said Nick.

The lieutenant walked over to the officer, who said, "Lieutenant, this is Mrs. Krebbs. She found the body."

Marian Krebbs looked to be in her seventies. Her short white hair framed a wrinkled face as she looked at the detective through silver-rimmed glasses. "I'm Lieutenant Greer. Are you all right, ma'am? Can we get you anything? A glass of water or something?"

She shook her head. "No, thank you. I'm fine. I'm just a little shook up, but I'll be okay."

"Can you tell me what happened?" Nick asked.

"Well, I had just gotten my mail." Her hand shook as she held up an envelope for the detective to see. "I was on my way back to my unit. I'm on the second floor. I pushed the button, and the elevator opened. That's when I saw him on the floor. I grabbed my cell phone and called nine-one-one." She pointed to the cell phone on her lap. "I take it with me wherever I go. I don't use it much. Sometimes my son or one of my grandkids call, but I have it mostly in case of an emergency."

Nick could see she was a talkative lady. "Did you see anyone else? Maybe someone leaving in a hurry or perhaps someone getting into the other elevator?"

She thought for a moment, then answered, "Now that you mention it, I saw someone going that way." She pointed to the other end of the walkway. "But I didn't see his face."

"You say 'his' face," Nick responded. "Are you sure it was a man?"

"Oh, well, I think so. It looked like a man. All I saw was his back. But he had on one of those, what do you call them? . . . Oh, yeah—hoodies."

"What color was it?"

"Uh, it was dark. Blue, I think. Yeah, blue."

"Can you describe him? How tall was he?"

She looked up at the lanky detective. "Not as tall as you."

She pointed to Bruce Mannion and Sonny Madison who were standing about twenty feet away and were talking to each other. "Uh, see those two men over there?"

Nick nodded. "Yes, ma'am."

"He was about the same height and build as the one on the right."

Nick nodded toward Bruce Mannion. "Did you see anything else, or hear anything? A car, or someone running maybe?"

"No, sir. Like I said, I was on my way back to my unit. I'm on the second floor, you know. When the elevator opened, I saw him lying there. There was blooood everywhere. I'm a retired surgical nurse. I worked at four different hospitals. In my day, I've seen my share of blood, but this—"

"I understand, ma'am." He wanted to keep her attention on the subject, but he did not want to appear rude. "I see there are two elevators next to each other. Do you remember which elevator you used when you came down from your unit?"

"The same one. The one on the right."

"Good. Now, can you tell me, how long you were gone? From the time you got out of the elevator until the time you got back, how much time would you say it took you to get your mail?"

"Well, let me see. I'd guess about twenty minutes, or maybe a half hour."

"Uh, twenty minutes to a half hour?" Nick questioned as he looked out across the parking lot and saw the mail cluster box was only about thirty yards away, next to the recreation center. "Is your mailbox there?" He pointed to the cluster. She nodded. "Did you stop somewhere in between?"

"I stopped by the rec center on my way back. I had a cup of coffee with Cori Mac. Corrine McGrady. We call her Cori Mac." She whispered as if telling a secret, "She's the complex gossip. She knows all the good stuff." She sat up straight as she crossed her arms. "I don't listen to that stuff! I make it a point to mind my own business." She smiled as she continued in a normal voice, "We talked for a bit, and then I came home."

Nick smiled. "Thank you, ma'am. Please give your contact information to the officer, in case we have any more questions."

Nick walked over to Sonny and Bruce. "Anything more?"

"Nada," Sonny responded. "The team is checking for any evidence on the sidewalk, but thus far there's nothing."

"What about foot prints?" Nick asked. "There's enough blood here. Some should have been transferred."

"Here's mine," Bruce said, as he bent down and removed his shoes. "Since I was inside, I'm sure there's blood transfer on them. You'll need them for elimination."

Sonny motioned to one of the CSIs, who handed him a clear plastic bag. As he did, they heard a voice from the elevator: "Detectives, you need to see this."

Nick walked over to the elevator. A CSI was pointing to a small piece of paper about the size of a business card. He said, "I found this under the body." Using tweezers, he held it up by the corner for the detective to see. A small amount of blood had stained the edge of the paper, but the four letters glued on it were easily visible: NEMO.

Nick motioned for Bruce and Sonny to come over. He pointed to the paper, still being held by the CSI. Mannion and Madison looked at each other, then back at the lieutenant, who looked at the CSI and said, "Bag it and tag it. See that Sue Kim gets it." The CSI nodded.

The deputy chief and his two detectives walked away in silence. By now, a small crowd had formed. It seemed as though none of the three cops wanted to be the first to speak the obvious. As they neared the parking lot, Bruce Mannion finally spoke, "Well, Detectives, it looks like we have another serial killer."

Sonny responded, "You could have gone all night without saying that!"

Nick took a deep breath, shook his head, and exhaled as he said in a forced whisper, "Yeah."

"I'm going back to my place and put on another pair of shoes," said Mannion. "Then I gotta call Helen."

"Helen?" Nick questioned.

"Helen Cavallo, Rich's wife," Mannion answered matter-of-factly.

"Oh, yeah. That's right. Where is she?" Nick asked.

"San Antonio," Bruce responded. "Her sister took ill. Cancer, I think. She flew down there to help out." He took in a deep breath and let it out. "Goddamn, what am I going to say to her?"

"What about other family? Are there any kids, siblings?" Sonny asked.

"They have three kids—all live out of state. They're scattered around the country. I think he has a sister somewhere in the Northeast. Ohio, or Pennsylvania, maybe."

Bruce Mannion's eyes appeared sad as he looked at his two detectives. "You know, I have a thirty-year-old bottle of scotch sitting in the closet in my condo. The seal has never been broken. Before I call Helen, I think I'll open it. Rich would want it that way. Would you gentlemen like to join me?"

Both detectives declined the invite. Nick said, "We'll get together and have a drink in his memory another time—after we put away the bastard who did it. We're going to question some of the residents here before we leave. Maybe we'll find something. Bruce, you go back to your condo and toast your friend. Then call his wife. We'll take it from here."

The deputy chief nodded and turned to go back to his unit. "Bruce, hold on a sec." Nick said.

Mannion stopped and turned back toward the detectives. "Yes?"

"How did you come across the body? Which way were you going?"

"I just got home. I was heading for the elevator. I came from that way." He pointed to the end of the walkway where Marian Krebbs was still sitting. "I heard her scream."

"Okay," said Nick. He turned to Sonny and said, "Let's start with the rec center. Perhaps someone there saw something."

A uniformed police officer was waiting in the Harbor House rec center as the two detectives entered. There were two ladies sitting at a table to the right side of the room. The officer said, "I'm glad to see you detectives. Those two women are giving me grief about having to stay here, especially the blonde."

"We got it," said Sonny.

As they approached the two women, the younger of the two, who looked to be about forty, stood and said, "My name is Laura Pate.

Which one of you is the officer in charge, and why are we being detained here?"

Nick held up his badge. "I'm Lieutenant Greer. This is Sergeant Madison."

"I'm sorry, ma'am," said Nick, "but there has been a murder. We need to secure the scene and talk to everyone who may have seen anything."

Her blonde bangs contrasted against her dark brown eyebrows as she shook her head. "Murder? Here? Who?" She sat back down at the table.

"Did either of you know Richard Cavallo?" Nick responded.

The older lady's eyes widened, and her mouth opened in surprise. She covered her mouth with her hand, looked at her friend, then at Nick, and exclaimed, "The judge?"

"Yes, ma'am."

"Who would want to kill the judge? He was such a nice man."

"That's what we are trying to find out."

Nick looked at his partner, who said to the younger woman, "Ma'am, can we go to another table and talk?" She nodded and followed Sonny to a table on the other side of the room.

Nick sat down across from the older lady and asked, "Ma'am, what is your name?"

"Corrine McGrady, but you can call me Cori." She appeared to be in her early sixties. She was holding onto her coffee cup with both hands. "Would you like some coffee, Detective?"

"No, thank you, Ms., excuse me, Cori. Would you be the one they call Cori Mac?"

"The one and the same!" She smiled.

"Tell me, did you see or hear anything that may help us find out who killed the judge? Did you see anyone running or maybe a car or perhaps a truck leaving the parking lot in a hurry?"

"No, sir. I've been in here playing gin with Laura most of the evening."

"I was hoping you could help me with the time of death." She looked puzzled as he continued, "I understand you know Marian Krebbs."

She nodded. "What would Marian Krebs have to do with it?"

"I understand she was in here a little while ago. I believe it happened between the time she left her condo and the time she got back. Can you tell me how long she was here and about what time she left?"

"Uh, I'd say fifteen, maybe twenty minutes. We had a cup of coffee, talked a bit and she left." Cori pointed to an empty coffee cup on the table. "She could have cleaned up after herself. There's a dishwasher right over there." She pointed toward a small kitchen in the back corner of the room. "She always does that." She shook her head. "Some people have no respect. She's a busybody, too. She knows everybody's business. And gossip—"

"Yes, ma'am," Nick interrupted. "I understand." He smiled as he remembered Marian had said the same thing about Cori Mac.

Sonny had finished his interview with Laura Pate, who had waved goodbye to Cori as she left. He shook his head as he sat down between Nick and Cori. The head shake told Nick that Sonny had found nothing.

"Okay, Cori, thank you. Is there anything else? Have you seen any strangers snooping around?"

"No, sir. Nobody."

Nick gave it one last effort. "Is there any reason you can think of that anyone might want to hurt the judge, anything at all? Think hard, Cori. This is important."

"Well . . . no. Nothing except . . . no."

"Except what?" Nick asked.

She shook her head and pursed her lips. Sonny said, "You know, I'll bet you've been here a long time."

"Seventeen years!" she said proudly. "I've been here longer than anybody! I was the first one in here after they turned this place into condos."

Sonny smiled. "I'll bet you know everybody here."

"Yep! Most of them, anyway."

"I think you were going to tell us something a moment ago, weren't you?"

"It's none of my business!" she said as she crossed her arms.

"I understand, but we really need your help," Sonny continued. "Please tell us what you were going to say. It may be nothing, but it may be important. Maybe you can help solve the case. Wouldn't that be great? You'd certainly be a hero around here."

Her eyes darted back and forth between the two detectives. She uncrossed her arms, leaned forward, and said in a whisper, "You didn't hear it from me, but I think the judge's wife was messing around."

The two detectives looked at each other and back at Cori Mac. Sonny leaned toward her and matched her whisper, "Why do you think that?"

Even though there were just the three of them in the room, she looked around as if to see whether anyone else was listening. Still speaking in a whisper, she said, "I saw them."

"Who?" Sonny asked.

"The judge's wife and that policeman. My son took me to dinner a couple of weeks ago. It was my birthday. We went to Linetti's. That's my favorite restaurant, you know. Have you ever been there?"

Sonny nodded. "Oh, yeah, several times. So tell me who you saw and what they were doing."

"I saw them all alone, back in a corner. They were having dinner and drinking wine." She crossed her arms again and sat up straight. "They were looking pretty cozy, if you ask me."

"Uh, do know the policeman's name?"

"I forget his name, but he's on the HOA board. Her name is Helen. She's a nice lady."

Nick and Sonny looked at each other and back to Cori. "Thank you, ma'am. We appreciate your time," Sonny responded. "If you want to go back to your unit, we'll have an officer escort you."

"Yes, thank you," she said as Nick motioned toward the uniformed officer at the door, who came over to them.

Cori Mac got up, took the coffee cups over to the dishwasher and put them in. Both detectives heard the humming of the machine as it started. She turned and walked toward the young police officer, put her arm in his, and, with a big smile, said, "Take me home."

As the detectives left the building, Nick said, "Uh, it kinda looks like we might have a slight problem."

"Ya think?"

CHAPTER 15

The Chief

Neither detective had slept well that night. For each, especially Nick, visions of their boss and friend, Deputy Chief Bruce Mannion, haunted their dreams. April Madison was asleep when Sonny finally got home, and though he tried not to disturb her, she felt her husband toss and turn all night.

Before they went to bed, Sue Kim had remarked to Nick that he had been unusually quiet. He dismissed her comment with, "I'm just tired, baby. It's been a long day." Though he knew Sue Kim was a professional, he didn't want to say anything that could possibly prejudice her findings. Nick had trouble falling asleep, and he woke up in the middle of the night in a cold sweat.

Sonny Madison was typing away on his keyboard. Nick Greer was reading over reports and notes, and at times consulting his computer. Both were anxiously awaiting the forensic results from the night before.

The loud slam of Sonny's drawer startled Nick. "Goddamn it! It's almost noon! They should've had something by now," Sonny exclaimed.

"It'll come, Sonny. Have patience. Did you find anything?"

"Patience, my ass! I didn't sleep last night. I kept seeing myself putting cuffs on Mannion and him looking at me and saying, 'Great career move, Madison!' This whole thing sucks! And, no, I didn't find anything. As far as I can see, there is absolutely no relationship between the first two victims and the judge, nor can I find where Bruce ever even met the first two victims."

"Look, let's go get some lunch. Maybe when we get back, we'll have some good news."

"I'm not hungry," Sonny stated as he looked back at his computer screen.

"Whoa! What's that I heard? Are my ears deceiving me, or did Sonny Madison say he's not hungry?" Nick smiled. "That's one for the newsletter."

Sonny didn't look up. His elbows were on the desk, and his head was cradled in his hands. Nick was about to go over to him when his cell phone rang. He retrieved it from his desk and looked at it. The text from Sue Kim read: *Results r in. U better come.*

Nick looked at Sonny. "It's the lab."

Sue Kim was waiting for them as they entered the crime lab. The look on her face served as advanced warning that they weren't going to like what they were about to hear. She pointed to two chairs in front of her desk and said, "Have a seat, guys."

There were three files on her desk, and as they sat, she tossed a file in front of each of them. "One for each of you," she said as she took her seat behind the desk. She waited patiently as the two detectives thumbed through the pages. After about a minute, Nick tossed his file onto the desk, leaned forward, put one elbow on the desk, and rested his chin between his thumb and index finger. He let out a long breath of which somewhere in the middle Sue Kim heard a weak, "Fuuuuck." Nick looked over to his partner, who just shook his head.

"There's no chance of a mistake?" Sonny asked.

Sue Kim shook her head. "I ran the tests myself, Sonny, twice. I'm afraid they're accurate."

Nick and Sonny stood up. "Thanks, babe," Nick said.

"Good luck," she responded.

"Yeah, we're gonna need it," said Sonny.

They returned to the Special Investigations Unit. Both detectives sat at their desks. Neither uttered a syllable. After about twenty minutes, Sonny finally spoke, "You know what we gotta do, Gumby."

"Yeah, I guess we better go."

Tricia was at her desk and greeted the detectives as they came through the door. "Well, SIU's finest. Welcome."

"Uhh," Sonny said, "we're SIU's only."

Tricia shrugged and smiled as she picked up the phone, pushed a button and said, "Detectives Greer and Madison are here to see you." She hung up the phone and said, "Go on in."

As Nick and Sonny sat in front of their boss's desk, Mannion looked at the file in Nick's hand and said, "Whatcha got for me?"

"Uh, this is a little awkward, Bruce, but, well, take a look at this." He handed the file to his boss.

Bruce Mannion read it over carefully and said, "Okay, why is it awkward?"

Nick let out a breath and said, "Well, Bruce, there are a couple of things that need to be cleared up."

Mannion leaned back in his chair. "Okay, go ahead."

"First of all, as you can see, they found a partial shoe print matching yours in size and type. It had the victim's blood on it."

"Well, yeah. I was in the elevator, remember?"

"I do, but it was found eleven feet to the west of the elevators, and then a smaller trace about sixteen feet away. You stated you came from the east side. When you took your shoes off, you went back to your place. We were wondering how the blood transfer got that far to the west."

"Uh, I don't know. I bought those shoes at Payless. They're a common-type loafer. There are probably thousands of them."

"Okay, good," said Nick. "Next, how about a hoodie? Do you own one?"

"Yeah. Actually, I have a couple of them. What are you getting at here?"

"Just doing my job. Would you want it any other way?" He didn't wait for an answer. "Bruce, what colors are your hoodies?"

"Uh, one is gray and the other one is navy blue."

"Where is it, the blue one?"

"I suppose it's at home in the closet."

"Can we go and see it? We'd like to check it for blood spatters, you know, so we can eliminate you."

The deputy chief looked at his detective. "Eliminate me? Where the hell are you going with this line of bullshit? You don't think I'm good for this, do you? Rich Cavallo was my best friend, for Christ's sake!"

"Bruce, Marian Krebbs said she saw a man fitting your height and weight and wearing a blue or black hoodie fleeing the scene just as she came to the elevator. Look at the file. Your shoes match the print on the sidewalk. Stop for a minute and put yourself on this side of the desk. Wouldn't you be asking the exact same questions? Do I think you did it? Hell, no! I know you. But I have to do my job. You've always taught us to ignore emotion and look at the facts, haven't you? That's exactly what we're doing."

The deputy chief pursed his lips and a frown appeared on his forehead as he stared at his detective for a moment. If looks could kill, the coroner would be on his way, thought Nick. Finally Bruce leaned back, took a deep breath, and said, "Yes, I did. I taught you well it seems. You have my permission to search my condo. You won't need a warrant." He reached for his keys and began to remove his house key. "But I have to ask you a question. What about motive? Why the hell would I kill one of my best friends? Have you thought about that?"

Sonny, who had been silent during the whole conversation, finally spoke, "Bruce, we kinda have one more question."

"Go ahead," Mannion said.

"Uh . . ." Sonny looked at Nick. The look on his face said go ahead. He turned to the deputy chief and asked, "What was your relationship with Helen Cavallo?"

Mannion looked surprised at the question. "Relationship? What do you mean by relationship?"

"Were you two having an affair?"

"Absolutely fucking not! How dare you—"

Sonny continued, "Okay, then help us understand why you were seen a couple of weeks ago in a quiet corner of Linetti's restaurant. You apparently were drinking wine and, as we were told, you were being cozy with Helen Cavallo."

"I see," said Mannion. "Cori Mac. Ms. Busybody." He shook his head in obvious disdain. "Next month will be, excuse me, would have been, Richard Cavallo's sixty-fifth birthday. Helen was planning a surprise party for him. She wanted me to see if I could find a couple of his friends from college. We met at Linetti's to discuss it. We had dinner. We both like wine with dinner. There was nothing cozy about it."

Nick and Sonny looked at each other. Mannion continued, "You can ask her. She'll verify it all." He looked at his detectives. "Now, Detectives, is there anything else?"

Nick shook his head. "No, I guess that's all."

Mannion tossed his key to Nick. "Here, do what you have to do. It's unit 312. The alarm code is 9876. Reset it when you leave. The closet is on the left as you go in the door. Check out anything you want. Don't fuck up my condo. Get the key back to me before I get off tonight."

The detectives left their boss's office.

The condominium complex was about a twenty-minute drive from the SIU. On the way, Sonny asked, "Do you really think Bruce is a serial killer?"

"Hell, no," Nick responded. "But we have to cover all the bases."

The east elevator was disabled, and yellow police tape was strung in an X over the door as the two detectives approached. Red stains were still soaked into the rug and blood splatters were still on the walls. An odor was beginning to form.

Nick pressed the up button on the west elevator, and the door immediately responded. They rode to the third floor. Unit 312 was the fourth unit down. Nick inserted the key, opened the door and went in. The beep from the alarm pad caught his attention. He punched in the numbers 9876, and the alarm was silenced.

Sonny had gone ahead into the living room while Nick was tending to the alarm. He stood in the center of the room with his hands on his hips and looked around. His eyes scanned the entire room from floor to ceiling.

"Here's the closet," Nick said as he opened the door. Sonny watched as Nick went through the items hanging from the rod that spanned the small closet. There was only one hoodie, a gray one. The black letters on the front said PPD. "Uh, this is all I can find here," he said.

"I'll check the bedroom," Sonny responded.

Nick and Sonny checked every closet and every drawer in the condo. They checked under the beds and in the hamper—nothing. No blue hoodie. Where was it?

Nick set the alarm, locked the door, and the two detectives left the condo and headed back to the SIU. Upon arrival, they went straight to the deputy chief's office. As they entered, Tricia nodded and pointed for them to go on in. Bruce Mannion was sitting behind his desk and looked up as they walked in.

Nick handed his boss his key. "Here ya go, Bruce. Don't worry, we didn't toss the place."

"Did you find what you were looking for? I suppose you sent it to the lab already?"

"Uh, no," Nick answered. "We couldn't find a blue hoodie, only a gray one."

"That doesn't make any sense. It should be in the closet next to . . . Oh shit! I forgot."

"Forgot what?" Nick asked.

"I forgot I threw it out a couple of months ago. I never wear them anymore. The blue one was getting pretty ratty, so I tossed it. Sorry. I didn't mean to send you on a wild goose chase."

"So you don't own a blue hoodie?"

"Guess not." Mannion smiled. "Now, if there's nothing else, Detectives, I have reports to go over."

The detectives turned and left the deputy chief's office and went back into the SIU where they both sat at their desks. "Well, what do you think?" asked Sonny.

"I told you he didn't do it," Nick responded.

"Uh, yeah, I guess," said Sonny.

"Yeah," Nick said. "What do you mean, I guess?"

Sonny looked up. "Look, Nick, I've known Bruce longer than you. He's always upheld the law. I remember once when his wife, God rest her soul, got a speeding ticket. He could have fixed it, but he didn't. I remember how pissed she was when he made her go to traffic school. But I gotta ask you, if he were a stranger, a normal citizen, would you back off so soon?"

Nick put his elbow on his desk, rested his chin on the heel of his hand, looked at Sonny, and lifted his middle finger.

Sonny grinned. "Thought so." He thought for a moment, then said, "Do you think he purposely sent us on a wild goose chase?"

"Huh?"

"Come on, Nick. You don't really think he had forgotten he tossed the hoodie, do you?" Nick shrugged. "I'll bet he sent us there to punish us."

Both detectives went back to what they had been doing. About five minutes later, the phone on Nick's desk rang. "Lieutenant Greer."

"Lieutenant, Sergeant Thomas is here. He says he needs to see you."

"Send him in." Nick hung up the phone.

About a minute later, a uniformed police officer came into the SIU. Sonny greeted him, "Hi, Chris. Welcome to our humble abode."

"Hey, Sonny," he answered. "Hi, Nick."

"So what brings you to our digs?" Nick asked.

Thomas stood with his hands on his hips and looked all around the room. "So this is the infamous SIU. With all the hoopla going around about it, I thought you'd have fancy desks and hot and cold running secretaries or something. It looks like any other squad room." Thomas looked around the room again and added, "But without anything on the walls."

"Yeah, We're still waiting on the decorator," said Sonny.

Nick said, "Yeah, the only thing I have to look at is him." He looked at Sonny.

"Wow, if I were you, I'd ask for hazardous duty pay," the officer said.

For the first time today, Nick laughed. Sonny looked at the officer and said, "I'm hurt."

"I doubt you came on a sightseeing tour," Nick said. "What's up?"

"Well, you remember the newsgirl the other night?" He didn't wait for an answer. "You had me do a couple of interviews for you."

"Yes, we have the reports," said Nick.

The officer sat down in the chair next to Greer's desk and looked back and forth between the two detectives as he spoke, "Well, as you know, I interviewed one of the producers, a Karen Pellegrini. It didn't seem to matter at the time, but I've been thinking about it. Since the cameraman was killed, I think it may be something you guys might want to know."

Sonny leaned forward in his chair. Nick said, "Go ahead."

"She mentioned that Katy McKenna was having an affair with one of the cameramen. I didn't think anything of it at the time, so I didn't put it in the report."

"Was she sure? Did she say who?" Nick questioned.

"She seemed pretty certain. I remember she said, 'They were having an affair.' Not 'I heard they were having an affair.' And no, she didn't say who. But she did say he was married."

Nick and Sonny knew Katy McKenna was married to a successful contractor. "Anything else, Chris?"

"That's all I got."

"Thanks, Officer. Good job," Nick said. Thomas left the SIU.

Nick said, "Well, buddy, it looks like we're heading back to the McKenna place."

Sonny picked up his keys and said, "Yeah, and I guess I'm driving!"

"Why mess with history?" Nick chuckled.

CHAPTER 16

The Affair

Sonny Madison brought his car to a halt in front of the residence of Katy McKenna. The two detectives got out, walked to the front door, and rang the doorbell. A white-haired man, who appeared to be in his early sixties, answered the door. "Can I help you?"

Nick removed his gold shield from his belt and held it up. "I'm Lieutenant Greer, Phoenix PD." He gestured toward Sonny and continued, "This is my partner, Sergeant Madison. We would like to speak to Katy McKenna, please."

"I'm her husband. What do you want her for?"

"It's a police matter, Mr. McKenna," Nick answered. "Is your wife here?"

"My name is Vincent Peruzzi. McKenna is my wife's professional name. She's busy right now. Once again, what do you need her for?"

"It's okay, Vince." The voice came from behind him. "You can let them in."

He reluctantly opened the door, and the detectives entered the home. "Please excuse my husband, Detectives, he was just being protective of me," Katy said. "In my business, we get a lot of people coming around. Most of them are harmless, looking for autographs; you know the type. But ever since Marti was killed, we, well, we just want to be careful, that's all. I'm sure you understand."

Peruzzi extended his hand and shook with both of the detectives and said, "Come on in. Make yourselves comfortable."

Katy led them into the living room where they all sat down. "Can I get you something? Tea? Water?"

"No, thank you, ma'am," Nick responded. "We're still following up on your colleague's death, and we had a couple additional questions for you if you don't mind."

"Sure, go ahead," she said.

Nick looked at her husband as he stood up and took a seat in the chair next to her. "Uhm, ma'am, this is kind of a private matter."

She looked at Peruzzi, then back to the detectives. Something about the look on Nick's face told her this conversation should be between her and the detectives. "Okay, let's go out on the patio." She looked back toward her husband. "It's okay, honey. We'll be fine."

She led the detectives out through the French doors to the patio where they all three sat down. Nick got straight to the point. "Ms. McKenna, what was your relationship with William Scanlon?"

"Bill Scanlon was one of our cameramen. He's been at the station for a long time."

"I'm aware of that," Nick said. "But what about your personal relationship with him?"

A look of defensiveness descended upon her face and she stiffened as she answered, "Personal? What do you mean by personal? He was a camera operator at the station."

"Yes, I understand, but were you close to him?"

"Close? Please explain close?"

"Were you sleeping with him?" Sonny jumped in.

She sat up in her chair, pursed her lips, and looked at her accuser. "Excuse me?" She paused for a moment as she glared at Sonny. "I am a married woman!"

"So was he!" The look on the detective's face and the tone of his voice was challenging. "Not a woman, but he was married," he added.

Katy's eyes widened. "How dare you! Do you know who I am?"

"Yes, ma'am, I do," Sonny responded with a pretend smile. "You are a celebrity who has been caught with her panties off and doesn't want her husband to know it." He looked into her hostile eyes and asked, "How am I doing so far?"

The look on her face was irate, and her eyes looked like they could melt an arctic iceberg as Sonny continued, "Look, we understand. That's why we asked to speak to you in private." He raised his voice just a little louder. "Now, you can continue . . ." He looked at the closed glass doors behind him, raised his voice a little more and said, "Uhm, I wonder if the glass in those doors is soundproof."

Her eyes widened as she looked through the glass and saw her husband, still sitting in the living room. "Please, I beg of you. Please, don't do this."

Sonny was unceasing as he continued pressing her. "Ms. McKenna, we have credible information that says you and Mr. Scanlon were getting it on." He raised his open palms in front of him. "Look, we're not here to judge you nor to jeopardize your marriage or your career, though that ship seems to have sailed."

The fire in her eyes looked like it wanted to turn Sonny into toast, but, knowing he was in total control, he kept pressing. "But there have been three murders, and it's our job to find out who perpetrated them. In order to do so, we need all the information we can get. Now, once again, Ms. McKenna, the truth. Were you and William Scanlon lovers?"

"Three murders?" she questioned.

"You don't know?"

"No." She shook her head. "I haven't watched the news."

"A Phoenix judge was murdered. He was killed the same way as your reporter and your cameraman. But back to my question: were you banging your cameraman?"

She was silent. Nick's face was expressionless as he motioned toward where Peruzzi was still sitting and said quietly, "I assume your husband is not aware of the late-night visits while he was out of town. That's why we wanted to speak with you privately. So, how do you want to handle this? There are two options: we can talk here, or there are plenty of private rooms at the police station."

She hung her head. The only sound was from an airliner overhead that was descending into Sky Harbor Airport from the north. "How did you know?" she asked Nick.

"It's my job. It's what I do."

"Look, I love my husband." Nick and Sonny nodded. "It just happened. I went on scene to cover the Yarnell Hill fire and the deaths of those nineteen hot shots. We were all beat. Marti was tired and went back to her motel room. Bill and I had dinner together and one thing led to another. And, well, I don't know, like I said, it just happened. It wasn't my finest hour."

"I understand," Nick said. "So how serious were things with you two?"

"We got together a few times, mostly here, like you said. Vince travels a lot." She looked into Nick's eyes. "But it was over. We agreed not to see each other anymore."

"Who broke it off?"

"I guess we kind of both did. Rumors were beginning to spread around the station. Neither one of us wanted to jeopardize our marriages or our careers, so we agreed to break it off."

"How long ago?"

"A couple of weeks ago."

"Did his wife know about you two?" Nick questioned.

"I don't think so."

"Thank you, Ms. McKenna. We appreciate your time," Nick said as he and Sonny stood. They started to leave, but Nick turned and said, "One more thing, Ms. McKenna."

"Yes?"

"Were you in love with him?"

She shook her head. "No."

"Was he in love with you?"

"I don't think so."

"Thank you. We'll see ourselves out."

They thanked Vincent Peruzzi as they left. He asked, "Is everything all right? Is Katy in some kind of trouble?"

Nick looked at Sonny who answered, "No, sir. Not with us. We just needed her to verify some stuff, that's all. Thank you for your time."

As the car began to pull away from the McKenna-Peruzzi home, Nick said, "Not with us? Good answer."

Sonny grinned. "She may have some explaining to do to her husband."

"Probably not," said Nick. "He seems clueless."

"So, you think Shannon Scanlon knew her husband was fooling around, but she had the wrong woman?"

"Possibly, but why Judge Cavallo? What would he have to do with her? I couldn't find anything to show they ever met."

"I don't know. I can't figure it out either. Maybe it's a copycat or something. By the way, Gumby, how did you know about the late-night visits?"

"I didn't, but it made sense. She did the ten o'clock news, so she probably went home around eleven. His wife worked nights. I figured Katy's husband was out of town a lot, so I took a shot."

"You hit a bull's eye."

Nick heard his cell phone ring. The caller ID read: Cassie. "Yes, Cassie. What do you want?"

"We're here."

"You're here? I wasn't expecting you for a couple of hours."

"Where are you?"

"I'm on my way back from Scottsdale. My car is at the precinct. I'll be at least forty-five minutes."

"Hold on a sec," Cassie responded.

Nick waited a moment, and a familiar voice came on the phone. "Hi, Dad."

"Hey, princess. I can't wait to see you. I'll be there as soon as I can."

"It's okay, Dad. I have a key, remember?"

"Oh, yeah." He remembered he had given his oldest daughter a key to his townhouse in case of an emergency. The alarm code was her birthday. "You remember the code?"

"Of course, Dad."

"Okay, I'll see you soon."

Sonny motioned toward the chase lights switch. "You want me to punch it?"

"No, we're fine. Kelly has a key."

The detectives arrived back at the precinct. Sonny said, "I got this, Gumby. Go see your kids. Give them a hug from their Uncle Sonny."

"Thanks, pal. See you Monday."

CHAPTER 17

A Surprise Awaits

Kaitlin, the youngest of the Greer girls, was waiting outside on the front steps when Nick arrived at his townhouse. She saw him park his car and ran to him. He picked her up, and hugged her tight. "How's my peanut?"

"I'm fine, Daddy. I was waiting for you."

"I see. That's good. Where are your sisters?"

"They're inside with Mommy."

The girls were glad to see their dad and ran to him as he came through the door. Cassie nodded at him and said, "I'm glad you could finally make it." She stood up and said, "Give me a hug, girls. I have to go. I'll see you Sunday."

"Where are you going to be staying?" Nick asked her.

"Vegas. We're leaving right away. I'm already late, thanks to you."

"We?" Nick questioned. Cassie was silent.

"Mommy has a boyfriend," Kasey whispered in a tone like she was telling a secret.

Nick looked at his ex-wife. "Good. You should get out once in a while." Cassie shook her head, smiled, and left the townhouse.

"Where's Sue Kim?" asked Kelly.

"She's still at work. She'll be home soon," Nick responded.

Nick noticed Kaitlin and Kasey were sitting on the sofa playing with what appeared to be iPads. Nick asked Kelly, "Uh, who got them the iPads? Grandpa?"

"Jeff."

Nick was puzzled. "Jeff? Who's Jeff?"

"Mom's boyfriend. He gave me one, too." She pointed to an iPad setting on the kitchen table. "Isn't it nice?"

Nick thought for a moment. Jeff? "Uh, Kelly, do you happen to know Jeff's last name?"

"Winters, I think. Yeah, Jeff Winters."

Nick pursed his lips as his mind went into rewind mode to that fateful day a little over two years ago. He had been ill and had gone home early only to find his wife in bed with another man. The man turned out to be her boss, Jeffrey Winters.

Nick had moved out the next day. He stayed with Sonny and April Madison for a few days while he found an apartment. A few months later, he'd bought the townhouse.

Cassie had been a real terror throughout the entire ordeal. She did everything she could to blame Nick for their breakup, and she fought him all the way on every little item involving the divorce. But it was the move to Prescott that caused the biggest wound to his heart.

Under the disguise of a visit to her parents' home in Prescott, Cassie had enrolled the girls in school. After doing so, she called Nick and informed him they were staying there permanently. The divorce decree stated she couldn't move them more than one hundred miles away without his permission. Though Prescott was a little over one hundred miles from Phoenix, he decided not to fight it. The kids had been through enough, and the more he and Cassie fought, the more chance there was of the girls finding out what really had happened to cause their breakup. As far as they knew, their mom and dad just didn't love each other anymore. Nick preferred to leave it that way.

Nick made the trip every other weekend. Most of the time he would stay in a hotel, but sometimes he would bring them back to Phoenix. He knew they missed their friends, especially Kelly. Sometimes, if he was on a tight schedule or working an important case, Sue Kim would drive up and bring them to back to Phoenix.

The girls took to Sue Kim right away. Kelly once said to her dad, "We girls had a talk. We like Sue Kim. We decided to keep her, so don't mess it up."

His mind fast-forwarded back to the present. Cassie had claimed it was all over between her and Jeff. Apparently not, he thought, as he looked at Kelly and asked, "Uh, how long has your mother been seeing this Jeff guy?"

"I don't know, Dad," she answered. "I think for about a year, maybe longer. It was shortly after we moved to Prescott, now that I think about it. He comes up a couple of times a month. Sometimes Mom goes to Phoenix. She thinks we don't know," she whispered as she put her index finger to her lips.

"I never saw him there."

"I think he came on the weekends you weren't there. I think Mom wanted it that way."

She saw the concerned look on her father's face and said, "Dad, it's okay. You can let go. We're okay with it. He's a nice guy. We like him." She reached out and gave him a huge hug. "But you're our dad and we love you."

"I love you, too, princess."

The door opened and Sue Kim came through the door. She almost spilled the bags she had in her arms as the younger two girls ran to her. Kelly looked at her dad and smiled. "See, everything is fine."

Nick and Kelly helped Sue Kim with the load in her arms. Kelly gave her a hug and said, "KFC, my favorite. Did you get extra crispy?"

"Just for you," Sue Kim answered.

After dinner, Kelly asked, "Dad, can I go see Brittany?"

Nick knew Brittany and Kelly had been and still were best friends. "Do you want to call her and see if she's home?"

"I already did. She's waiting for me. She said her mom will bring me home."

Nick grabbed his car keys and they headed for his car. Shortly after they pulled out of the parking lot, Kelly removed the phones from her ears. "Dad, there's something I think you should know."

"Okay, what?"

"Did you see Mom's hand? Actually her finger?" She pointed to the ring finger on her own left hand. "She forgot to take it off. She turned it inward so you couldn't see it."

"What are you talking about? Turned what inward?"

"Mom turned the diamond, or the rock, as Grandpa calls it, down so you wouldn't see it."

Nick slowed to a stop as he saw the red light in the intersection ahead. He looked at his daughter. "Uh, how long has she had it?"

"I think she's had it for about a month. She finally showed it to us last week. I think she was afraid to tell us."

"So, what do you think about that?" Nick asked as the light turned green and he stepped on the gas.

"Well, I don't know about my sisters, but I think it's all good. It's kind of weird though."

"Weird? Why weird?"

"Well, think about it. Both my mom and dad are in love—but not with each other. Both my mom and dad are engaged—that's kind of weird." She reinserted the earphones and resumed listening to her music.

Nick looked at his daughter and thought how she had grown up.

CHAPTER 18

Family Time

The Sunday morning sun was just beginning to blaze its path across the southern sky as Nick Greer sat at the table on his patio. He took a sip of coffee and opened the morning paper.

"You know, this is the twenty-first century. Most people I know get their news off of the Internet or their smartphones," Sue Kim commented as he opened the paper to the sports page. "I can already tell you they won last night." She giggled as she added, "Uh, I got that from my smartphone."

Nick looked at his little fiancée and smiled. "This is relaxing to me. I prefer the morning sun, a hot cup of coffee, and the printed version of what's going on in the world."

"How about some hot pancakes?" Sue Kim asked. "I put cinnamon in them."

"Sure," he said, "if the girls haven't scoffed them all down."

She smiled. "I'll be right back."

Nick heard a noise and saw his three daughters come through the door with their plates in their hands. As they crowded themselves at the table with him, Kasey said, "Why are you out here all by yourself, Daddy?" She pointed to Sue Kim as she backed through the door with a stack of hot cakes and a bottle of maple syrup. "Want some?"

Sue Kim went back into the kitchen and soon returned with a tray holding a pitcher of orange juice and five glasses. "I thought you'd want something to wash it down with."

They talked; they ate. Suddenly, Kelly looked at Sue Kim, then at her father and said, "Dad, we just want you to know, we talked it over, and we've decided we're gonna keep her."

"Uh, okay. . . . What about me? Can I keep her?" Nick asked.

Kelly looked at her sisters, who both smiled and nodded. "You will if you're smart," she responded.

Sue Kim looked at each of the girls, then at her fiancé, and asked, "What about me? Do I have any say in the matter?"

There was silence as they all looked at her with questioning eyes. She looked around the table at the eight eyes that were all staring at her in unison. Finally, she smiled, got up, walked around the table and kissed each of the girls on the forehead and said, “Okay, I’ve decided. I think I’ll let you keep me.” They all laughed.

A buzzing sound came from inside the townhouse. Sue Kim got up and went into the kitchen. Nick’s cell phone was setting on the counter, vibrating. She looked at the screen as she picked it up. It read: Sonny. She brought the phone to Nick and said, “It’s for you. It’s your brother from another mother.”

Nick took the Android.

(Sonny) *No luck yet. Taking a break. Talk tomorrow.*

(Nick) *Don’t you ever sleep?*

(Sonny) *Sleep is overrated. I’ll sleep when I’m dead.*

Nick shook his head. “That Sonny Madison is a workaholic.”

Sue Kim giggled. “Listen to the workaholic pot calling the workaholic kettle black!”

CHAPTER 19

Where Is Cassie?

Nick walked out onto his patio and stretched his long arms as he looked up at the dark and overcast evening sky. He checked his watch for the umpteenth time. It was eight-fifteen and Cassie had not yet shown up to pick up the kids. He had called her cell phone three times, but each time it went straight to voicemail. He was beginning to worry. There was a huge thunderstorm coming in, and he didn't want her driving back to Prescott late at night with the kids in the car, nor did he want them to miss school tomorrow. He thought it odd she didn't answer her cell phone or return his call. He decided to take a quick shower.

Sue Kim heard the sound of the doorbell. Remembering that Nick was still in the shower, she began to stand, but Kelly beat her to the door and opened it wide. The air was thick, and Sue Kim could smell the dust as it seemed to rise into battle against the raindrops that had challenged its resting place. Cassie stood in the doorway. Sue Kim said, "We've been worried. Nick called you a couple of times, but your phone went to voicemail."

Cassie's tone was sharp and venomous as she shut the door and marched into the room. "And why, pray tell, would you care?"

Sue Kim got up, opened the door and pointed outside. "That's why, pray tell! Because it's getting late, a storm is coming, and you still have to drive the girls back to Prescott." She almost slammed the door.

"Yeah, well, that's none of your business. Where's Nick?"

Sue Kim didn't want a scene with the kids there, so she paused long enough to regain her composure. "He's in the shower."

"I want to talk with him," Cassie stated.

"Like I said, he's in the shower," Sue Kim repeated.

"I have ears!" Cassie's eyes widened as she almost yelled, "Tell him I want him." She looked at the girls. "Are you ready?"

Kelly looked at her mother and said, "Well, Mom, it looks like you're in a great mood. Maybe we should stay here tonight."

Nick had just gotten out of the shower when Sue Kim came into the bedroom. "The bitch-in-the-box is here. She wants you." She rolled her eyes. "Now!"

Nick smiled as he pictured a large white box with the word bitch written on it in big red letters. Its red handle was turning, and the melodic sound of "Pop Goes The Weasel" was ringing in the air. All of a sudden, up popped Cassie with a green face and a long, black pointed hat. His smile widened as he pictured her with her arms flailing and obscenities flowing out of her mouth like a dam that had just sprung a leak.

"What are you smiling about?" Sue Kim asked.

He chuckled. "You. Bitch-in-the-box? You nailed it."

"I call 'em as I see 'em," she stated.

He hurriedly got dressed and went out into the living room. "I called you a couple of times. I left messages. Why didn't you answer? Why didn't you return my calls?"

Cassie answered, "You never called. The phone never rang!" She reached into her purse and pulled out her cell phone. When she saw the black screen, her face reddened. "Shit! I guess it was off."

Nick shook his head. Though Sue Kim never uttered a word, the combination of the smile on her face and the gleam in her eyes said it all.

The girls hugged Sue Kim, and Nick accompanied them to Cassie's car. After the girls had gotten in the car, Nick asked his ex-wife, "What the hell is going on with you, Cassie?"

"What do you mean?" she asked.

"You're really in a bitchy mood. I don't like you driving back to Prescott with the girls in the car when you're in this kind of mood. And you look fatigued, too. Perhaps they should stay here tonight. You can stay with your boss, excuse me, your boyfriend, or should I say your fiancé, and pick them up in the morning. They won't mind missing a day of school." Her hands were on the steering wheel, and he saw for the first time the sparkling ring on her finger.

Kelly said, "That's okay with me." The other two girls were in the back seat listening to their music and didn't hear the conversation.

"I'm fine. I'm not fatigued. I'm just pissed!" Cassie answered.

"Should I ask why?" Nick questioned.

She paused for a moment. "It's Jeff! All he did was gamble the whole time we were there."

"Uh, you were in Las Vegas. That's what people do there."

"Not like that! He has a problem. I know he lost a good ten grand at the blackjack tables, and then he spent the rest of the time at roulette and craps. I'll bet he dropped at least thirty grand. And if that wasn't enough, I heard him talking to his soon-to-be ex-wife. He sure was talking sweet to her."

Nick shrugged his shoulders. "I don't know what to tell you, Cassie." He grinned. "Maybe he's trying to get rid of his money before she takes it in the divorce."

"That's not funny!" She hung her head like she was looking for sympathy. Seeing none, she reached toward him like she wanted a hug, but he took a step back.

"You be careful driving to Prescott. It's starting to rain. It's coming from the south, so you should be able to stay ahead of it. Have Kelly call me as soon as you get home, so I know you're all safe."

"Yeah," she responded as she turned on the ignition, rolled up the window, and backed out of the parking spot. Nick could see the girls waving at him from the back seat as the car rolled away. He waved back and threw them a kiss.

Sue Kim had been watching the whole thing from the front window and smiled when she saw him back away from Cassie.

Later, Nick and Sue Kim were sitting in the living room. The Channel Four ten o'clock news was just coming on. He heard: "We're telling it like it is; but first, breaking news." The large red letters BREAKING NEWS rolled from left to right across the screen, and then it showed a young reporter with a microphone in his hand, standing in front of the Phoenix Police main building. Nick didn't recognize him.

The reported said, "Do we have another serial killer in our midst? According to sources inside the Phoenix Police Department, we do. They even have a name for him. They call him Nemo.

"It appears the vicious slaying of two of Channel Four's own, Action News reporter Marti Montgomery and camera operator William Scanlon, and last night's brutal killing of District Court Judge Richard Cavallo, are related. Someone who calls himself Nemo appears to be responsible.

"Originally Scanlon's wife, Shannon Scanlon, was arrested, but the charges were later dismissed. The killer is believed to wear a dark hoodie. Be on the lookout." He paused for a moment, then said, "Back to you, Clint."

The shot went back to the news desk as the anchor said, "If you have any information, call the Phoenix Hotline or Silent Witness at the numbers on your screen." A picture of Marti Montgomery and William Scanlon appeared on the screen.

"Shit!" Nick exclaimed as he aimed the remote at the television and shut it off.

Sue Kim said, "Why did you turn it off, baby?"

"It's attached to the wall; I couldn't throw it out the goddamn window!"

"Good thinking." She giggled. "Cheaper, too."

"How the hell did they find out about Nemo? That was not supposed to be public knowledge. Now we'll be getting calls and emails and false confessions up the wazoo!"

"What are you going to do?" she asked.

"I don't know. Deal with it, I guess."

Just then Nick's cell phone rang. The caller ID read: Sonny. "Yeah."

"Have you seen the news?" Sonny asked.

"Yeah."

"What the hell is going on?"

"It looks like we got a leak!" Nick answered.

"There's always a leak, but how did it get out so soon?"

"I don't know. I'll talk to you tomorrow." He disconnected and immediately his phone buzzed again. It was a text from Bruce Mannion: *My office. 8 a.m.*

He showed the text to Sue Kim, who said, "I guess he saw the news, too."

CHAPTER 20

The Leak

Tricia looked up at the detectives as they entered Deputy Chief Bruce Mannion's office. "Enter at your own risk. He's super upset about something. I wish I could offer you a hard hat, but we're fresh out."

Nick and Sonny went into their boss's office and sat down. Mannion got straight to the point. "We got a goddamn leak, and I want to know who it is!"

"Uh, okay, I guess," Nick responded.

"You guess? You guess?" The chief was borderline yelling. "Didn't you see the news last night? And this morning? It's all over the goddamn place! All the stations have it. TV, radio—we got another serial killer! That's all I heard driving in this morning. They're making us look stupid." By now he was at a full-throttle yell. "And how the fuck do they know about Nemo?"

The lieutenant shrugged. He looked at Sonny, who also shrugged but remained silent. "No clue, Bruce. We're as surprised as you."

The deputy chief pursed his lips and stared directly at his lieutenant. His piercing eyes focused on Nick's like a laser. "Find out who the goddamn leak is! There are only a few people who knew about it. I want the name of the leak, whoever he or she is!" He paused for a moment, then said, "That will be all, Detectives!"

They turned to leave, but Nick motioned for Sonny to go on ahead. Nick waited until he was sure Sonny had gone before he turned, looked at his boss, and said, "Bruce, I know you're pissed. I don't blame you. So are we. But you're just making our job harder. You need to back off and let us focus on finding the killer."

The deputy chief stood up. His face was red with anger. "Back off? Who the fuck are you to tell me to back off? I'm your boss!" He pointed to his nameplate sitting in the middle of his desk. "I created the SIU, and I can disband it with the stroke of a pen. Then, both you and Madison can go back to homicide and deal with your buddy, the drill sergeant."

Nick well understood the threat to which his boss was referring. Captain Spencer Lovett had taken over command of the homicide squad after the retirement of the previous commander. He was a highly disciplined ex-marine and a taskmaster who had it in for Sonny from the first day he met him. Nick also knew the Special Investigations Unit was the deputy chief's pet project and that he had worked long and hard to get the okay to form it. Should it disband, especially while still in its infancy, it would not look good for the deputy chief, especially since he was on the short list to replace Chief Morris, who, according to the rumor mill, was considering retirement life.

"Yes, Bruce, you're right. You are my boss. And, yes, you can disband the SIU and send us back to that asshole Lovett, but you won't. And you're still out of line, and what's more, you know it." The chief's eyes widened. He was about to speak, but Nick kept on going, "You've never before been this concerned about a leak. They happen all the time. What's really bugging you? Are you still pissed about our conversation the other day?"

Again Mannion looked like he was about to speak, but Nick didn't allow it. "We're doing our jobs, Bruce. And you know it. Tell me, should I ignore the facts just because you're my friend? Or should I not question you just because you're my boss? You didn't train me that way. Put yourself on my side of the desk, and tell me you wouldn't handle it the same way I am, and I'll shut up."

Mannion sat back down, exhaled loudly, and leaned back in his chair. Silence ruled the office as he looked around the room, then back to his detective. He closed his eyes as he shook his head and let out a breath. "Yeah. I guess you're right, Nick. I've been struggling with this whole thing. I've never been a suspect before, and I don't like it. I don't know whether to send it to Internal Affairs or not."

"First of all," Nick responded, "no one said you were a suspect. Should you become one, I'll call IA myself. And as for the leak, it didn't come from Sonny or from me, and certainly not from Sue Kim. It could have come from anywhere: the morgue, a secretary, a lab tech, or some house mouse could have overheard someone's conversation." Mannion knew house mouse was police slang for cops who worked inside the station. Nick continued, "Personally, I don't give a shit who leaked it. It's done. It's not like it's the first leak we've ever had, and it surely won't be the last. What's out is out. I'll file it under 'shit happens' and get on with it. All I want to do is catch the bastard who's slicing our citizens' throats—before he strikes again."

Nick waited a moment for a comment. Finally, it came with the trace of a smile. "I taught you well, Lieutenant."

Nick got up and left. As he walked back to the SIU, he thought, I wasn't completely forthright with Bruce; he is a person of interest.

Sonny was sitting at his desk and said in a mocking manner, "Good morning, Detectives. How is the case going? Oh, by the way, it appears we have someone with a big mouth within the department. While you're at it, see if you can find out who it is. Oh, and have a nice day."

"He's pissed."

Sonny's eyes widened as he looked up at his partner. "Uh, ya think?"

Nick grinned and changed the subject. "So, what do you think? Any ideas?"

"I don't know who the leak is and I don't give a flying—"

"No, Sonny. I could give a shit about the leak. I'm talking about the killer. Do you have any idea who our killer is?"

"I don't know, Nick. I thought for sure the wife was good for it, but now I don't know. I've searched all over the place and found absolutely nothing that would connect her or her husband to Judge Cavallo."

Nick reached into his desk and pulled out a yellow pad. "Okay, let's see what we got."

Sonny got up and went over to Nick's desk and sat in the chair beside it. "Talk to me."

"Okay," Nick said as he picked up a pen, "let's start with Shannon Scanlon." He wrote her name on the paper.

"Like I said, I've searched and searched," Sonny said, "but I found no connection to her and the judge. She's never been in court as far as I can tell. She's had a couple of speeding tickets, but nothing criminal. Nothing she would've gone before Judge Cavallo for."

Nick shook his head. "She's got quite a temper." He rubbed his cheek.

"That she does, your Gumbyness, but having a temper isn't enough to convict her." Sonny thought for a moment. "Okay, let's look at anyone who would've known about the broken security system. Someone either got lucky or knowingly took advantage of the security cameras being out."

"Uh, the station manager put out a memo to all employees about it. Everybody knew, I guess. Scanlon could have told his wife. We should keep her on the list."

"Yeah, I agree." Sonny stroked his chin. "What about Munder? He sure had opportunity. He could have sliced her and broken the window himself."

"But why? There doesn't appear to be any motive. Besides, if you had seen him puking his guts out, you would've laughed. Blood is not his thing. I would think, even if he did kill Montgomery, he wouldn't have the stomach to do it again."

"Maybe he faked it."

"Faked what?"

"Getting sick. Barfing."

"You're reaching, Madison."

Sonny shook his head as he went back to his computer, typed something, and said, "According to the info, he works three-thirty to midnight. He was working the night Scanlon was killed. There's plenty of time to get to the Scanlon place by two a.m."

"Did you find any connection to Cavallo?"

Sonny frowned as he shook his head. "No."

Nick scribbled on the pad. "Okay, I'll put him down, but I doubt he did it." He looked at Sonny. "How about Katy McKenna? What's your take on her?"

Sonny thought for a moment and rubbed his chin. "I wouldn't a hundred percent rule her out. She was really worried about her hubby finding out she was fooling around on him. Maybe Montgomery found out and was going to say something. Hey, maybe she was blackmailing her. It's obvious McKenna didn't like the kid. Maybe it wasn't jealousy at all. Hey, maybe Scanlon was in on it, too." He thought for a moment, then continued, "But she is rather small. She doesn't fit the height in the ME's report. I . . . I can't see her mustering up the strength to do it, can you?"

"Not really, but stranger things have happened." said Nick. "And how does she fit with Cavallo? Were you able to find any connection?"

"Not yet, but I'm still working on it."

"You know, we still can't completely rule out Bruce," Nick said.

"Yeah, I know. I was afraid you were gonna say that." Sonny slowly shook his head as he continued, almost whispering. "I can see a possible motive for him if he was banging the judge's wife, but what connection could he possibly have to the other two?"

"Keep looking. Let me know what you find." Nick stood and headed for the door.

"Where ya going?" Sonny asked.

"I'm going for a walk. I need to think."

* * *

As Nick walked into the crime lab, Sue Kim was sitting at her desk, reading files and entering information into a computer. "Well, good morning, Lieutenant Greer. To what do we owe the pleasure of the presence of one of our SIU's finest?"

"Uh, there's only two of us."

She giggled. "Yeah, I know."

"I don't know. I had to get out of the SIU. I need to think."

"And you thought you could think better here?" She giggled again. "I'll put you to work. Hand me that file over there on that table."

Without thinking, Nick walked across the room, took a file from the table and brought it back to her. "I guess you could always work here as an assistant." She laughed.

He sat in the chair next to her desk. "This whole case is screwy. What do you have on the judge? Is there anything different? Anything at all that may help?"

"I'm entering it into the system now. By the looks of things, I'd say it was the same perp on the first two for sure. Probably a male, about five-ten to five-eleven. The weapon looks the same. Probably a common everyday utility knife or box cutter. The attacker came from behind, did his thing and left. It was very quick."

"Could it have been a woman?"

"I suppose so, but didn't one of the witnesses say she saw a man leaving the scene of Judge Cavallo's murder?"

"She saw the perp from the back. She assumed it was a man, but it could have been a female." He thought for a moment. "Uh, you said the first two? What about the judge? Is there something different there?"

"The wound was a little different on the judge. Whoever sliced up the reporter and the cameraman was definitely right-handed, but I'm not positive about the judge."

"Annnd?"

She showed him the pictures of the three deceased victims' throats and pointed to the wounds. "The cut on the first two definitely traveled from the left side to the right, but the wound on the judge could have come from the other side."

"You sound like you're not sure."

"No, I'm not. The cut extended slightly further on the right side of the first two victims. This leads me to believe he or she inserted the weapon on the left side of the neck and pulled it across as a right-hand dominant person would if he or she reached across from behind. The judge, however, was almost the same on both sides, but the deepest part was on the right."

Nick added, "But since it was in an elevator, and it may have started the descent or stopped just as the knife was being inserted, the actual line could have been a little different. Or perhaps he was attacked from the front."

"Exactly!" As she nodded, her long black hair fell over her left shoulder and covered her name badge causing Nick to remember the first time he had seen her. It was in the morgue, and, just as today, her hair had fallen over her shoulder, but that day he had brushed the hair from the name tag in order to see who she was. She's just as beautiful as the first day I saw her, he thought.

His trance was broken when he heard her say, "Hey, Detective, are you with me here?"

His attention snapped back to the present. "Oh, yeah, I was just thinking about what you said," he lied. "It's safe to assume the perp was in the elevator with the judge. He probably was waiting for him, or entered at the same time and rode down with him. Who knows, they may have even known each other."

"Yeah, and it's only one floor, so he would've had to have struck quick," Sue Kim added.

"So if you had to bet, what would you say?"

She thought for a moment and looked at the pictures again. "I don't know, Nick. I really don't know. If I had to bet, I'd say left, but I couldn't swear to it."

He looked at Sue Kim. "Got anything else?" The look on his face said, give me something, anything. "What about footprints?"

"Just what I already told you."

"Anything on the Nemo paper?"

"Nemo was glued to a cut piece of ordinary, white printing paper. The perp used normal glue like you can buy in any Walmart. There were no prints and no DNA."

"He probably wore gloves," Nick said as his cell phone buzzed. The text was from Sonny: *Got something.*

Nick didn't say a word as he immediately jumped up and hurried back to the SIU.

* * *

He was barely through the door when he said, "Whatcha got?"

Sonny looked up at his partner. "I couldn't find anything connecting any of the victims or any of the suspects to Judge Cavallo, however"—he grinned as he looked at Nick like a kid who had just brought home a report card with all A's—"it appears the judge and our ex-anchor's husband have a bit of history."

Nick grabbed the chair next to Sonny's desk and stretched his lanky frame to get an optimal view of the computer screen. "Talk to me."

"Well, it seems a few months ago there was a massive lawsuit against Peruzzi Construction for breach of contract. The completion time was four months' late, and the cost overruns were staggering. He blamed the property owner and they blamed him. He lost. It cost him over a million and a half."

"Who was the plaintiff?"

"The city of Phoenix. Peruzzi Construction was the general contractor on terminal four at Phoenix Sky Harbor Airport," Sonny said.

"Oh, yeah. I remember that. It was all over the news."

"Uh-huh, and guess who the judge was."

"Uh, Richard Cavallo?"

"Yep. You're smarter than you look, college boy." Sonny grinned.

"So, are you thinking what I'm thinking?" Nick asked.

"Uh, it depends on what you're thinking. Impress me. Tell me what's going on way up there in that belfry of yours."

"Okay, Peruzzi found out his wife was spending more than just camera time with Scanlon. Then he finds out she's losing her job to Montgomery, so he decides to take them both out. First he does Montgomery, then Scanlon. He sees we arrested the wrong person and has an attack of conscience, so he comes up with the Nemo thing. He has a vendetta for the judge so he adds him to the list, figuring what's one more. This time he leaves his calling card."

"Yeah, sure. That's what I was thinking, I guess."

"Think about it, Sonny. We have motive. Now we need to find out where he was when each vic was killed. What do you say we go for a ride?"

"I know," Sonny said as he shut down his computer and grabbed his keys, "I'm driving!"

* * *

For the third time, Lieutenant Nick Greer found himself ringing the doorbell of the McKenna-Peruzzi residence. Vincent Peruzzi answered the door and said, "What do you want now? Why can't you cops leave my wife alone?"

"We're not here to see your wife, sir," Nick said. "We have some questions for you. May we come in?"

"I guess so. What's this about anyway?"

They sat in the living room, and Nick got straight to the point. "Mr. Peruzzi, where were you last Saturday evening, let's say between six and eight?"

"I was in Tucson. I have a project down there, and I was checking on it. I was there the whole weekend. Why do you ask?"

"When did you go there?"

"Thursday afternoon."

"When did you come back?"

"I got home Sunday afternoon around three o'clock. Why?"

The detective ignored the question. "Where were you Sunday night?"

"Here. Right here. Why are you asking me these questions?"

Again, Nick ignored his question. "Mr. Peruzzi, how well did you know Marti Montgomery?"

"I didn't. I've seen her on TV, but I never met her."

"How about William Scanlon?"

"What about him? I never met him either." He looked at the detective. "I don't like this line of questioning. What the hell is this all about? Do I need a lawyer?"

"This is America; everybody needs a lawyer," Sonny said as he took over the questioning. "Mr. Peruzzi, do you recognize the name Richard Cavallo?"

Peruzzi's lips pursed and his brows furled. Sonny continued, "I'll give you a hint. He's the judge who presided over your little disagreement with the city."

"Yeah, I know who the son of a bitch is! He cost me almost two million dollars after court costs and attorney fees."

"He's dead," Sonny stated.

"Yeah, I know. I saw on the news that someone aced him. Good. They should give the person a medal!"

Nick saw the fire beginning to ignite in his partner's eyes. He looked at Peruzzi and said, "Richard Cavallo was a well-respected judge and a personal friend of mine—"

"And mine," Sonny interrupted. "So I'd be careful what I say if I were you."

Nick took over. "Where were you Wednesday, around six p.m.?"

"He was right here with me." The familiar voice was Katy McKenna. She came into the room and sat beside her husband. Her eyes showed signs of recent tears. "He hasn't left the house since Sunday." She reached for his hand. He seemed reluctant to take hers, but he did. "It's okay. He knows. I told him everything after you left yesterday. We're working things out." She looked at him as she spoke. Both detectives thought by the look on his face, combined with his body language, that he didn't appear as eager to work things out as she did.

"Is there anyone else who can collaborate that you were here all night?" Nick asked.

Peruzzi stood up. "This is absurd! You're acting like I'm a suspect." The look in his eyes was challenging as he looked at Nick. "Am I a suspect, Lieutenant? Are you here to arrest me?"

"We're here to ask you questions, sir. That's all for the present," Nick responded.

"You're goddamn right, that's all," he yelled. "You're done asking either one of us questions! Please leave! If you ever come back here, you'd better have a fucking warrant! I know my rights. My brother is a lawyer!"

"You have my condolences," Sonny retorted. The detectives got up and left the home.

On the way back, Sonny noticed a trace of a smile on Nick's face. "What do you look so happy about, Gumby?"

"You. I was just thinking about what you said."

"Uhh, like what?"

"You have my condolences! I thought it was funny. Appropriate, but funny."

"Yeah, remind me to send him a sympathy card on his brother's birthday!"

"Do you think he's good for the murders?" Nick asked.

"I don't know. When we get back, I'll check his credit cards. He could have easily driven back up from Tucson and gone back. It's only a little over an hour. There was plenty of time to come up here, whack the girl, and drive back. But if he did, maybe it wasn't on one tank of gas. Did you see that gas-guzzler in their driveway?"

Nick remembered the Chevy Silverado one-ton crew cab that was parked in their driveway and nodded. "Yep. I sure do." He added, "Don't forget to check with the hotel. See if they know anything about his comings and goings."

"Of course!" Sonny said. "This isn't my first rodeo, you know."

"I'm sorry. I know you know what you're doing."

"Do you believe her?" Sonny asked.

"Who?"

"Katy McKenna. When she said he never left the house, did you believe her?"

"I don't know," Nick responded. "Right now, she's in deep shit with her husband. Did you see them when they held hands?"

"Yeah, he looked like he didn't want to touch her."

"I think she'd say or do almost anything to save her fractured marriage."

That night, a little after nine o'clock, Nick received a text from Sonny. It only contained two words: *Peruzzi lied!*

CHAPTER 21

Double Image

Sonny Madison was already typing away at his computer when Nick Greer walked into the SIU. "Happy Tuesday, your Gumbyness."

Nick tossed his car keys on his desk and laid his Android beside them. "Whatcha got? Your text said Peruzzi lied! What were you doing last night anyway? Don't you ever sleep, watch television, get laid or something?"

"Yeah, I do most of that stuff, some more than I used to, some not so much anymore."

"Uh, I think I'm sorry I asked."

"Yeah, when you're married as long as—"

"Now I know I'm sorry I asked!" Nick interrupted. "What did Peruzzi lie about?"

"I couldn't get this case out of my mind, so I just kept digging. Take a look at this."

Nick got up and walked over to his partner's desk. Sonny handed him a printout of a credit card report. Nick read it and said, "Good work, Sonny. I guess we ought to pick him up—for questioning, at least." He thought for a moment and added, "You know, he was not very happy with us the last time. Do you think we have enough for a warrant? I'll give Shelley a call."

"I'm way ahead of the Great Gumby. Shelley is waiting for us in the chief's office."

As they entered the outer office of Deputy Chief Bruce Mannion, Tricia waved them on, pointed to the open door to her right, and said, "I believe they're waiting for you."

The chief and Assistant District Attorney Shelley Kisler were waiting for them as they walked in. "Have a seat, Detectives," Mannion said. "I just read the report." He pointed to Shelley. "She's going over it now."

Shelley raised her hand in acknowledgment, but her eyes never left the page as she continued reading the document in her hand. Sonny had been thorough in his outline of the evidence against Vincent Peruzzi. The detectives sat and waited as she turned the pages. Finally, without looking up, she broke the silence. "The credit card receipt shows he bought gas at the Quick Trip three miles from his home at eleven-thirty-three the night of the first murder. Your statement says he claimed he was in Tucson the whole time."

"Yeah," Sonny said. "It kinda looks like he lied a bit."

Shelley said, "We looked pretty stupid when we arrested the Scanlon woman and then had to let her go. I don't want that to happen again. We need to be sure we have the right perp this time." She looked at the detectives. "Convince me."

Nick spoke first, "Okay, let's start with motive. Peruzzi's wife was being pushed out of her job and out of the limelight by Marti Montgomery. Next, we have opportunity. Peruzzi was in town, and the fact that he lied about it doesn't help him at all. Why would he lie unless he was hiding something?"

Sonny added, "I think Peruzzi knew his wife was fu . . . , excuse me, having an affair with the second victim."

Shelley smiled for the first time. "I've heard the word before, Sergeant."

Sonny continued, "He admitted he was in town when Scanlon was sliced."

Shelley said, "According to your report, his wife said he never left the house."

"Uh, like she would be the first wife ever to alibi her husband? And don't forget, she was already in deep shit with him for banging the cameraman."

Mannion added, "Your report says he emphatically stated his disdain for Judge Cavallo."

He looked at Sonny, who nodded, and said "Oh, yeah! The arrogant son of a bitch said the judge's killer should get a medal. I felt like knocking him on his pompous ass right there in his own home."

"Your restraint is admirable," said Shelley. "I'd have scratched his eyes out. Richard Cavallo was a good man and a damn good judge."

Sonny looked at Shelley, then at Mannion. "Okay, here's what I think. Peruzzi wanted to take out Scanlon. When he found out about Montgomery taking his wife's job, he figured why not kill them both? He probably figured the cops would be looking for a stalker or someone at the station. When the security system went out, McKenna probably told him, and he figured it was the perfect time to strike. He could've easily gotten into the parking garage. He may have even used his wife's car. He probably arranged the trip to Tucson for an alibi. Then he went to the Scanlon place, found him lounging in the hot tub, and he became victim number two."

Mannion said, "Then he took out Judge Cavallo?"

Sonny nodded. "Yeah. I don't know if he was a part of the original plan or an afterthought."

Nick said, "He came up with the Nemo thing to keep us thinking there was a serial killer. Either he had an attack of conscience when he heard the Scanlon woman was arrested, or he wasn't finished with his vendettas and still wanted to take out the judge who had cost him two mill. Who knows? Maybe there's more."

"What about the security guard's sliced tires?" Shelley asked.

"I don't know." Nick shrugged. "I'd imagine Peruzzi had some knowledge of the station's operations; after all, his wife was a big celebrity there for a long time. Maybe he somehow knew Cardinale was scheduled, and maybe he just got lucky. Maybe someone else sliced the tires. I don't think that's a biggie." He looked at the ADA. "What do you think, Shelley? Can you work with what we have?"

"I'd feel better if you could put him near the Cardinale place when the tires were cut, or at least prove he knew about the schedules or where Cardinale lived."

"Look, Shelley, he fits the height, weight, and build of the man our witness saw leave the Cavallo scene," Mannion said.

She closed the folder and said, "Okay, pick him up. Let's hear what he's got to say."

Mannion said, "I'll call for the warrant."

"By the way, Shelley, do you know any lawyers named Peruzzi?" Nick asked. "He says his brother is a lawyer."

"The only one I know by that name is a junior partner with Fisher and Tannehill. I've been up against him before—not impressed."

"Just thought I'd ask."

The two detectives got up and left the chief's office. As they walked back to the SIU, Sonny said, "Uh, let me guess, I'm driving." Nick grinned.

* * *

They arrived at the Peruzzi-McKenna residence, and, once again, Nick rang the doorbell. Katy McKenna came to the door, partly opened it, and asked, “What do you want this time? I’m busy. I really don’t want to talk to you right now.”

She started to close the door, but Nick said, “Ms. McKenna, we’re not here for you. Is your husband here? We’d like to speak with him.”

Sonny held up the warrant. “He said we would need one of these if we wanted to talk to him again, so we decided to accommodate him.” He grinned. “It’s official, see?” He pointed to the signature line. “It’s signed by a judge and everything.”

A look of worry descended upon her face as she said, “Uh, he’s not here.”

“Where is he?” Nick asked.

“He’s at his office, I guess. What do you want him for anyway?”

“Ma’am, can we come in for a moment? Perhaps we should talk.”

Katy paused for a moment. “Okay, I guess.” She opened the door all the way.

Nick and Sonny followed her into the living room, and they all sat down. Nick began the conversation, “Ms. McKenna, we wanted to double check on something, if that’s all right.” He didn’t give her a chance to object as he continued, “You stated previously that your husband was here all day and all night the Sunday before last.”

She nodded. “That is correct.”

Nick pressed on, “Are you one hundred percent sure? Is there any possibility he could have gotten up during the night and left?”

“I’m a light sleeper, Lieutenant. If he even got out of bed to go to the bathroom, I would’ve known it. What’s this all about? Are you thinking my husband committed murder? You gotta be out of your mind! Please leave immediately.”

The detectives got up and left the home.

* * *

It was about thirty minutes later when Sonny parked his car in front of the office building that housed Peruzzi Construction. He and Nick entered through a set of large glass doors and took the elevator to the fourth floor. They were greeted by a young lady. “May I help you, gentlemen?”

Nick said, as he and Sonny displayed their badges, "We'd like to see Vincent Peruzzi. Is he here?"

She didn't look at all surprised as she pointed to her right and said, "The second office on the right."

The door was open and the two detectives entered. Vincent Peruzzi was sitting behind a large oak desk. Another man was standing beside him. Nick assumed it was his brother as the black wavy hair, larger than average noses, and the eyes were identical. If not for the mustache on the attorney, one couldn't tell them apart. He was not surprised to see the brother there as he figured Katy would have gone straight to the phone and warned her husband after the detectives left her home, but he was surprised to see they were twins. The brother spoke first, "I'm Victor Peruzzi. Please tell me why you have been hassling my client, and why you are here."

Nick and Sonny looked at each other. Nick said, as he handed the barrister the warrant, "We're taking him in for questioning, Counselor. Please step aside."

The attorney looked at the warrant and stepped out of the way. Sonny went behind the desk. The suspect bent over as Sonny frisked him, cuffed him, and said, "Vincent Peruzzi, you have the right to remain silent. Anything you say can, and will be used against you in a court of law. You have the right to an attorney. If you cannot afford an attorney, one will be appointed for you at no charge, or you can use your brother here. Maybe he'll give you a family discount. Do you understand these rights?"

"We got it," replied Victor. "What is he being charged with exactly?"

Sonny looked at Nick, grinned, and said as he ushered the suspect away, "Having a lawyer for a brother."

"I'll meet you there," Victor said to his brother. "Don't worry about anything. Don't say a word until I get there. It'll all be fine. You'll be home for dinner."

CHAPTER 22

The Story

Lieutenant Nick Greer, Sergeant Sonny Madison, Deputy Chief Bruce Mannion, and Assistant District Attorney Shelley Kisler were standing outside the interview room as Victor Peruzzi approached. He nodded to the ADA. "Ms. Kisler."

She nodded back. "Counselor. We've been waiting for you."

He looked through the one-way glass window and saw his brother sitting there alone at the table. Shelley handed him a folder. He glanced through it and said, "This is a bunch of crap!"

"We don't think so," Sonny said as he opened the door. Nick and Victor Peruzzi followed him into the interview room.

The suspect's handcuffs had been removed, and he seemed fairly confident as he sat at the gray table. The two detectives sat across from the suspect, and Victor sat down next to his brother. He began the conversation, "What exactly are you charging my client with?"

Nick looked at the lawyer. "How does murder sound?" He looked at the suspect. "But first, we have some questions. Mr. Peruzzi, you stated the other day when we spoke to you at your home that you left for Tucson Thursday and you didn't return until Sunday. Is that correct?"

"Yes, that is what I said."

"Do you want to change that statement?"

"No."

"Then how do you explain this?" He handed a copy of the gas receipt from that Saturday night to the attorney.

Victor's eyes widened as he read the date, time, and location of the purchase, which were all highlighted in yellow. He looked at the detective as if the information meant nothing. "My client has no comment at this time." He handed the paper to his brother, who looked at it and handed it back.

Vincent put his elbows on the table, leaned forward and hung his head. He let out a deep breath and said, "I can explain."

"Oh, I'm sure you can," Sonny said as he leaned back in his chair and crossed his arms. "Let's hear it."

The two brothers whispered back and forth into each other's ears. Finally Victor said, "You don't have to say anything. This is nothing. I'll get it thrown out."

"Uh, yeah?" Sonny said. "It certainly does mean something. It means your brother lied to us about where he was when a murder was committed. And as far as getting it thrown out, good luck at that. We got a warrant for his credit card records. Do you wanna see it?"

He looked at the suspect. "The only thing that's getting thrown anywhere is you—thrown into a cell a lot smaller than that nice big home you have in Scottsdale. You know, I'll bet your closets are bigger than your cell is gonna be. And the food? That's not so good either, is it, Nick?"

Nick answered, "Oh, come on, Sergeant. I'll bet he'll get used to green bologna sandwiches after a while. They say it's not so bad once you get used to it." They all knew he was referring to the green bologna sandwiches served to the inmates at the well-known Tent City jail in Phoenix.

Sonny looked at the suspect. "And I'll bet you're gonna miss that beautiful view from your patio." He grinned. "But I'm sure you'll get used to fences and razor wire. Some say they're not so bad after a while."

Vincent said, "Okay! Okay! I was in town. I lied."

Sonny looked at Nick. "Did you hear that, Lieutenant? The man said he lied. Oh, I'm shocked." He looked at the suspect. "Tell us something we don't know. Like, oh, how about why you lied."

The suspect hung his head for a moment, then he looked at his brother, who nodded. He looked at the detectives and said, "I was watching the house."

"Uh, you were watching your house?" Nick asked.

"Yes."

"Why?"

"I thought my wife was seeing someone. I told her I wouldn't be back until Sunday. I knew she didn't do Saturday night newscasts, so I set it up. I drove back up from Tucson, and I sat there all evening. She even called me on my cell while I was sitting there. She talked about getting replaced by Marti Montgomery. She was pretty distraught. We talked for about twenty minutes when she said she was tired and she wanted to go to bed.

"I figured that was it. He was coming. So I sat there and watched the house, but no one came, and she never left. The lights went out around eleven-thirty. I sat there until a little after midnight. Then I left. I stopped at the QT, got gas and a cup of coffee, then drove back to Tucson."

"Wow! That's a pretty good story. And I suppose you expect us to believe you," Sonny said.

"It's the truth."

The attorney said, "If that's all, we'll be leaving now." He began to stand.

"Sit down, Counselor. We'll tell you when we're finished," Nick said. He looked at the suspect. "Where were you between six and seven Wednesday evening?"

"I was in a meeting."

"What meeting?"

"Knights of Columbus."

"Where?"

"At my church."

"What time did it start?"

"The meeting starts at seven o'clock, but I got there at six-thirty. I helped set up."

"Help set up?" Nick questioned.

"I'm the Deputy Grand Knight."

Sonny said to Nick, "That's next in line to the Grand-Poobah Knight."

Vincent Peruzzi said, "Look, there were about thirty other people there who can vouch for me."

"What church?" Sonny asked.

"St. John's, Scottsdale."

Nick asked, "How do we know you didn't leave during the meeting? With all those people there, you could have snuck out and come back."

Victor spoke, "Obviously, the lieutenant has never been to a Knights of Columbus meeting. My brother is a chair officer. He never left the room from the time the ceremony started—seven o'clock—until it was over a little after eight-thirty. I was there the whole time. I saw him and so did about thirty other people. I guarantee you we can prove he never left his chair."

The door opened. The deputy chief said, "Detectives, can I see you for a moment?"

"Excuse us," Nick said as he and Sonny got up and left the room.

Shelley had been listening and watching through the one-way glass. She looked at Nick and at Sonny and said, "Thirty witnesses would be hard to dispute, and it would be a stretch to kill the judge and make it to St. John's by six-thirty. With no traffic and hitting all green lights, it's still at least a twenty-minute drive."

"A stretch? Yes, but not impossible. Maybe he drove fast," Sonny said.

Shelley lowered her head and her blue eyes stared at Sonny over her black-rimmed glasses. She shook her head. "And I suppose you think I can sell that to a jury. His brother isn't very good, but even a first-year law student could overcome that."

Sonny was about to speak when a uniformed officer came up to them. "I'm sorry to bother you," she said, "but I was told to give you this." She handed Shelley a folded paper. "Oh, by the way," she added, "by any chance, would your suspect be the husband of Katy McKenna, the Channel Four newscaster?"

Shelley nodded her head. "Why?"

"She's outside. She wants to see him."

Bruce said to the officer, "Keep his identity under wraps. I don't want a bunch of reporters to deal with, not right now." He thought for a moment and added, "And put Ms. McKenna some place private. I don't want anyone seeing her here either."

"I'll put her in interview room two," the officer responded.

Shelley handed the paper to Nick. "It's a warrant to search his home, car, and business. We've got crews on the way now. Let me know what you find. You got your twenty-four." They all knew what she meant. Statutes allow for a suspect to be held up to twenty-four hours without filing charges.

Nick and Sonny went back into the interview room. Nick tossed the warrant onto the table as they sat down. The attorney read the warrant and looked at Nick. "You gotta be kidding me. You're really going to push this? Are you that hard up for a suspect?"

Nick was confident in his response. "Your client had both motive and opportunity. Marti Montgomery was replacing his wife in a high-profile job. His wife was having an affair with the second victim, and Judge Cavallo cost him millions. He even admitted he hated the guy."

Vincent Peruzzi looked up and leaned forward. His eyes widened, and his face became as white as snow. He looked at Nick. "Are you saying the person my wife was seeing was Bill Scanlon?"

A look of shock descended upon the face of each of the detectives as they looked at each other. Nick was the first to recover. "Uh, are saying you didn't know who it was?"

"No. She wouldn't tell me. And I didn't really want to know, I guess. I thought it was Rick."

"Rick? Rick who?" Nick questioned.

"Rick Janetic. He used to be her producer until he moved to Los Angeles. He came back here about six months ago." He looked over to his brother. "That's when things started to get different between Katy and me." He looked back and forth between the detectives and said, "Scanlon has got to be at least fifteen years younger than Katy." He looked at Nick. "Are you sure?"

Nick and Sonny were silent as they got up and went out into the hall. The look on Shelley's face told the detectives she was not sure. "Either he's not our perp or he's a damned good actor," she said. "Let me know what the search teams come up with—a dark hoodie with blood on it would be nice." She turned and walked away.

The deputy chief spoke, "We got twenty-four hours, actually less than twenty-two now. I'll send him to holding."

Nick said to his partner, "Sonny, ride herd on the search teams."

"What are you going to do?" Sonny asked.

"I'm going across the hall!"

Katy McKenna was sitting at the table in the interview room when Nick walked in. "Ms. McKenna, I'm sorry we had to put you in this room, but due to your notoriety, we thought it would be best for you not to be seen."

"I understand," she responded. "Thank you for that. Can I see my husband now?"

Nick ignored the question and said, "I need to ask you a couple questions, if that's okay."

"Questions? Don't you think you've asked us enough questions? Don't you think you've caused enough damage to my marriage?"

He thought, You've caused your own damage by sleeping around. "It involves Rick Janetic."

"Rick? What does he have to do with anything?"

"How well do you know him?"

"Quite well. He was my producer for several years until he moved to LA."

"I understand he's back in town."

"Yes. He came back a few months ago."

"Were you having an affair with him?"

She shook her head. "Lieutenant, Rick and I are friends, that's all. I know you may think I'm a loose woman, but I have been true to my husband, except for what I did with Bill. I'm not proud of it and I wish I hadn't. All I want to do is take my husband home so we can try to salvage our marriage. Please, Lieutenant, can I see him now?"

"I'm sorry, but he's being held for a while until we sort things out."

"Held? On what? Sort what out?" she asked.

"We're holding him under suspicion of murder."

Tears began rolling down her cheeks as she stated, "Vincent didn't murder anyone. He was in Tucson when Marti was killed, and he was with me when Bill was killed. Why are you doing this, Lieutenant?"

Though Nick considered telling her to ask her husband where he was that Saturday night, he thought better of it. Instead, he said, "Ms. McKenna, it's my job. I'm thinking you probably should go home. When the news channels get wind of this, you're going to be busy. You're going to be the subject of the news instead of reporting on it." Nick liked Katy McKenna. He felt a little sorry for her and said in almost a whisper, "Ms. McKenna, I think it's best for you to go home. Prepare yourself for what's coming." He turned and left the room.

* * *

Nick was right in his assessment of the media. All the stations covered it on the evening and nightly news. The headlines read: Husband of Channel Four News Anchor Held as Person of Interest in Slayings.

He and Sue Kim were watching the Channel Four news as they aired interviews with one of Peruzzi's neighbors. One of the reporters did a field report and showed the sign on the Peruzzi Construction office door. She ended her report by saying, "Katy McKenna was not available for comment."

Nick shook his head. “Reporters! They’re like some sharks. What are they called? Oh, yeah, the sand tiger shark. They eat their own species.”

Sue Kim added, “Do you know where the word shark came from?”

“Enlighten me.”

“It’s German for greedy parasite.”

Nick smiled. “Works for me!”

Nick’s cell phone buzzed. He picked it up and Sue Kim watched his face turn white as he read the text. “What’s wrong, baby? Are the girls okay?”

He looked at Sue Kim. The look in his eyes told her something was terribly wrong. He couldn’t speak. His hand shook as he handed the Android to her. She read the text from Deputy Chief Bruce Mannion addressed to both Nick and Sonny: *Another one. Joshua Tree Apartments. It’s ADA Shelley Kisler.*

A stunned Sue Kim stared at her fiancé. They could see the shock of disbelief in each other’s eyes. “I’m coming with you,” she said as she hurriedly grabbed her forensics kit. They ran to his car. He fired up the engine and hit the chase lights. Sue Kim pulled her seat belt as tight as she could as the Ford Taurus shot like a laser through the streets of Phoenix.

CHAPTER 23

Shelley

The tires on Nick Greer's Taurus squealed he turned into the parking lot of The Joshua Tree apartments. He felt his heart flutter when he saw an ambulance sitting in front of the building entrance. Parked next to it was Sonny Madison's car. He killed the engine, got out of the car and ran full throttle toward the ambulance. Sue Kim was at his heels as he flashed his badge to a uniformed police officer, who pointed to three cops standing and talking to each other. Two of them were uniformed police officers; the other was Sonny Madison dressed in shorts and tennis shoes.

Sonny saw his partner approach and said, "She's in the laundry room. The medics are with her."

"She's still alive?" Nick questioned.

"Yes. She's still alive. It looks like the attacker was scared away by one of the tenants. He also happened to be a paramedic, and he got to her right away."

As Sonny spoke, two paramedics came out of the building pushing a gurney. A third one was walking alongside and holding an IV in the air. As they were about to lift her into the ambulance, Nick stopped them for a moment. He looked at Shelley and reached out and took her hand. "You're gonna be okay, Shelley. You're gonna be okay. Did you see who did this?"

Her eyes were barely open, and she looked like she was trying to speak. Nick lightly squeezed her hand, bent down, and put his ear as close to her lips as he could. He could barely make out what she said as she whispered, "Po . . . lo." She let out a breath and closed her eyes. He felt her hand go limp.

"We have to go, sir," one of the EMT's said, and they quickly loaded their patient into the ambulance and closed the doors. Moisture came into the detective's eyes as he watched the red and blue lights from the ambulance disappear from the complex. He continued to stand there, and a tear rolled down one cheek as he listened to the siren fade away.

Nick wiped his cheek with his finger and regained his composure before he walked back over to his partner, who was talking with one of the uniformed first responders. He looked at Sonny's bare legs.

"Hey, I didn't have time to change," Sonny stated.

"Does anybody know what happened? Were there any witnesses?" Nick asked.

"We don't know much yet, but it looks like one of the tenants went into the laundry room and caught the perp in the act. I guess he spooked him, and the attacker took off. Fortunately, he's a paramedic and he knew what to do. From what I understand, he saw her throat was bleeding profusely. I guess he grabbed a T-shirt, pressed it onto the wound, and called nine-one-one. I heard one of the EMTs say he probably saved her life."

"Where is he?" Nick asked.

"In the ambulance. He went with them."

"Where? What hospital?"

"Banner Thunderbird is the closest trauma center."

"Sonny, do your thing here. I'm going to Thunderbird. Meet me there when you're finished."

"Keep me posted. Let me know if she . . ." Sonny hung his head.

Nick nodded. "I will."

Sue Kim followed Nick back to the car. They got in and Nick fired up the engine, pulled out into the street, and hit the chase lights. On the way to the hospital, Nick asked, "What are her chances? Do you think she'll survive? I mean, if her throat is cut, can she make it?"

"It depends. If both carotids aren't severed and she hasn't lost too much blood, there's a chance. As long as they can keep oxygen flowing to the vital organs and prevent hypovolemic shock, she might make it. If the guy who came upon them hadn't been a medic, she'd probably already be dead. That's the only thing that might save her."

"Are you saying she might not make it?"

Sue Kim didn't answer as they pulled off of Thunderbird Road and into the Banner Thunderbird Medical Center.

As Nick pulled into the hospital parking lot, he saw the red and white ambulance parked in front of the emergency room entrance. Its dual rear doors were still open. Nick drove straight to a spot reserved for police and pulled into it. Holding hands, they ran together across the asphalt to the emergency entrance. The doors opened automatically and they hurried through them. Nick saw a nurse coming out of a room, and he flashed his badge as he approached her. "The ambulance outside . . . they just brought a woman in. Where is she? How is she?"

The nurse replied, "The doctors are working on her now. They just ordered an operating room."

"Is she going to be all right?"

"I don't know, sir, but the fact that she's here is in her favor."

Nick's eyes scanned the room. "Where are the paramedics who brought her in? I need to speak with one of them."

Just then, one of the paramedics came through the door. It was the man they had seen walking with the gurney. Nick said, "Sir, I need with speak with you."

He looked at Nick and said, "In a minute. I've got something I gotta take care of first."

Nick held up his badge. "Now! Unless it's life-threatening."

"Uh, yeah, it kind of is. I really gotta piss!"

Sue Kim giggled as the man turned, hurried down the hall and went into the restroom. She looked at Nick and giggled again. "Uh, I guess that could be considered life-threatening at times."

A few minutes later, the man came out of the restroom and walked up to Nick. "Okay, how can I help you, Officer?"

"It's Lieutenant. Lieutenant Nick Greer, and this is CSI Sue Kim Lee."

He extended his hand, shook with Nick, and nodded toward Sue Kim. "Ms. Lee," he said, "I'm Ed Kramer." He reached out and shook her hand, then looked at the lieutenant. "What can I do for you?"

Sue Kim said, "I'll be back. I need to use the ladies' room."

Kramer smiled. "Maybe it's something in the air." He watched her as she walked down the hallway, then turned to Nick. "Wow, she's a fine-looking chick. Is she seeing anyone?"

"Yeah, kind of. She's engaged."

"There's one lucky guy hittin' that," Kramer commented. "Fine-looking stuff."

Nick glared at the man. "That lucky guy would be me."

Kramer saw the look on Nick's face and said, "Oops!"

Nick changed the subject. "Thank you for your quick response. I understand you saved Shelley."

"It's no big thing. I'm an EMT. It was lucky I was there, that's all."

"Can you tell me what happened?"

"Sure. I went into the laundry room. I had a load to wash. As I walked in, I saw a man with his back to me, and he was doing something to the lady. I didn't know what, but it didn't look good, so I said, 'Is everything okay?' The guy turned and that's when I saw the razor knife in his hand. He let her go and she fell to the floor. He knocked me over as he ran out. My first reaction was to chase after him, but I saw the blood gushing from her neck. I knew he had cut an artery, so I grabbed a T-shirt, pressed it onto the wound with one hand, and grabbed my cell phone with the other and called nine-one-one. Thank God, they got there fast. Otherwise, she wouldn't have made it."

"So, she's going to make it?" Nick asked.

"I'm not a doctor, but I think I got the bleeding slowed down enough to give her a fighting chance at least. The cut didn't look real deep. I think I got there just in time. Do you know who she is?"

"Yeah, I do. She's an assistant district attorney. Did you get a look at the attacker?"

"You know, it all moved pretty quick, but I'd say he was white, about five-ten, maybe one hundred sixtyish pounds. Mustache."

"How was he dressed?"

"He wore dark glasses, rather large ones, and a white ball cap pulled down low."

"Was he wearing anything else, like maybe a hoodie?"

Kramer closed his eyes like he was reliving the incident in his mind. He opened them, shook his head, and said, "No, sir, he had on a blue polo shirt and jeans. That's all I can remember."

"How about his hair? What color was his hair?"

"Uh, brown, I think."

"How about his face? Did you see his face? Were there any marks? Could you ID him?"

"I'm sorry, Lieutenant, but I only saw him for a split second, and like I said, the hat was pretty low. He knocked me on my ass as he took off, and I couldn't see much from the floor."

The detective noticed he was rubbing his left wrist. "Are you okay?"

"Yeah. I think I may have jammed my wrist, but it's nothing to worry about."

"Think you could identify the attacker if you saw him again?"

He thought for a moment. "I don't know for sure if I could pick him out of a lineup, if that's what you're asking."

Sue Kim joined them and said to Kramer, "I just talked with one of the EMTs. She said it looks like you got there just in time. You saved her life. You're a hero."

"It was just luck. I was off shift. As you probably figured, I'm an EMT." He looked at Nick. "You know, I think I've seen you before. Weren't you on a case a couple of months ago where we pulled a guy from a pool? I remember it because the guy's finger was missing."

"Yeah, probably. You have a good memory."

"Uh, it's not hard to remember someone as tall as you."

Nick said, "I need your contact information." He reached into his shirt pocket for a pen, but it was empty. Sue Kim opened her purse and pulled out a pen and a small notepad. She handed them to the EMT, who took them and wrote his name and contact information and handed it to Nick.

"Here ya go."

"Thank you," Nick said.

"Let me know how she turns out," Kramer said. "I'm gonna head back. I still have laundry to do, and I may need to wrap my wrist."

"You'll have to wait on the laundry. You won't be able to get in there. It's still a crime scene and will be for a while."

"That's right. Is there any chance I can have my clothes? Perhaps I can at least take them to a laundromat."

"Maybe. When you get back there, see Sergeant Madison. It's his call." Nick thought for a moment. "By the way, do you need a ride?"

"No." He pointed to the two EMTs standing by the door. "My friends are waiting to take me back."

Nick and Sue Kim went into the waiting room and sat down. Nick took turns pacing and sitting. A short while later, Deputy Chief Mannion came in. "How is she? I was in Gilbert when the call came in, and then there was an accident on the freeway."

Nick brought his chief up to date on the situation. "I hope she got a good look at him," Mannion said.

Sue Kim pointed to a door that had just opened, and Nick turned around. A man in green hospital scrubs came through it. "Are you the detective?"

Nick showed his badge. "Lieutenant Nick Greer, PPD. How is she?"

"The left external carotid was cut, but, fortunately, it was not completely severed. We were able to repair it. She's in recovery. She'll be in ICU for a couple of days, at least. We'll see what happens from there, but I think she'll make a full recovery."

"When can I see her? I need to talk with her," Nick said.

"She's resting right now, Lieutenant. We should be moving her out of post-op in about an hour. You can see her once she wakes up, but only for a very short time."

"Thank you, Doctor."

"Don't thank me. Thank that paramedic. If it weren't for him, I would never have seen her."

Nick was about to speak when Sonny came through the emergency room doors. "How is she?"

"She just got out of surgery. It looks like she's gonna make it," Nick answered.

"Thank God!" Sonny said.

"Thank Kramer. He saved her life."

"Yeah, him, too," Sonny replied. "Have you talked to her at all?"

"I'll try in a little while. She's still in recovery. What did you find out at the apartment?"

"No one saw anyone go into the laundry room, or come out. A couple of people heard tires squealing right about the time it happened. It probably was the perp booking out, so I don't think he lives there. One resident said he was almost hit by a pickup as he was coming into the complex."

"Did he get a description?" Nick asked.

"Uh, white, that's it."

"White . . . the pickup or the driver?"

"Both."

"I don't suppose he saw the driver long enough to get a description, or anyone got a plate, even a partial?"

"You don't suppose correctly."

"Shit." Nick shook his head.

A nurse came up to them and said, "I was told to let you know as soon as Ms. Kisler was awake."

Nick responded, "Good. Can we talk with her?"

She nodded. "Yes, but please be brief. She's been through a lot, and she'll be in and out for a little while."

They all got up and headed for the recovery room. The nurse held both of her hands up in front of her—palms out. "Hold on, everybody! You can't all go in there. Just one of you."

They all looked around at each other as if to decide who should go. When they looked back, Nick was gone.

Shelley Kisler was lying in a small hospital bed. The left side of her throat was covered with a white bandage. An intravenous line was running down into her arm, and a tube was running down her throat. A nurse, who was busy reading a printout from a monitoring machine on the other side of the bed, heard Nick come in and looked up. "Can I help you, sir?"

He showed her his badge and asked, "Can she talk?"

"She's asleep, but I think when she—"

Just then, Shelley slowly opened her eyes.

"Hey, Shelley. Welcome back." He gently took hold of her hand. "Are you able to talk?"

The nurse said, "No, sir. She has an endotracheal tube in her. She won't be able to talk for a while."

"She can nod her head, right?"

"Gently."

He looked closely at the patient and asked, "Shelley, do you have any idea who attacked you?"

She barely shook her head. She looked like she was trying to speak, but couldn't. She closed her eyes.

The nurse said, "Like I said, she'll be in and out for a couple more hours, I suppose. I think that's enough for now. She needs to rest."

Nick turned and went back out into the waiting room.

The first one to speak was Sonny. "How is she?"

"She's sleeping. She'll be okay, I think. She's pretty tired. I don't think she saw her attacker. He probably came from behind—total surprise."

"Just like the others," Sonny added.

Nick thought for a moment, then said, "Before she was put into the ambulance, I think she was trying to tell me something. She said the word or words, 'po . . . lo'. I think she meant polo, but I don't know of any polo fields around here, do you?"

"Yeah," Sonny said. "The Arizona Polo Club in Scottsdale."

"Oh, yeah, that's right. I wonder what she was trying to say. Maybe she knows him. Perhaps he is a polo player, or maybe he works at the polo club. We should check it out."

They heard a giggle, and they all looked at Sue Kim.

"Uh, what's so funny?" Sonny asked.

She said, "What a typical male response! And I thought you two were supposed to be super cops."

The detectives looked at her in silence as if they were waiting for a news bulletin to flash across a television screen. Confidence emitted from her as she stated, "I don't think Shelley was talking about horses, divots, or chukkers."

Sonny bowed to her. "Enlighten us, oh little one."

"I'll bet her attacker wore Polo cologne. His face would've been right next to her. She probably could smell it on him."

The two detectives and Chief Mannion looked back and forth at each other. Mannion shrugged and said, "Makes sense."

Sonny said, "Great! Now we got it. Case closed! Let's get an APB out on a white male driving a white pickup. He's wearing a blue shirt, a white hat, maybe sunglasses, and Polo cologne." He looked at Mannion. "Goddamn, Chief, let's stop all the white pickups in town and smell the drivers!"

The fire from Sue Kim's eyes could have ignited an inferno. She was a proud woman and didn't take kindly to being made fun of.

Nick had witnessed her ire in the past. He remembered seeing his ex-wife lying on her parents' patio floor, bleeding from a right cross that Sue Kim had landed perfectly. Cassie would now think twice about ridiculing this little lady.

Sonny looked at her and grinned in a way that only he could. "You know I'm just messin' with ya, little one."

She calmed down immediately. There was something about the way Sonny called her little one that made her feel good. Perhaps it had something to do with her childhood. She remembered her father used to say to her almost every morning, "*Oyahou! Chiisana ohimesama!*" In English it meant: good morning, little princess. Maybe that was why. Besides, she knew Sonny and understood how he approached life. Some people thought he was a smartass, but she knew him well enough to know he was just being Sonny.

She held up a fist and smiled. "Do you want a knuckle sandwich, Detective Sonny?"

He grinned again. "On rye, and hold the pickles."

Mannion shook his head and smiled. "You guys find this guy. I don't care what you gotta do. Find the bastard!"

Nick said, "You know, Bruce, once he finds out she's alive, he may be back."

"I'll put a twenty-four on Shelley. I'll see you in the morning."

Nick looked at his boss. "Uh, Chief, what about Vincent Peruzzi? I'm thinking it would've been kind of hard for him to have attacked Shelley from lockup."

"Shit!" Mannion replied as he rubbed both sides of his graying temples. "You're right." He looked at Sonny and asked, "Did your team find anything at the Peruzzi place?"

"No. His office was clean, too."

Mannion took a deep breath and let it out. "It looks like we gotta let him go." He shook his head and let out another breath. "I'll make the call." As he reached for his cell phone, he shook his head and sighed again. "We don't just have egg on our faces—we're swimming in it!"

CHAPTER 24

Clink, Clank, Cassie

The door of the SIU opened, and the two detectives looked up. It was Rick Yeager. He had worked along wtih Nick and Sonny in the homicide unit before they formed the Special Investigations Unit. "Hey, Rick, happy hump day. To what do we owe the pleasure?" Sonny asked. "How are you and the drill sergeant getting along? Has he got you guys spit shining your shoes yet?"

Yeager knew what Sonny meant by "drill sergeant." Captain Spencer Lovett had become the homicide commander a few months ago. He was a real bulldog: an ex-marine who ran his unit like a boot camp. "He hasn't changed," Yeager responded. "He's still a prick. I try to stay away from him as much as possible."

He looked at Nick. "Hey, Nick."

"Hey, Rick. What brings you to our little corner of the world?"

"Uhm, Nick this isn't a social call." The look on his face was serious.

"Okay. What's up?"

"I figured I should let you know, uhh, . . . we're bringing in your ex-wife. A unit picked her up in Prescott this morning. They should be arriving any time now."

Nick was silent for a moment as he looked at his visitor. "Cassie? You picked up Cassie? For what? What the hell could homicide possibly want with my ex-wife?"

Again, there was momentary silence. "Nick, she's being brought in for questioning in a homicide."

"Homicide? Who? Where? When?"

"Nick, do you recognize the name Jeffrey Winters?"

"Uh, yeah, I do. He's supposedly going to marry Cassie. What's going on? What does he have to do with it?"

"He doesn't have much to do with anything anymore. I'm sure you heard about the body that was found in a motel room off of I-17 yesterday?"

Nick nodded. "Yeah. I saw something about it, but I didn't pay much attention to it. This Nemo case, and what happened to Shelley, you know."

"By the way, how is Shelley?"

"We're going to see her today. She's in ICU, but they say she'll make a full recovery. So what about Jeffrey Winters?"

"Jeffrey Winters was the victim," Yeager responded.

"No shit?" Nick didn't like Jeff Winters. He didn't know whether to smile, or to be sad for Cassie. He once again remembered the day he'd gone home and found them in bed together. "What happened?"

"It looks like somebody busted his skull with a lamp!"

"Okay, so what's Cassie got to do with it?"

"Uh, sorry to tell you, buddy, but she's our prime suspect."

Sonny had been listening and said, "You gotta be shitting me! Cassie Greer? Murder? Huh-uh. Insult a Walmart greeter, yeah, but murder, no fucking way."

"Sonny's right," Nick added. "Cassie has a mouth on her that sometimes gets out of control, but she isn't capable of murder. So tell me, what's this about Jeff Winters? How the hell do you figure my ex-wife is involved?"

Yeager took a breath and exhaled. "The body of Jeffrey Winters was found in a motel room that was paid for with a credit card belonging to Cassandra Greer."

"Goddamn!" Sonny exclaimed. "That's it, Judge. It was her credit card. She did it. Guilty!"

Both Nick and Detective Yeager looked at Sonny, who grinned. "Uh, I'm just saying."

Yeager continued, "Witnesses heard her and Winters arguing. A couple from Indiana was in the room next door and heard them; well, they said they heard the woman yelling. I guess it got pretty loud. They said they saw a woman fitting Cassie's description leave the motel room in a huff, then get into a car and take off fast. As one of them said, she was as 'mad as a hornet.' They remembered her plate number."

Nick nodded. He knew Cassie had special plates—CASMAR1, for Cassandra Marie. "Go ahead. I'm listening."

"Well, a couple of hours later, one of the maids opened the door and saw the body. She screamed and they called nine-one-one. We found the victim with the side of his head bashed in and a broken lamp on the floor. There was blood on the lamp, and it matched the victim." He looked at Nick, then to Sonny, then back to Nick. "I'm sorry, but Cassie's prints were on the lamp."

Nick knew Cassie had a real estate license; thus, her prints were in the system.

"I'm sorry, Nick, but this is a cut and dried case." The detective handed Nick a file. "Here, see for yourself." He sat next to Nick's desk.

Nick sat down and began reading. The man and woman's statements matched. Cassie's fingerprints matched those on the broken lamp. Nick recognized Cassie's signature on the credit card receipt.

He closed the file and handed it to Sonny who had come over and joined them. The room was silent except for the sound of pages turning as Sonny read the file. When he finished, he handed the file back to Detective Yeager. "I still don't believe it."

The intense look on his partner's face caused Nick to realize how serious this really was. "Rick, I know I gotta stay away from this, but she is the mother of my children."

"Yeah, Nick. I understand," Yeager answered. "That's why I'm here. I thought I'd give you the courtesy of a heads-up."

"Do you have any other suspects?"

"No."

"Are you looking for any?"

He looked at his colleague and said, "Nick, I'm sorry, but this one looks like a slam dunk. We have our perp. I'm sorry, but the best thing you can do for her is find her a good lawyer."

Nick understood. He rubbed his mustache and shook his head. "When do you expect they'll be bringing her in?"

Just then Detective Yeager's cell phone buzzed. He pulled it from his belt and looked at the text message. "Uh, they just got here. Interview room one. There's an ADA on his way. Do you want to observe?"

Nick took in a deep breath, let it out, and nodded. "Yeah, of course. Who's the ADA?"

"Clark Cordova drew the case."

Nick's eyes widened. "Clark Cordova? You gotta be shitting me!" He knew Cordova was trouble. He was proud of owning the highest conviction rate in the county.

Shelley Kisler was one of the best prosecutors there was, but at least she had a conscience. This guy only had a nickname, and Sonny blurted it out, "Nero, the persecutor?"

Rick was right, Nick thought. Cassie, if she was charged, would need a damn good lawyer.

CHAPTER 25

You Have The Right . . .

Nick and Sonny were standing outside the interview room when ADA Clark Cordova approached. "Well, Detectives Greer and Madison, to what do we owe the pleasure of the presence of Phoenix's Special Investigations Unit? And both of you, at that."

The two detectives looked at each other and then at Cordova. Nick said, "Uh, you don't know?"

"Know what? This looks like a normal murder case. Nothing to involve the SIU. . . . Wait a minute." He looked up to the ceiling. "Greer? Cassandra Greer?"

Sonny pointed to Nick. "Ex-wife."

Cordova looked at Nick. "You know you can't—"

"Just observing, Clark. Just observing."

"Uh, which side are you rooting for?" Clark asked. Nick looked puzzled. "Well, I mean, she is the ex."

"She's also the mother of my children," Nick stated.

The ADA could see by the seriousness of the detective's face that he had better drop it, so he turned and they all watched through the one-way window and listened to the conversation between Detective Yeager and Cassie Greer.

Cassie was yelling. "I didn't do anything. Why did you bring me here? You wait until my Nick gets here. Nick Greer! He's a big detective, and he'll teach you idiots a thing or two!" She tried to stand up. "I'm leaving right now!"

Detective Yeager said, "Ma'am, you need to sit down. You're not going anywhere until I say you can."

"You can't treat me like a common criminal. I'll have your badge. You'll be shoveling garbage somewhere when I'm done with you."

Cordova looked at Nick, who shook his head and continued listening to the interview.

Yeager said, "I understand you were at the Valley Motel yesterday. Is that correct?"

"Yeah, and your point?"

"You were there with a Jeffrey Winters?"

"Yeah, if that's any of your business. Hey, wait a minute. Did Nick put you up to this?"

"Lieutenant Greer has nothing to do with this. Now, tell me, exactly what was your relationship with Mr. Winters?"

"What do you mean, was? Jeff is my fiancé."

"Okay, so why were you and he at the motel?"

"Why the hell do you think we were there?"

"You tell me, Mrs. Greer."

"We were fucking! What the hell else do you do in a motel?"

Sonny tried to hold back, but Nick and Clark could hear him chuckle. They saw traces of a smile appear at the corners of Rick Yeager's mouth, but he regained his composure and continued questioning his suspect. "Okay, I guess that makes sense," Yeager answered. "Mrs. Greer, there was a broken lamp in the motel room. Do you know anything about that?"

"You brought me all the way down here from Prescott for a stupid broken lamp? Fine, I'll pay for the goddamn lamp! How much was it? The goddamn motel probably wants five times what they paid for it."

"Can you tell me how the lamp got broken?"

"Yeah. I threw it at the bastard!" She looked at the detective and thought about what she had just said. "Why? What did he tell you?"

"Ma'am, he didn't tell us anything. He's dead."

Cassie's eyes grew as big as ping pong balls as she gasped, "What? . . . Dead? . . . Jeff is dead?"

"Yes. ma'am, he's dead. Now, would you like to tell me exactly what happened? You can begin by telling me why you killed him."

Tears began to well up in her eyes as she stared at the detective. "I . . . I . . . didn't. I threw the lamp at him, that's all, and I left. I didn't . . ."

"Ma'am, the murder weapon, the lamp, had the victim's blood on it. You were seen running from the scene at the time of death. All I want to know is why. Why did you kill Jeffrey Winters?"

Tears were streaming down her cheeks as she leaned back in the chair. "I told you I didn't kill him." She crossed her arms and stated, "I want a lawyer!"

Detective Yeager stood up and walked behind Cassie. "Please stand up, ma'am." As she stood, he took a pair of handcuffs from his belt and pulled her hands behind her back. She felt the cold metal surround her wrists and lock into place. Tears flooded her eyes. "Cassandra Greer, you are under arrest for the murder of Jeffrey Winters. You have the right to remain silent. If you give up your right to remain silent, anything you say can, and will be used against you in a court of law. You have the right to an attorney. If you cannot afford an attorney, one will be appointed for you at no charge. Do you understand these rights?"

Cassie sobbed as the detective escorted her out of the room. She saw Nick standing there and realized he had been watching her all along. "Nick! Nick!" she cried as she was led away. Suddenly she stopped, jerked her arm from the detective, turned, and yelled at Nick with fire in her eyes, "You son of a bitch! You did this! You'll never get away with it!"

Cordova looked at Nick. "She's your ex, huh?"

Nick nodded.

"Congratulations," Cordova remarked.

"Uh, why?"

"On the ex part."

Nick smiled slightly. "Let me know when she's gone through the matrix. I want to see her after she's booked."

Neither detective spoke a word as they went back to the SIU and sat at their desks. Sonny was the first to break the silence. "What the hell is going on, Nick? We both know Cassie can be a shithead at times, but she's not a killer. Are you gonna look into it? Do you want me to do it?"

"I'll do what I can, but it's Yeager's case. I need to talk to Cassie as soon as I can though. I need to find out what happened in that motel room."

"Let me know what I can do."

Nick nodded. His cell phone rang. It was a text from Sue Kim.

(Sue Kim) *Is it true?*

(Nick) *News travels fast.*

(Sue Kim) *Did she do it?*

(Nick) *Yeager thinks so.*

(Sue Kim) *What do you think?*

(Nick) *Don't know. Doubt it.*

(Sue Kim) *Wow. Can I help?*

(Nick) *Help what? Put her away?*

(Sue Kim) *LOL. Only if she did it.*

Just then the phone on Nick's desk rang. He answered, "SIU, Lieutenant Greer."

"Nick, it's Yeager. She's done. She's in holding."

"Thanks."

Nick texted to Sue Kim: *Gotta go. Talk later.*

Sonny said, "I'm coming along."

"There's no need, Sonny, I got it."

"Uh, did you detect a question in there somewhere? That wasn't a request," Sonny stated as he followed his friend out the door.

CHAPTER 26

Cassie's Story

Cassie was standing in the back of the cell when she heard the metal door open. Detective Yeager walked in and Nick and Sonny followed. She looked beyond Yeager as if he was invisible and said, "Nick! Thank God, you're here! I knew you'd come. Take me out of here." She ran to the front of the cell and wrapped her arms around her ex-husband, hugging him hard.

Nick gently pushed her away. "Cassie, I can't take you out. This is serious. You're being charged with homicide."

"Those idiots have no clue what they're doing. I didn't kill Jeff. Get me out of this hole, now!" She grabbed onto his arms and tried to shake him. "Let me out of this goddamn cage," she yelled. "I don't belong here. This is a place for criminals. You're a goddamn cop. Get me the fuck out of here!"

Nick took a step back and said, "Cassie, calm down. You don't seem to realize what's going on here. This is very serious. You're in big trouble. You're being charged with murder. Do you understand me? Do you know what that means?"

She looked at Yeager. "Yeah, it means he's stupid!" she said to Nick.

"Damn it, Cassie, you aren't helping yourself at all. You need to calm down. I won't even talk to you until you do." He paused as he looked into her eyes. "Now, can you do that? Can you calm down?"

Cassie squeezed her hands into fists and nodded.

Nick looked at the two detectives. They both understood. Yeager looked at Sonny and then at Nick, cocked his head, widened his eyes slightly and smiled. "Uh, I think we should leave you two alone for a bit."

As they walked away, Yeager said to Sonny, "I wouldn't want to be in his shoes." Sonny was silent. His face showed no emotion.

Cassie sat down on the steel bed, and Nick saw a tear begin to well up in one eye as he stood there. "Okay, now tell me exactly what happened at the motel. But before you do, listen to my words carefully." Though her face was looking at him, her eyes seemed to be looking beyond him. "Cassie, did you hear me?" He waited a couple of seconds, reached out and took ahold of her chin, and said, "Goddammit! Look at me, woman!"

She nodded and her eyes focused on those of her ex-husband. "Okay."

He took a couple of steps back and said, "All right. Now, before you say a word, remember I am an officer of the law. You are no longer my wife, so there is no spousal privilege afforded here. Do you understand that?" She nodded. "Okay, I need you to speak slowly and quietly, and if I tell you to stop—you do just that—stop talking immediately. Don't say another word unless I tell you to. Do you understand me?"

"I . . . I . . ."

Nick stared into her eyes. "Cassandra, do you understand me?"

The serious look in his eyes told her she had better do what he said. She actually seemed a little humble as she nodded.

Nick said, "Okay, now tell me exactly what happened."

She took in a deep breath and exhaled. "We met at the Valley Inn. We meet there once in a while to, well, you know."

"Yes, Cassie. I know."

"Everything was fine until after we made love, then Jeff said he had something to tell me." Her knuckles turned white as she gripped the metal bed.

"What? What did he want to tell you, Cassie?"

"The son of a bitch said he was going back to his wife. He said they had reconciled. He said he loved me, but he was in financial trouble, and he couldn't handle the cost of a divorce. He said he owed some people money."

"Some people? What people?"

"I don't know. He just said people."

Nick remembered what Cassie had told him about Jeff's gambling spree in Las Vegas. "The report said you hit him over the head with a lamp."

"The son of a bitch said we could still see each other. He said his wife didn't need to know. He said that's why he had me get the motel room, so she wouldn't see it on his credit card. I told him I wasn't anybody's mistress! I don't know what happened. I remember I grabbed the lamp and threw it at him. It hit him in the nose, but it didn't kill him. He laughed and said, 'I'm sorry babe, don't be mad,' and he reached out to try to hug me. I pushed him away and got dressed. He tried to hug me again, but I slapped him across the face and pushed him onto the bed. I took off his stupid ring and threw it at him. Then I picked up my purse and left. Nick, he was fine when I left. He was sitting on the bed. I don't even think his nose was bleeding."

"You said you threw the ring at him?"

"Yeah. I should have thrown it out somewhere, or sold it at a pawn shop, but I was pissed. Nick, he used me! I'm such a fool. I should have never got involved with him." She started crying, almost sobbing. "Nick, I'm so sorry for what I did to you. I should have never let you go. I love—"

"Cassie, I want you to listen to me. This is very important, do you understand?" She nodded. Tears were streaming down her face. "What did he do with the ring?"

"I don't know. It was in his hand when I left."

"You're sure he was alive when you left?"

"Yeah. He called after me as I opened the door. 'I love you,' he said. 'Don't be mad.' Yeah, right. All he wanted was to get laid!"

"Okay, Cassie, that's enough for now. They'll be coming to move you soon. Do us all a favor and lighten up on them. Your dad will get you a lawyer. I'm going to check on the kids. Where is your dad anyway? I'm surprised he isn't here."

"He's in Chicago, I think. Some sort of conference or something. Mom has the kids." A look of concern came over her face. "Nick, they saw it all."

As he turned to leave, he heard her cry out, "Nick. I love you." He stopped for a moment, then he continued out of the area and went straight to the crime lab.

CHAPTER 27

Something Missing

Sue Kim was sitting at a desk, typing something into a computer, when she looked up and saw him. "What's going on, Nick? How's Cassie?"

"I don't know, but I thought I'd check and see if you might know anything. The vic's name is Jeffrey Winters."

"Uh . . ."

"Yeah, that one," Nick affirmed.

"Wow! This could get interesting. Does it look like she did it?"

"Yeager thinks so."

"And what does Nick think?"

"No."

"I don't have the case, at least not yet. The ME has him. He's still in a drawer. We're pretty busy, you know. That's why they sent me down here." She added, "You know, since I do all this double duty, maybe I should ask for a raise."

"Yeah, good luck on that!" They both knew the recent budget cuts would put the skids to that effort.

"What about his personal effects? Is the inventory available yet?" Nick asked.

Sue Kim picked up the phone on her desk, dialed, and waited. "Lisa, Sue Kim. . . . Fine. . . . You have a Jeffrey Winters in your guest room. He checked in yesterday. How is he coming along?" There was silence as she listened for a moment. "Uh-huh. I see. What about his personal effects? Are they processed yet? Good, can I see the inventory? See you then, and thanks."

She hung up the phone and said, "Lisa is bringing them up right away." She asked, "Are you okay? How are the girls? This must be traumatic for them."

"I'm okay. I haven't spoken with the kids yet. I'll call Prescott now." He removed his cell phone from his belt and found the Metzler number on speed dial.

"Hello." Nick recognized the voice of his ex-mother-in-law.

"Dolores, it's Nick."

"I know who it is. What do you want? What did you do with my daughter?"

"That's what I'm calling about. First of all, I didn't do anything with or to her, but it looks like Cassie is in big trouble. She's been arrested."

"I know that. They came to the door and took her away this morning. It was horrible. The girls were here. They saw it all."

"How are they handling it?"

"Kelly stayed home with me. Kasey and Kaitlin are in school. I don't think they understand what happened. Frankly, neither do I."

"Let me talk to Kelly."

He waited a moment. "Hi, Dad. What's happening to Mom?"

"I don't exactly know, princess, but she's all right. I just talked to her. She's a little shook up, but she's okay for now."

"Why did the police take her away?"

He thought for a moment and decided his oldest daughter was mature enough to understand. "Kelly, you know Jeff, right?"

"Yeah, of course."

"Honey, Jeff died."

Silence entered the conversation, and then Kelly spoke, "Died? Jeff? How? What happened?"

"Sweetie, I need you to be strong, okay?"

"Okay," she answered in a soft voice.

"Jeff was murdered." Nick could hear her breathing into the phone, but there was no other sound. "Kelly? Kelly?"

"So, why did they take Mom away?"

"Sweetie, they're saying your mother killed him."

Nick could tell by his daughter's tone that she was crying. "Dad, what are you going to do? You gotta bring Mom home. Please, Dad, please bring Mom home." By now she was sobbing.

"Honey, I would if I could. But right now I have to think about this whole thing. I'll do everything I can to help. I promise. Your mom needs you to be strong. I need you to be strong. I don't want you to tell your sisters yet. I don't know how Kasey will react, and I don't think Kaitlin is old enough to understand. You're my big girl, okay?"

Her sobbing had let up some. "Okay, Dad. I understand."

"Let me talk to Grandma."

“What’s going on, Nick?” For the first time since Nick and Cassie’s separation, Dolores spoke to her ex-son-in-law in a civil tone. “Why did the police take my daughter away?”

She listened intently as Nick explained what he could to her. When he was finished, she said, “Nick, I know Cassie has a temper, but she didn’t kill anyone, especially Jeff. She loves him. They were going to be married. You gotta get this thing fixed.”

“I’ll do what I can; I promise. But I need to talk to Rod. He’ll need to get her a good attorney. Is he there?”

“No. He had a meeting in Chicago. He’s flying back Friday morning. I’m supposed to pick him up at nine-fifteen. He doesn’t know about this yet. Maybe I should’ve told him. I’m so confused. I don’t know what to do.” She began to cry.

“Dolores, the first thing you need to do is show strength in front of the girls. You’re all they have right now, and they shouldn’t see you crying. They need a rock to hold onto, and that rock has to be you. There’s no one else. I can’t come up there and get them and work on the case at the same time. Can you handle it?”

“I think so.”

“I know you can. Now, give me the flight number. I’ll pick Rod up at the airport. I’ll tell him what happened. He’ll figure out what to do. You stay there and take care of the girls, okay?”

“Okay, Nick.” After she gave him the flight number, she said, “Cassie still loves you, you know.”

He didn’t answer. He disconnected the call.

CHAPTER 28

The Visit

Assistant District Attorney Shelley Kisler was partially sitting up in her hospital bed when Sonny Madison walked in. The endotracheal tube had been removed and had been replaced by a nasal cannula. Shelley smiled when she saw her visitor.

"Hey, beautiful," Sonny said. "How ya feelin'?"

She said with a labored whisper, "I wanna go home."

"Uh, I'm sure you do, but I imagine it'll be a few days before you get out of here," he said as he took her hand. "You've been through a lot, you know."

She nodded. "Did you get him?"

"No. He got away. I hoped maybe you could help. What can you tell me about your attacker?"

"Was it Nemo?"

"We think so. It's the same MO."

"Uh, I didn't see him, but I'd say he was about five-ten." Sonny looked puzzled. She explained, "I felt his chin on the back of my head as he held me."

Sonny nodded. "That's pretty good. Is there anything else you can think of?"

"I don't think so. It happened so fast."

"Do you remember talking to Nick?"

She lightly shook her head. "Where's Nick?"

"Uh, he sort of has a family problem. He sends his love."

"Family problem? The kids?"

Sonny responded, "I'll tell you about it later. Right now I need to know about your attacker. When you were being put into the ambulance, you said something to Nick about Polo. Do you remember?"

"Oh, yeah. It was his cologne. He wore Polo cologne. Lots of it."

"Hmm, . . . Sue Kim was right."

"Huh?"

"Never mind. Is there anything else? Anything at all?"

She shook her head. "I'm sorry."

He thought for a moment. "Shelley, of course you knew Judge Cavallo, but had you ever in any way met or spoken to either of the other two victims? Marti Montgomery or William Scanlon?"

"No. I don't think so."

"That's okay. We'll figure it out."

"What happened to Nick?" Shelley asked with concern.

"He's at the station, I guess. His ex-wife kinda got arrested."

"Really? Why?"

"Uhm, she's being charged with homicide."

Shelley's eyes opened wide. "What? Who? How?"

"Her fiancé. A lamp."

"Really?"

"Yeah." Sonny explained the whole story to her.

"Who's the ADA?"

"Cordova."

"Ouch!"

"Yeah, I know."

"Tell him good luck."

"Who? Cordova?"

She smiled. "No, silly, Nick."

Sonny bent down and kissed her on the forehead. "I'll see you later." He left the hospital room.

CHAPTER 29

Where's The Glitter?

Lieutenant Nick Greer and CSI Sue Kim Lee entered the motel room. As they stepped inside, they stood still for a moment as all four eyes scanned the small cavern. It was a normal motel room with a king-sized bed in the center. To the right, a mirrored dresser supported a television. Next to it was a door leading to a bathroom. To the left sat a small round table with two chairs.

Sue Kim reached into her purse and handed Nick a small flashlight. Detective Rick Yeager had accompanied them. "Are you looking for anything in particular?" he asked.

"Maybe something shiny," Nick answered.

Yeager stood in the doorway and watched as they inspected the room from top to bottom. They removed the mattress and searched all the nooks and corners. They checked under the bed. Sue Kim pointed to a couple of blood droppings on the carpet and on the bed, then to a small splatter on the wall. Nick nodded. After checking the bathroom, he asked her, "Anything?"

Sue Kim said, "There's a lot of blood for a nose bleed."

When they were finished, Yeager asked, "Did you find what you were looking for?"

Nick shook his head. "Nope."

"Sorry, Nick." Yeager seemed sincere.

"That's actually a good thing, Rick. It's what we didn't find that concerns me."

Yeager stepped inside the room. "What do you mean? What didn't you find?"

"Anything shiny."

"Huh?" Yeager was clearly puzzled.

"You see, Rick, Cassie was wearing a diamond ring—a big one. I saw it. I'll bet it was worth close to ten grand. She told me she threw it at him, and he had it in his hand when she left. Yesterday we checked the inventory, and there was no mention of a ring in Winters' personal effects. So I began to wonder—if the crime team didn't find it and he didn't have it—what happened to it? You just watched us scour the whole place for it; it's not here. So again I must ask what happened to it?"

"If you're thinking robbery-murder, I don't think so," Yeager responded. "Maybe the maid who found the body took it."

"Well, I guess that's possible, but according to your report, the maid never went into the room. The report says she opened the door, saw the body and screamed, and the folks in the next room came out immediately and called nine-one-one. So no one entered the room, at least not according to your report."

"Maybe the maid lied," Yeager said. "Maybe the folks from Indiana took it. Anyone could have found it. Hey, maybe one of the crime scene techs found it and—" He stopped when he saw the look on Sue Kim's face. Her eyes looked like fire was about to erupt from them. He said to her, "I'm just saying something that valuable and so easily pocketed could be a temptation to almost anyone. It wouldn't be the first time—"

She put her hands on her hips and stated, "Not any of our people!"

Nick decided to change the subject before it got out of control; rather, before Sue Kim got out of control. "Rick, there's one more thing you should know. Cassie and Jeff went to Vegas last weekend. Cassie told me he lost a ton of money while they were there. She said she thinks he has a gambling problem. Also, he told her he owed some people money, but he didn't say to whom. Perhaps he was in over his head, they came to collect and it got out of control. That would explain the missing ring."

"Okay, Nick, I understand where you're going with this, but I still think she's good for it. She got pissed off because he dumped her. She felt used. She wouldn't be the first jilted girlfriend, wife, or whatever, to smash a perfectly good lamp over some sleazeball's head. Besides, we have no proof she even had the ring with her. Hey, maybe she lost the ring. Maybe that's what they were fighting about. He spent a lot of money on a ring and she lost it. I'd be pissed, too. Or maybe he did owe on gambling debts. Maybe he wanted the ring back to pay them. Look Nick, I don't think it was premeditated. The charges will probably be man-one and maybe Cordova will take a deal to man-two."

"Rick, would you check it out? I'd appreciate it. I don't want to get involved if I don't have to."

Yeager knew what the lieutenant meant. If he didn't do it, Nick would. "Okay, Nick. I'll put the description of the ring out to the local pawn shops." He looked at his colleague. "I'll need some kind of a description. What does it look like?"

"Uh, big."

"It was a princess cut—a full carat, I'd say," Sue Kim added. "White gold."

The two detectives looked at each other and then at Sue Kim who, when she saw the surprised look on their faces said, "What? I'm a girl. We know that stuff!"

"I'll put it out to the pawn shops," Yeager said. "A ring that size should be easy to spot."

"I'd appreciate it," Nick replied.

As Nick and Sue Kim left the scene, her cell phone buzzed. She answered. "Uh-huh. Now? Okay." She put the phone back into her purse. "I need to get back right away."

"What's the hurry?"

"Dr. Graves is getting ready to examine Jeffrey Winters' body. I thought you might want me to be there to assist."

"Oh, for sure."

"It looks like I'll be late getting home."

CHAPTER 30

Good News/Bad News

It was after seven p.m. when he heard his Android ring. It was a text from Sue Kim.

(Sue Kim) *The results are in. On my way home. You hungry?*

(Nick) *What ya got?*

(Sue Kim) *Chinese.*

(Nick) *I mean results?*

(Sue Kim) *When I get home.*

He was waiting for her as she came in the door. "Whatcha got for me?"

"Well, good evening to you, too," she said sarcastically as she dropped the paper bag of Chinese food on the table.

He got up and gave her a long kiss. "Ummm, now that's better," she said.

She opened the refrigerator, pulled out two bottles of Bud, sat down at the table and slid one over to him.

He asked, "Okay, what do you have for me?"

Sue Kim opened the bag and said, "Well, it looks like there's some moo goo and . . ." She looked up at him and giggled. "Okay, what do you want first, the good news or the bad news?"

"The good, I guess."

"Cassie didn't do it." She began removing the food from the bag and handed Nick a set of wooden chopsticks. "At least not with the lamp."

"Are you sure?"

"Oh, yeah. The blood on the lamp was the victim's all right. His nose was cut, but not broken, and the traces of blood on the lamp are consistent with her story. I can't say for sure that Cassie didn't kill the guy, but the fatal wound certainly didn't come from that lamp."

"Uhh, and you know this because?" Nick asked.

"First of all, there were only traces of blood on the lamp, and there was no hair on it at all."

"Hair?"

"Yeah, hair. It looks like someone bashed in the side of his head, and I'm certain it was not with that lamp."

Nick leaned forward and watched as she began eating. Sue Kim looked up at him and asked, "Aren't you gonna eat? I thought you said you were hungry."

"You're having fun with this, aren't you? Are you enjoying yourself?"

She looked at him, took a swig of beer, and nodded. "You betcha!"

The look on Nick's face told her the fun time was over. She said, "Okay, the murder weapon was metal and had an angle to it. I'm thinking something like a tire iron or a jack handle was used to bash in the left side of his head."

Nick smiled. "That's great news! So what's the bad news?"

"I just gave it to you." She giggled. "The good news is Cassie didn't do it. The bad news is, tomorrow they'll let her out, and she'll be free and running her mouth off again—bummer!" She took another taste of beer and giggled again. "Hey, you're a cop. You got some clout. Can't you keep her in lockup for a couple of extra days? Consider it a contribution to society."

Nick smiled widely. "You know, this is really funny."

"Okay. Let me in on the jocularity."

"You don't like her."

"And your point?"

"I'm gonna tell her she got freed all because of you."

"Don't you dare," she said as she flung some rice from her chopsticks at him. Nick laughed. "You know, your buddy Yeager isn't going to be thrilled when he gets the news," she added.

"*Que sera, sera*, I guess."

CHAPTER 31

Lieutenant Who?

"Where are you?" Sonny asked Nick.

"I'm on my way to the airport to pick up Rod."

"How's the traffic?"

"Friday light, I guess."

"Have you heard anything more on Cassie's release?"

"I'm still waiting for Fourth Avenue to call. It should be any time now. Hey, after we get her out, I think I'm going to drive them up to Prescott. I want to talk with the kids about all of this, and I don't want to wait until the weekend. You can handle it for the rest of the day. Let me know if you get any breaks."

"Uh, you're going to ride all the way to Prescott with your ex-wife in the car? Must I remind you she hates you? Hey, do you need an extra pair of bracelets? How about some duct tape?"

"Her father will be in car with us. I imagine she'll behave herself."

* * *

Rod Metzler's flight was on time. Nick had left him a text message stating he would be picking him up instead of Dolores, and he would explain when they met.

Rod handled the news well. He had always been one who was practical and handled crises calmly. He told Nick if they didn't let her go, he would get his daughter the best lawyer money could buy.

As they drove to the station, Rod said, "Nick, I appreciate what you're doing for Cassie. Though she won't admit it, I think she still cares for you."

This was the third time he had heard this; first from Cassie, then from Dolores, and now from his ex-father-in-law. Nick was emotionally conflicted. He was silent as he looked ahead at the road and continued driving.

"I just thought you should know, just in case you two ever, well, you know," Rod added.

Continuing to look forward, Nick responded, "It ain't gonna happen, Rod. It's over between Cassie and me."

Rod Metzler had always liked Nick. Though Rod had never made it known, somehow Nick knew his ex-father-in-law was aware that what happened between Nick and Cassie was all on her.

Nick said, "Cassie was my wife. I loved her at one time. She's the mother of my children. There will always be a place in my heart for her, but I don't love her anymore, Rod, at least not that way."

"I understand," he answered. Nick could sense the disappointment in his voice.

Just then Nick's cell phone buzzed. He pulled it from his belt. It was a text from Sonny: *4th Ave called. She's ready.*

He showed the text to Rod, who asked, "Are there any car rental agencies on the way?"

"Yeah. There's one about a mile up the street, but I planned on driving you both back to Prescott. I want to see the girls. I want to be sure they're okay."

"Are you sure?" Rod asked. "I mean, you and Cassie together in a car for over an hour?"

"I'll drive fast."

"You got any duct tape?" Rod grinned.

Nick smiled. "Yeah, there's a roll in the trunk. I have handcuffs and a Glock 17, too."

Rod laughed out loud. "That ought to work."

* * *

Detective Rick Yeager was waiting for Nick as he walked into the Fourth Avenue jail. "Good morning, Detective Greer."

"Hey, Rick. Sorry about all this."

"No, you're not. You're just being polite."

"Yeah, well."

Yeager shook his head. "Hey, don't worry about it. It looks like you were right. I should've known it was too easy. I scratched the charges. She should be out soon. Are you gonna wait for her?"

"Yeah. Her father is outside. He's on the phone talking to his wife. I'm taking them back to Prescott."

"Your little girlfriend is a pretty sharp cookie."

Nick smiled. "Yeah, she seems to know what she's doing." Nick didn't want to insult his fellow detective by saying this one was easy, and he shouldn't have arrested Cassie in the first place.

"You know, this is weird."

"Why?" Nick asked.

"Well, your girlfriend—"

"Fiancée," Nick corrected.

"That's right. Once again I stand corrected. That makes it even weirder. Your fiancée is the one responsible for setting your ex-wife free. They must get along pretty well."

Nick laughed. "If you only knew." He shook his head and repeated, "If you only knew."

Just then Rod Metzler came in. "Uh, that's him now," Nick said to the detective. He decided not to introduce them. Rod was not happy about what his daughter had gone through, and, though he was normally mild-mannered, Nick was afraid he might go off on the detective, especially if he knew he was the one who arrested his daughter.

"Is she ready yet?" Rod asked.

'Uh, not—" He stopped as he heard a buzzer and saw Cassie being led through the door by a matronly officer.

She ran straight to her father and hugged him. She was crying, and her father said, "It's okay, baby. It's over now. We're gonna take you home."

She broke away, looked at Nick and went over to him. She put her arms around his neck and hugged him tightly. Yeager, Metzler, and the female officer all watched as Nick gave her a courtesy pat on the back. She tried to hang onto him as best she could, but, as he gently pushed himself away, she looked at him and said, "I knew you'd get me out of here. I knew you would rescue me. You're my hero!" She reached out and tried to hug him again, but he stepped back out of her reach. Disappointment showed on her face.

The female officer handed Detective Yeager a clipboard. He took it and scribbled his signature on it. He looked at Cassie and said, "Mrs. Greer, you are free to go. Please accept my apologies and those of the city of Phoenix."

She glared at Yeager. The look on her face could have stopped a clock as she pursed her lips and furled her brow. "You ought to be sorry! If I have anything to do with it, your next job will be as a mall cop!" She looked at her ex-husband and said, "I want to file a complaint!"

"You'll get a survey in the mail," he responded. "Now let's get you out of here."

As Cassie stormed out of the Fourth Avenue jail, her father and ex-husband followed. Rod whispered to Nick, "Maybe you should have kept her a couple more days."

Nick smiled. "Wait until she finds out who was really responsible for getting her out."

"Who?"

"You don't want to know."

"Yes, I do."

"My fiancée."

Metzler's eyes widened, and a smile came across his lips. "No shit?"

"No shit."

"I hope I'm there when she finds out."

For some unknown reason, Cassie was completely silent during the whole ride to Prescott. Rod asked her a couple of questions and all she did was nod. She never uttered a word. Nick wondered if she was just tired or if she was plotting something.

* * *

The phone rang and Sonny picked it up from its cradle, "Sergeant Madison."

He recognized the voice of Tricia, the assistant to Deputy Chief Mannion. "The chief wants to see you when you have a minute."

"Okay, but Nick isn't here right now. He's getting his ex-wife out of lockup. Do you want me to wait?"

"No, Sergeant. Lieutenant Greer isn't involved in this. The chief made it perfectly clear; you are to come. Just you, alone."

"Okay. I'm on my way." What the hell did I do now? he wondered.

Though she tried to hide it, the smile on Tricia's face told Sonny he was not in serious trouble. "You can go on in, Sergeant. He's waiting for you." Sonny wondered why she had put extra emphasis on the word Sergeant.

As Sonny entered the room, the chief said, "Have a seat, Sergeant. This will only take a few minutes."

The chief had a personnel file in his hand. Sonny could see the name on it—Madison, Jasper J. The stern look on his boss's face gave Sonny concern that he may have misread Tricia. "What's up, Chief?"

The deputy chief said, "Sergeant Sonny Madison; that's what's up." He looked at Sonny and continued, "Do you like being a sergeant in the Phoenix PD?" He didn't give Sonny a chance to answer. "Well, that ship has sailed. Give me your badge!"

Sonny squinted and furled his brow. "Huh?"

"Give me your shield, Sergeant!" Mannion ordered.

Sonny reached into his pocket and laid his badge and identification on his boss's desk. He reached to his side and began to remove his gun, but Mannion said, "I didn't ask for your piece, just your badge."

A look of confusion was all over Sonny's face. He knew if he was being fired or suspended, he would have to surrender his service weapon.

Mannion held Sonny's badge out, looked at it, shook his head, and said, "Nope, this is all wrong." He reached into his drawer and pulled out another gold badge and handed it to Sonny.

Sonny took it, and a wide smile came across his face when he saw it was the same badge number, but this one read: Lieutenant.

Deputy Chief Bruce Mannion reached out his hand and said, "Congratulations, Lieutenant Madison. It's about time."

Sonny shook his boss's hand and said, "I didn't get the results. I didn't even know I passed."

Bruce smiled. "I knew it a week ago, but I didn't tell you. I wanted to wait until I had the badge in my hand and surprise you. You deserve it, Sonny. You're an asset to the department."

He picked up a pen with his left hand and signed a form. "This makes it official."

"Tell me Nick doesn't know," Sonny said.

"I figured you could tell him."

Sonny smiled, took the badge, breathed on it, and rubbed it against his chest. "I'll do just that. Thanks, Chief. I thought you were calling me in about Nick's ex."

"Nick's ex? What about her?"

"Uhm, you don't know?"

"I may be Chief of Detectives, but I am not privy to all my detectives' family matters."

"She was arrested."

"Oh? What did she do, insult a Walmart greeter?"

Sonny chuckled as he shook his head. "That's what I said, but it's a little more serious than that. She was charged with homicide."

"Cassie Greer? Murder? No way! Who?"

"That guy at the Valley Motel."

"I heard they brought someone in on that one. Cassie Greer? Really? I still don't believe it."

"I don't either, but Yeager thought it was a slam dunk case. The dead guy was her fiancé."

"How is Nick handling it?"

"He's waiting for her father to show up and take her back to Prescott, I guess."

"She got bail? How the hell did she do that?"

"She got freed. Yeager's squelching the arrest. The autopsy showed she didn't do it, or at least gave enough doubt. You'll probably get the report later today. All I know is what Nick told me."

"Well, Lieutenant Madison, you've got your work cut out for you. You and Nick have a serial killer to find. Once again, congratulations, Lieutenant."

"Yeah, thanks, Chief," he responded as he turned and left the office.

On his way out, Tricia said, "Congratulations, Lieutenant. This is for you." She handed him a new nameplate for his desk. It read: Sonny Madison, Lt.

Sonny thanked her and went back to the SIU. Nick still hadn't returned, so with an enormous smile on his face, he removed the old nameplate from its holder and slid the new one in. He wondered how long it would be until his friend noticed. He sent a text to April.

(Sonny) *I'm taking you out to dinner tonight.*

(April) *Why?*

(Sonny) *Got something to celebrate.*

(April) *What?*

(Sonny) *It's a surprise.*

(April) *K.*

CHAPTER 32

The Vixen

The morning was cool and a gentle breeze teased the pines that adorned the mountains as Nick pulled his Taurus up to the Metzler home. It was Saturday morning. He had spent the night at Bucky's. He wanted to stop and say goodbye to the girls before heading south to Phoenix. He got out and as he began to follow the sidewalk to the front door, Kaitlin ran to meet him. He picked her up, gave her a big hug, and swung her around. "Wow, you're getting big. Pretty soon I won't be able to pick you up." She giggled. "But you'll always be my Katy Bug," he said.

He carried her up the sidewalk. The door opened before Nick had a chance to touch the doorbell. Dolores Metzler was holding the door. Surprisingly, she had a smile on her face. "Good morning, Nick. Welcome!"

He didn't know what to make of her attitude. This was uncharted territory for him. If it were not for his daughter in his arms, he would have thought he was dreaming.

"Good morning, Dolores. How are you?"

"Oh, some aches and pains here and there, but nothing for you to be concerned about. Come on in. I'm glad to see you."

Now Nick knew there was something wrong. Had he somehow been transported into a parallel dimension where his ex-mother-in-law was actually a nice person? Or maybe she thought he had pulled some strings to get Cassie out of jail, though he doubted it was that.

"Would you like something to eat or drink?"

Nick shook his head as he put Kaitlin down. "No, thank you. I had breakfast at the hotel. I just came to say goodbye to the girls. I'm heading back to Phoenix."

"Kelly is getting ready, and Kasey is out on the patio with Cassie. You can go on back. I hope you all have a good time."

A good time? Nick wondered what she was talking about. He failed to notice the picnic basket sitting on the kitchen table as he made his way out to the patio.

The whole aura around the Metzler home was different. The fact that for the first time since he and Cassie's separation his ex-mother-in-law treated him like a normal human being and actually tried to make him feel welcome caused his "WTF" antennas to extend to full length. Did Dolores Metzler have an epiphany over her daughter's arrest? Maybe it had something to do with the kids. Perhaps Rod had ripped her ass. Whatever it was, he was sure of one thing—he didn't trust her. Women like her do not change overnight and neither do their daughters, he thought.

"Hi, Daddy," Kasey said as she ran to him and gave him a big hug. "Are you ready? Kelly is late as usual."

"Uh," he looked at Cassie. "Ready for what?"

"Mommy says we're all going to the lake. We're gonna have a picnic, just like we used to when we lived in Phoenix," Kasey answered.

"A picnic?" He looked at his ex-wife.

The smile on her face looked innocent as she answered, "We thought it would be nice if we all went on a picnic together. The kids think it's a great idea. I packed some sandwiches and chips. I baked some cookies, too. You know, those chocolate chip ones you like so much? And Mom made potato salad. There's soda and beer in the cooler. We just need to stop somewhere for ice, if that's okay. It's going to be a nice day. We should have fun."

Nick sat down in one of the patio chairs. He had intended to work on the Nemo case, and he had told Sue Kim he would be back today. He looked at his ex-wife. His mind was in a spin. He wondered what was going on. Did she want something, or did her arrest actually bring her around? She wants something, he thought. Yeah, she wants something. I'd better be on guard.

"Cassie, is there something going on here? What do you—?"

"Hi, Dad!" It was Kelly. He bent down, and she kissed him on the cheek and said, "Are we ready to go to the lake?"

Nick looked around. "Where's Grandpa?"

"Dad is in the Valley at a golf tournament," Cassie said. Nick knew Rod Metzler was an avid golfer, and he belonged to the Prescott Valley Country Club. Dolores called it his second home. Cassie stood and said, "Okay, let's go."

"Hold on. I need to make a call." Nick walked out to the yard where he could have some privacy and dialed Sue Kim's cell phone. He knew she wouldn't be able to join him, because this weekend *Swan Lake* was being performed at the Grady Gammage Auditorium in Tempe. Sue Kim, being the lead cellist, had to play with the symphony.

When Nick told her he was staying another day, there was no hiding the concern in her voice. Anger and sadness overcame her as she remembered what had happened a few months ago. Cassie had seduced Nick and caused the couple to break up.

Sue Kim shook her head and said, "Baby, I don't like this. You remember what happened—"

"Never! Never again will I ever allow that to happen. I promise. I love you, Sue, and only you. You know that, don't you?"

"I know that, Nick. I know you love me, but I just don't trust her. She's a vixen."

"I know. But it'll be okay. I promise. Besides, how can I say no to the girls? I'll be home tomorrow morning for sure. You can trust me. I promise."

"It's not you I'm worried about."

The tone in her voice told him his words had been little comfort. What he didn't tell her was Cassie had said he could stay at the house, but he had declined. He would procure a room at Bucky's for tonight and head out in the morning.

When he finished his call, he went back to the patio. Cassie and the girls were waiting for him.

Nick and the girls followed Cassie into the kitchen where she picked up the picnic basket and pointed to a cooler sitting on the floor. "Nick, would you be a dear and take the cooler to the car?"

A short time later, Nick pulled into the Circle K, shut off the engine and said, "I'll get some ice."

"I'm coming with," Kelly stated.

They went into the store and Nick grabbed two bags of cubed ice and headed for the checkout. They were last in a line of six. "What's going on, Kelly?"

"What do you mean, Dad?"

"Why are your mom and grandma being so nice to me? Why are we ALL going on a picnic?"

"I don't know," she answered. "I thought Grandma hated you, no offense."

"None taken. She does, or did."

"Maybe it has something to do with Mom's incident in Phoenix. They won't talk about it with us. Last night I heard them talking in the living room. But when I walked in, they stopped talking. What happened, Dad? What really happened to Jeff? Who really killed him? Why did they think Mom did it?"

They were now at the cash register, and Nick paid for the ice. "We'll talk about it later after we get to the lake."

* * *

They entered Goldwater Lake Park and found a comfortable spot. Cassie spread two blankets on the grass. A few scattered cotton clouds slowly drifted across the blue sky as they ate lunch and talked. The seventy-degree temperature, along with a slight breeze and the sound of the water lapping along the shore was peaceful and relaxing.

As they ate lunch, Nick and Cassie explained to the girls what had happened to Jeff. They told them someone had killed him. They didn't go into any major details—just enough for them to understand, at least Kelly and probably Kasey, they hoped.

They had finished lunch, and Kaitlin and Kasey were kicking a soccer ball across the green grass. Kelly was walking barefoot along the water's edge. Nick was sitting on the blanket and watching her. Once in a while she would pick up a stone and skip it across the water. It was very peaceful.

Cassie had been lying on the blanket, when she suddenly sat up and said, "Nick, can we talk?"

Here it comes, he thought. "Yeah, I guess."

She reached out her hand to his, but he pulled his hand away. "Nick, I wanted to thank you for getting me out of that horrible jail in Phoenix. Just as you've always been, you're still my hero." She took in a deep breath, and her partially unbuttoned tight blouse looked like it was about to pop open as her ample breasts fought to be released from their braless restraints.

She slid closer to him and reached for his hand once more, and again he pulled his away. He figured now was the perfect time to tell her. "Cassie, I think you should know it wasn't me who figured out that you didn't kill Jeff."

She looked puzzled. "Okay, so who was it? Was it Sonny?"

"No, it was someone in our crime lab."

"Well, tell him thank you for me."

"Uh, it wasn't a him; it was a her—Sue Kim." He waited for a comment, but she was silent though her face showed a sense of shock. He continued, "She figured out that the lamp was not the murder weapon. It's Sue Kim you should be thanking, not me."

Cassie's face was now expressionless, and she didn't say a word. It was like she was processing all this in the data files of her mind and waiting for the results.

"Perhaps the next time you see her, you might say thank you or something appropriate," Nick said.

Cassie was still silent. Nick didn't know what to think say or do. Finally she spoke, "Why would she do that? She hates me. She probably loved it when I was in jail."

"First of all, Cassie, Sue Kim did her job. No matter how she feels about you, she wouldn't let you go to prison for something you didn't do. And as far as hating you, she doesn't exactly hate you, but you certainly are not on her list of favorite people, and rightfully so. You haven't treated her very well, you know. And you say she loved it when you were in jail?" He nodded. "Probably."

"She came between us. You want to marry her."

Nick shook his head. "Cassie, Cassie! You know perfectly well Sue Kim didn't come between us; Jeff Winters did. If it weren't for him, we would probably still be together."

She reached out and took his hand and looked into his eyes. "We still can be, Nick. We still can be together; you and me and the girls, just like it used to be. We can be a family again."

She leaned forward and tried to kiss him, but he moved away from her. "Not this time, Cassie. It's over. You and me are no more. I love Sue Kim. I'm going to marry her and spend the rest of my life with her. Accept it!"

"Yeah, Mom, accept it." Neither Cassie nor Nick had seen Kelly standing there. They both wondered how much she had heard, or seen.

Kelly reached into the cooler and pulled out a can of soda. She snapped it open and began to walk away, but she turned and said, "Mom, Kaitlin, Kasey and I like Sue Kim. Isn't that important? We liked Jeff, too. Dad knew we liked Jeff, didn't you, Dad?" She looked at her father who nodded. "Dad also knew that no one will ever replace our dad, and you need to know that Sue Kim will not replace you, ever. You are our mom and we love you."

"I love you, too, Kelly." She reached out to her daughter.

Kelly held up her hand. "Hold on, Mom. I'm not done yet."

Nick watched as his oldest daughter knelt on the edge of the blanket and took control of the conversation. He held back a snicker as he saw the look of surprise on Cassie's face.

"I don't know what's going on with you and Grandma, but you both need to accept Sue Kim and be nice to her. Think about us. She will be our stepmother, and we like her. And Dad is right, you need to thank her for what she did and stop hating her. Without her, you'd probably still be in jail."

As Kelly walked away, Cassie looked at Nick and said, "I'm sorry, Nick."

The short ride back to the Metzler home was quiet until they heard Kelly's voice from the back seat. "Mom, Dad, I think I know what I want to be when I grow up."

Nick furled his brow as he viewed the reflection of his oldest daughter in the rearview mirror. Cassie turned around as Kelly said, "I want to go to criminal school and learn how to be a CSI."

Nick and Cassie looked at each other. Both of them thought the same thing. When she grows up? She already has.

CHAPTER 33

The Trail Reveals

It was ten-thirteen Sunday morning when Sonny Madison heard the vibration of his cell phone as it rattled against the kitchen counter. He picked it up and stared at it, wondering who would be calling him on Sunday morning. April and the kids were at church. I hope she isn't having car troubles again, he thought. "What the—" he said out loud. He stopped when he saw the readout: Chief Mannion. "Madison," he answered.

"Sorry, Sonny. I know it's Sunday, but it looks like we have another body."

"Fuuuck!" He breathed the word into the phone more than spoke it.

Sonny pulled the phone from his ear, held it in front of his face, and looked at it like he hoped it would disappear from his hand. He shook his head and put the phone back to his ear. He took a deep breath and said, "Where?"

"At the Peak."

"Throat cut?"

"Yep. Sounds that way."

"Shit! Have they ID'd the vic?"

"Not yet. All we know is it's an African American male. I guess some hikers found him. One of the uniforms called it in. He said we didn't need to bother the EMTs, but they're already on their way. I'll call for the wagon and get a crew out there. Then I'll head out, too."

"What about Nick? Does he know yet?"

"I haven't been able to reach him. He's not answering his phone."

"He's probably on his way back from Prescott. He said he was coming back this morning. He might be in a weak signal area, or maybe he has his phone shut off. I'm on my way. I should be there in twenty. Where exactly do I go?"

"Summit Trail. Uniforms are waiting for you. See Sergeant Joe Bernard."

"Got it."

"I'll try texting Nick. Sometimes it works better than voice. I'll meet you there as soon as I can."

* * *

Nick Greer was on his way home from Prescott. He was on I-17, about ten miles north of Phoenix, when he received the text: *Another one. Piestewa Peak. Summit Trail. Madison responding.*

Immediately Nick hit the chase lights and jammed the gas pedal to the floor. Since there was little traffic on Sunday morning, he figured he could make it in twenty to thirty minutes. He arrived in twenty-eight. He saw two helicopters hovering over the mountain long before he turned off of Lincoln Drive onto Squaw Peak Drive and pulled into the Phoenix Mountain Preserve.

The parking lot was crammed with cars and emergency vehicles. A uniformed officer was stationed on Squaw Peak Drive and was stopping cars and not allowing them access. He saw Nick's grill lights flashing and went over to him as he stopped. Nick rolled down his window and displayed his badge. "The place is packed," the officer said. "You won't be able to get your car in there."

Nick pulled to the side of the road and shut off the engine. He retrieved his Glock from the trunk and clipped it onto his belt, then walked about fifty yards to the entrance.

The insignia of the Phoenix bird showed prominently on the doors of the three police cruisers that were parked in various spots in the crowded lot, along with an ambulance and a crime scene van that had somehow squeezed its way in. Two uniformed police officers had a group of about a dozen people corralled together under a wooden ramada and appeared to be questioning them. Nick saw a group of people making their way up the rocky mountainside toting a stretcher, forensic bags and other equipment. The lettering on their backs identified them as EMTs and CSIs. Sonny Madison was talking to a uniformed officer as Nick approached. "What do we have?"

Sonny answered as he nodded toward the uniformed officer standing next to him, "This is Sergeant Joe Bernard."

Nick shook hands with the sergeant. "Lieutenant Nick Greer. What do we have?"

"A male body was found up on Summit Trail," the sergeant responded. He looked away for a moment, swallowed, and continued, "It appears his throat was cut. There are two officers up there now."

Sonny pointed to the group trudging their way up the trail and said, "A crime scene crew is already heading up there. A couple of EMTs are with them, but they may as well have stayed here." He shook his head. "Bruce is on his way." They could hear the sound of rotors chopping through the late morning air. Sonny looked up above the gray cathedral rock cliff, then back to Nick. "News travels fast."

Originally named Squaw Peak, this landmark towers twenty-six hundred feet over the city of Phoenix and is famous for its scenic hiking trails. Mostly composed of ancient metaphoric rock dating back to the Precambrian period, the alternating dark and light bands of gneiss and highly compressed layers of schist combine to give it its beauty. Several species of cacti make their home in this natural desert, but the statuesque saguaros that share the landscape with blue palo verde and mesquite trees seem to rule the mountain. Though long ago named Squaw Peak, the name was changed to Piestewa Peak in 2003 in honor of Lori Ann Piestewa, who was killed in the Iraq war. She is believed to be the first Native American female in history to be killed in combat on foreign soil.

Both Nick and Sonny knew there were at least eight hiking trails along this scenic mountain. The temperature was predicted to reach one hundred degrees today. Depending on where the body had been found, it could take up to an hour to hike up the mountain trail, providing the body was even on one of the trails at all. Adventurous hikers were constantly wandering off the trails in search of who knows what. Most of the mountain rescues were hikers who decided to blaze their own path and got lost, injured, or stranded. The detectives were also concerned that some of the carnivorous predators, indigenous to the desert mountains, were possibly snacking on the body. The mountain is a natural habitat for coyotes and turkey vultures, along with owls and hawks. Though they seldom came near humans, the aroma of fresh blood could be inviting to a hungry animal.

Sergeant Bernard said, "The body is about twenty minutes up Summit Trail. A couple of hikers found him lying behind some rocks." He pointed to a young couple sitting on the corner of a rustic wooden bench under the shade of the ramada. They were isolated from the rest of the crowd. "That's them over there."

"What do you know so far, Sergeant?" Nick asked.

"Not much, Lieutenant. The CSIs got here shortly before you guys. My partner went up in order to help protect the integrity of the scene as much as possible. There are a bunch of other hikers up there, you know. We're doing what we can to keep the looky-loos from getting in the way. Already, someone saw the body and puked all over the place."

"Yeah, I figured as much," Nick responded. "You did right, Sergeant." He looked toward the man and woman sitting on the bench. "Did anyone interview them yet?"

"Yeah, I did. They're pretty shaken up. From what I understand, they were hiking up the trail and stopped to rest. The female said she sat on a rock. When she glanced behind it, she saw the body and screamed. The guy said there was a lot of blood, and it looked like the victim's throat was cut. She got scared, and they both ran all the way back down the trail. He called nine-one-one from his cell. When I got here and found out the condition of the victim, I called Chief Mannion, just as we were instructed." The sergeant ripped a sheet of paper from a small notebook and handed it to Nick. "Their name is Bennett."

"It looks like there are a lot of people on the trails today," Sonny stated.

The officer looked at the array of vehicles parked in the lot and said, "It's Sunday morning. Half of the population is in church, the other half seems to be here." He waved his finger as he pointed around the parking lot. "Not an empty space to be found."

Both detectives knew the Summit Trail was the longest and highest reaching trail on the mountain, and the most popular. "I guess I'd better head on up," Sonny said. "I'll bet the scene is tainted with a bunch of people up there. I hope the uniforms made it in time to keep the contamination to a minimum."

Nick walked over to the couple and showed them his badge. "Mr. and Mrs. Bennett, I'm Lieutenant Greer. I'm a detective with the Phoenix Police Department. I understand you found a body up there?"

The young woman was shaking. The man took her hand and said, "Yes, sir. I'm Mario Bennett. This is my wife, Tracey."

The detective sat down. "Can you tell me what happened?"

Mario answered, "Like I told the officer, we stopped to rest a bit. We both sat on a rock. We heard a buzzing sound, and Tracey looked behind the rock and screamed. I thought she got stung by a bee or something until I saw it."

"By it, I assume you mean the body?"

"Yeah. The buzzing sound was flies. There was blood all over the ground, and his throat was cut. His eyes were wide open, but I knew he had to be dead, so we ran back down here and I called nine-one-one." He held up his cell phone.

His wife looked at Nick. Her voice was almost shattered as she said, "I'll . . . I'll never forget the look on his face. His eyes . . . they were wide open. He . . . he looked like something out of a horror movie!"

"I understand, ma'am. Something like this can be traumatic. I'm sorry you had to go through this." She nodded. "Can we get you anything? Water, maybe?" Nick asked.

"I'm okay," she answered as she shook her head and held up her own bottle of water.

Concern for her entered the detective's heart as he saw her hand shaking uncontrollably. "Ma'am, do you want me to have one of the EMTs check you over?"

"I'm fine. I just want to go home." Tears were rolling down her cheeks.

"In a moment, ma'am." Nick continued questioning, "Did either of you see anyone? Maybe someone leaving the scene in a hurry? Perhaps someone was coming down the trail as you were going up, someone who seemed to be in a rush?"

Mario shook his head. "No, sir. I don't think so. There were people coming down, but I didn't pay attention."

Nick continued, "Did either of you see anyone wearing a hoodie?"

"No, sir, not that I can remember," Mario answered. "There were lots of people going up and down. It's a little hot for a hoodie anyway, isn't it?" He looked at his wife and back at Nick. "Detective, my wife is a little shaken up, and, frankly, so am I. If you have nothing else, I really would like to take her home now."

"Are you okay to drive? I can have an officer take you home if you'd like," Nick offered.

"I'm okay. We just want to go home." He looked out into the parking lot. "How are we ever going to get out of here? Our car is buried."

Nick saw their dilemma. He thought for a moment. "Where do you live? How far from here?"

"In the corridor," Mario answered. "We're off of Northern and Eleventh Avenue."

Nick knew it was about fifteen minutes away. "Which car is yours?"

He pointed to the middle of the lot next to the road. "See that red Prius? It's pretty well penned in."

"Okay, I'll tell you what. Why don't you give me your car keys? I'll have an officer take you both home. As soon as we can, I'll have your car brought to your home. Will that work? It's the best I can do at the moment."

Bennett reached into his pocket, removed a key from his chain, and handed it to Nick. "Thank you."

"Okay," Nick responded. "If we have any more questions, we know how to reach you. Thank you for your help."

Nick turned and headed up the mountain trail. About halfway up, he felt his Android vibrate and pulled it from his belt. It was a text from Sonny. He shielded the face of the cell phone from the glaring sun so as to view the message. Nick quickened his pace as he read: *You need to get up here ASAP.*

Once he reached the crime scene, Nick bent his tall frame down and made his way under the yellow police tape that had been wrapped around trees and cacti. Both Sonny and Sue Kim were standing there. "Hey, babe, what are you doing here?"

"Sonny called me."

"I figured you'd want her here," Sonny said.

"You figured right," Nick answered. "Whatcha got?"

Sue Kim and Sonny looked at each other, and then Sonny pointed to the body lying on the rocky ground. Shock seized the detective, and his legs momentarily felt weak and wobbly as he recognized the face of the victim. He lay on the ground with one arm hanging over a barrel cactus and coagulated blood on his neck and chest. Nick shook his head, looked at Sonny, and then back to the body. "You gotta be shitting me."

James Holder had been a detective with the Phoenix Police Department for a little over five years. He had manned a desk behind Sonny when he and Nick were on the homicide squad. They had worked a couple of cases together. His throat had been cut all the way across, just like the others.

Sue Kim commented, "This one may be a little different, I think, but I won't be sure until the ME examines the body."

"Different? What's different?" Nick asked.

"I don't want to say yet, but I'll let you know when the exam is finished."

"I want you to assist the ME."

She looked at him and saluted. "Aye, aye, Lieutenant! I fully intend to."

He smiled. "What can you tell us for sure?"

"It appears the victim was coming down the trail." She pointed to three yellow tent markers on the ground a few feet up the pathway. "See the blood drops? It looks like he was cut there"—she pointed to the marker placed at the highest part of the trail—"and ended up behind those rocks. I'll let you know when all the tests are completed, but there is blood on both of his hands, and there are no visible drag marks. So my guess is he grabbed his throat, staggered over there and went down behind the rocks."

"Or perhaps he was pushed there," Sonny added.

"Possibly," she answered.

"How long ago do you think?" Nick asked.

"I'd say no more than two hours."

"Then I doubt if the perp is still be on the mountain," remarked Sonny. "He's probably long gone by now."

"I doubt it, too," Nick responded. "I don't think this guy would be stupid enough to stick around. He probably hit his mark, went down the trail and left. But who knows, maybe he tried to blend in with the crowd, so let's have the uniforms check everyone who comes off the mountain for weapons. Who knows, maybe we'll get lucky."

"Luck is sure something we could use with this one," Sonny said.

Nick pulled his phone from his belt and began typing a text to Bruce Mannion: *At the scene. The vic is Jim Holder.* He took a breath and pushed send.

Sonny called one of the uniformed officers over and said, "Radio down below and have everyone checked for weapons. No one leaves until they're checked out. Hold anyone with any kind of knives or sharp instruments until we get there. Then, I want you to check everyone up here before they go down. People are still coming down. Set up a spot about a hundred feet up and stop them. No one gets past you without being checked. The CSIs have luminol. They can check any knives for blood. If you find any blood residue, tag and bag the weapon and bring the person to me."

Nick walked over to Sue Kim and asked quietly, "Did you find a note?"

"None that I could find; but I'll have the team check around. There's a bit of a wind today. It could be anywhere." She looked up at him. "So how was Prescott?"

"Okay, I guess. We'll talk about it later."

Nick said to Sonny, "Let's head back down. There's nothing more we can do up here. Let's get out of the way and let Sue Kim and her crew do their thing."

"Here, you'll need some of this." Sue Kim held up a plastic spray bottle and handed it to Sonny. "I've got another bottle."

They knew it contained luminol. "Thanks, little one," Sonny said as he took the bottle from her hand. Nick was already about a hundred feet ahead of him as they made their way down the trail to the parking lot. All the way down Nick kept looking at the ground, hoping to find a piece of paper that read: NEMO.

Deputy Chief Bruce Mannion was waiting under the ramada when his two detectives came off of the trailhead. "Are you sure it's Holder?"

Nick nodded. "Yeah, it's him, all right."

"What the hell happened?" the chief asked.

"I don't know, Bruce." Nick shook his head. "His goddamn throat was cut."

"Nemo?"

"It looks like it," Nick responded. "We'll know more after the ME gets him."

"Was there a note?"

"The crime team is looking."

Mannion looked up to the sky and back to his detective. "It's a little windy today. It could have blown anywhere."

Sonny walked over to Sergeant Bernard, handed him the bottle of luminol, and said, "You know what to do." The officer nodded as he took the bottle, motioned to two of the uniformed officers to come with him, and walked over to the crowd of people who had been detained. It had grown since the two detectives had gone up the trail. A couple people were yelling and complaining about being detained, but, for the most part, the good citizens of Phoenix understood.

Chief Mannion said to his detectives, "I'll call the chaplain. Jim was single, but I believe he has a girlfriend who lives with him. I think his parents live in Sun City. We'll probably go there." He let out a breath and shook his head. "Goddamn! Sometimes I hate this fucking job!"

He began to walk away, but stopped, turned and looked at Nick, then at Sonny. "You guys figure out who's killing our people. This shit has got to stop!"

The road was lined with news vehicles, mostly satellite trucks whose crews were pushing and shoving, trying to get into the parking lot, but the uniforms were able to keep them at a distance. One reporter saw Nick and yelled, "Hey, Detective, is it Nemo?" Nick ignored the question. Already, the radio and television stations had aired the story that a hiker was found dead on Piestewa Peak and it looked like foul play. One of them even titled the report: Nemo Strikes Again.

Nick and Sonny spent the next couple of hours, along with the help of the uniformed officers, interviewing all those who they had found on the mountain, checking their pockets and backpacks for weapons. Several knives were found, but only three showed traces of blood. Those knives were confiscated and would be checked in the lab to see if the blood matched that of Jim Holder. Neither Nick nor Sonny were counting on any positive matches. They both figured the perp was long gone.

As far as witnesses, no one saw the attack or heard anything. The police checked all of the trash cans for weapons, but they came up empty.

Two people were arrested for possession of cocaine and one for an outstanding warrant. Sonny remarked, using his best imitation of Forrest Gump, "Mama says life is like a box of chocklits. You never know what yer gonna git."

* * *

That night Nick and Sue Kim were sitting on the sofa. She had laid her head on his shoulder, and they were watching the Phoenix Suns basketball game. She repeated her earlier question, "So, how was Prescott?"

"How was *Swan Lake*?"

"Uh, fine. How was Prescott?"

"Fine."

"The kids?"

"Fine."

"How was the picnic?"

She felt him stiffen up as he said, "Uh, okay, I guess."

She could sense he wanted to change the subject, but she kept pushing. "Just okay?"

"It was kind of awkward, I guess."

"Awkward? Awkward, you guess? I should think so; you and your ex-wife lying on a blanket all afternoon and her looking sexy and all."

"I did not lay down on the blanket. I sat the whole time. Who told you about the picnic, anyway?" He figured his fiancée had her own network of information and her name was Kelly.

The rest of the evening was silent.

CHAPTER 34

A Peek In The Closet

"How was your weekend?" Sonny asked.

"Fine. How are the background checks coming along?" Nick responded.

"They're mostly done," said Sonny as he got up from his desk and went over to the printer. "I'm printing them out now."

"Did you find anything interesting?"

Sonny removed the papers from the printer, walked over to his partner's desk and sat down. "Take a gander for yourself," he said as he inserted them into a manila folder and tossed it on the desk in front of his partner.

Nick opened the folder and removed the papers. He commented here and there as he read them. "Marti Montgomery looks clean, Bill Scanlon had a couple of speeding tickets; no big deal. Harlan Jacoby looks clean." He flipped the page. "Katy McKenna is good, but I expected that." His brow furled as he read further. "Hmm. Megan Findlay was arrested for assault five years ago?"

Sonny said, "Yeah. Take a look at the arrest report. It looks like she smacked some woman on the side of the head with an ashtray."

"It says the charges were dropped to trespassing, and she was assigned anger management classes."

Sonny laughed out loud. "Yeah, anger fucking management classes! What a bunch of BS!"

"It says she paid a hefty fine and the victim's medical bills. The victim filed a civil suit, but it was settled out of court."

"Yeah, according to the records, Megan Findlay's stepdaddy is Mason Stevens. How much do you wanna bet he paid them off?"

"THE Mason Stevens?" Nick knew Mason Stevens was a wealthy entrepreneur who owned a plethora of fast food restaurants throughout the state.

"Yup. That one." Sonny grinned. "He's got more money than God."

"Hmm." Nick shook his head. "She doesn't seem like the type."

"Read on, your Gumbyness. There's more 'she doesn't seem like the type' stuff in there."

Nick reread the arrest report and shrugged. "Okay, what am I missing here?"

"The bar. Look at the name of the bar." Sonny pointed to the name on the page.

Nick shrugged. "The Olive Branch. Okay, I don't think I've ever been there. What's so special about The Olive Branch?"

"I don't figure you would have been in there. It changed owners a couple of years ago. It's now called Busters."

Nick was still puzzled. "Yeah, I know Busters. I've seen it. It's a sports bar, isn't it? So what's so special about it?"

"When it was The Olive Branch, it was a different kind of sports bar."

Nick thought for a moment, then looked up from the file. "You mean a gay bar?"

"Ahh, your master's degree serves you well, Professor Gumby. It used to be a big lesbian hangout."

"You're kidding!"

"Nope. I kid thee not. It looks like our first victim and her assistant had more in common than just the news business."

Nick leaned back in his chair and stroked his mustache. "I guess we ought to make a visit to little Miss Findlay."

Sonny let out what was almost a snort. "Uh, ya think?"

As Nick continued reading the background checks, he said, "What about our security guard, Munder? It looks like he's had a DUI and a leaving the scene."

"They're four years old," Sonny commented. "He's been clean ever since, and there were no priors. Besides, the way he reacted to the first victim's blood, I doubt he could be our perp."

"Uhm," Nick said as he searched for another page. "What about Leo Cardinale? Did you check him out?"

"You know, that's the odd part." Sonny scratched his head. "He went to work for Secure-Max a year ago, but I found no trace of him before that. It's like he"—Sonny raised his hands in the air—"poof, just appeared out of nowhere."

"Keep on looking. You'll find him. Maybe the DOB is wrong. Maybe a number is transposed. The security company had to have run a background check on him. If you can't find anything, check with them. Get his sosh and run it."

Nick closed the file. “But first, let’s go talk with Megan Findlay. You got your keys?”

“Yeah, I got my fuckin’ keys, but you can drive.”

“Okay, what’s nibbling at your ass? You’ve been a little standoffish all day.”

Sonny reached to the front of his desk and turned his nameplate around. Nick’s face turned red when he saw it. He looked proudly at his friend who was holding up his new badge. “I’ll be dipped! Congratulations! I didn’t even know you took the test. Why didn’t you tell me?”

“I wanted to surprise you, and, besides, if I didn’t make I didn’t want you to know. Some detective you are; the nameplate has been sitting here since Friday.”

Nick shook his partner’s hand. “You and I and April and Sue Kim are gonna go out and celebrate. Dinner’s on me.”

“So is the driving. Got your keys?”

Nick nodded. Sonny grinned and said, “Good! Fire up the Gumbymobile and let’s go talk to Megan Findlay.”

CHAPTER 35

The Closet Reveals

Detectives Greer and Madison entered the KTPA studio and walked up to the reception desk. Sonny displayed his badge and said, "We would like to speak with Megan Findlay, please. I'm Ser . . . Lieutenant Madison, PPD." He nodded toward Nick. "This is Lieutenant Greer. Is Ms. Findlay in?"

"Hold on a moment, please." She brushed back her strawberry blonde hair with one hand, punched a number into the phone with the other, and said through her headset, "Two policemen are here for Ms. Findlay." She paused. "Thank you." She looked at the two detectives. "I'm sorry, but she isn't available."

Nick spoke, "Where is she? Is she in the building?"

"No, sir, she is not. She's out in the field."

"Out in the field?"

" Ms. Findlay is now one of our field reporters."

"How about Harlan Jacoby? Is he in?"

"Yes, sir."

"Tell Mr. Jacoby we're here and we want to speak with him," Nick ordered.

"Right here, Detectives." The voice came from Harlan Jacoby who had just entered the lobby. He looked at the receptionist and said, "It's okay, Lisa." He looked back at the visitors. "Welcome. Let's go up to my office."

The station manager's office was well designed for meetings. The large, round, glass cocktail table in the center was surrounded by four plush chairs. They all sat. Jacoby began, "What can I do for you gentlemen today? Please tell me you're here to inform me you have caught my niece's killer."

"I wish that were the case, sir," Nick responded. "We have some questions for Ms. Findlay. Do you know where she is or when she'll be back?"

"She's covering the rally at the Capitol. I believe it's over now, so she should be back soon." He stood, walked over to his desk, picked up the phone and said, "Buzz me when Megan returns." He put the phone back in its cradle and rejoined the detectives.

"I thought she was an assistant. Do assistants normally cover these things?"

"No, but we wanted to give her a chance. She wants to be a reporter. Since Marti's death, well, there's no way Katy is going to come back, so we promoted Brittany Hennessey to anchor, and we needed another field reporter to replace her. It's a good career move for Megan. She earned the opportunity."

Nick even surprised Sonny as he asked, "Mr. Jacoby, what can you tell us about your niece's sexual appetite?"

"Uh, I don't understand your question." Jacoby looked insulted and confused.

"I understand she preferred women over men. I'm sure you were aware of that."

"Where did you hear that? I don't be—"

"Believe it," Nick stated. "What about Megan Findlay?"

"What about her?"

"Does she like men or women?"

"I have no idea. Men, I assume. What difference does it make anyway?" Just then the phone buzzed. Jacoby walked over to his desk and picked up the phone. "Okay, send her up."

Harlan Jacoby looked at his guests and said, "You can ask her yourself. She's on her way up." He walked back and sat down. "What the hell does either of their sexual preferences have to do with my niece's death?"

Nick shrugged. "Maybe nothing, but we have some questions for Ms. Findlay."

Just then Megan Findlay walked into the room through the open door. The three men stood. She froze when she saw the two detectives. They could see she was frightened. "Is there something wrong?"

"No, ma'am," Sonny answered. "We just have a couple of questions for you."

Nick looked at the station manager. "Is there someplace private we can go?"

Jacoby understood. "I'll leave you three alone." He got up and closed the door behind him as he left the room.

Megan Findlay looked scared as she took a seat across from the detectives. She looked different than she had on the night of Marti Montgomery's murder. Today, she had on makeup and whoever styled her hair gave it the perfect amount of curl as it fell over her shoulders and down her back. The night of the first murder, the ponytail added a childish look to her, but today an attractive woman sat nervously on the edge of her seat.

Nick began, "Ms. Findlay, how did your report go today?" She seemed to relax a little, and he knew his question had put her somewhat at ease as she sat back a little in the chair.

"I think it went well. It was my first real televised report. I was a little nervous. I hope it doesn't show when it's aired tonight." Pearly white teeth showed through her wide smile.

"I'm sure it'll be fine. I can't wait to see it."

She was now sitting comfortably in the chair and the tenseness seemed to be waning. "Have you made any headway in finding out who killed Marti?" Her confidence was back, and she seemed to be assuming the role of a reporter interviewing the two detectives.

Nick and Sonny picked up on her demeanor and looked at each other, then back to Megan. Nick said, "We're working on it, ma'am. That's why we're here today. We have some questions, and we hoped you could help us."

"Sure, go ahead."

"Tell us, what exactly was your relationship with Ms. Montgomery?" Nick questioned.

"Well, as I told you that night, I was her assistant."

"I understand you were her assistant, but let's say on a more personal level, what was your relationship with her away from the station?"

"We really didn't have one. She had her life and I had mine."

"Did you go to lunch together at times or maybe dinner?

"Uh, we'd had lunch a couple of times, but only while on business."

"Ms. Findlay, do you remember our conversation the night Ms. Montgomery was killed? You stated that night that Bill Scanlon was not her type. Tell me exactly, what did you mean by that? Why was he not her type?"

Nervousness reappeared in her voice, and she stiffened up slightly as she answered, "Uhm, I meant he was married, I guess."

"Ms. Findlay, your exact words were: 'First of all, he's married. And, second, he's not her type.' So, once again, what did you mean by not her type?"

She shrugged. "I don't know. He's quite a bit older than she is; maybe that's what I meant. They were friends, that's all."

"So what was her type?" Sonny interjected.

"I don't know what you mean."

Sonny leaned toward her. "Would you be her type?"

She looked at Sonny, her mouth opened, and her head shook ever so slightly. She was sitting on the edge of the chair again.

"Ms. Findlay," Nick said. "I understand you were involved in an incident at The Olive Branch a while back. We also are aware it was a gay and lesbian bar, so I assume you prefer women. That's okay, to each his own."

"Or her own," Sonny added.

Nick continued, "We also know Marti Montgomery was a lesbian too, so it made us wonder about you and Marti and just how close you two really were."

Her mouth was closed, and the look in her slightly squinted eyes was defensive as she said, "That's a typical attitude from someone who doesn't understand the lifestyle. Tell me, assuming you are both heterosexual, do you think every male and female partner in your department sleep with each other? Huh? Just because Marti and I are lesbians doesn't automatically mean we were lovers. And I certainly did not kill her!"

"No one is saying you did," Nick stated. "What we want to know is why you didn't disclose your relationship with Ms. Montgomery."

"We had no relationship. It only happened once!" She looked like she wanted to reach out and grab her last words and shove them back into her mouth. The detective had caught her. He had worked her well. She looked at him, then to Sonny, and slid back in her seat. She suddenly looked relaxed. She hung her head for a moment and took a breath. "It was during the Yarnell Hill fire. The hotels and motels were booked so we had to share a room. One thing led to another, and the next thing we knew, well, you know." She hesitated for a moment. "We both went back to Phoenix the next day."

"So, what happened after that?" Nick questioned.

"What do you mean?"

He leaned toward Megan. "You made love and then you left. What happened when she got back? How did she react? Did you continue seeing each other in that way?"

"No, sir. We never even discussed it. It was like it never happened. We went on about our business. Marti never mentioned it, and I was afraid to."

"Afraid? Why?"

"She was my boss. I didn't know what to do or what to say or how to approach it, so I left it alone."

Sonny asked, "Are you telling us that you and Marti Montgomery got it on once, and that was it? That it was just a casual one-night stand? That you still worked together, and you both acted like it never happened? How can that be?"

"That's the way it is sometimes." She seemed sincere in her answer. "It was awkward for me at first, but it turned out okay. You would have to understand this business and especially understand Marti."

"How did you feel about that?" Nick asked.

"I accepted it.

"Did you love her?"

"No, Detective. I told you it was just a casual thing."

"Ms. Findlay, you told me you had heard rumors that Ms. Montgomery was having an affair with Bill Scanlon. Did that make you jealous? I mean, if she was, that would make her bisexual, wouldn't it?"

"No. I knew they weren't true. Marti only liked women!"

"Are you sure? Bill Scanlon was a handsome man. Maybe your mentor was bisexual. Maybe you were jealous, and you took them both out."

Both detectives could see the rage building up inside her as she began to stand up, but took a breath, and sat back down. "Detectives, I didn't harm Marti. Now, if you have no more questions, I have work to do."

She started to stand again when Nick asked, "Ms. Findlay, have you ever been to Bill Scanlon's house?"

"Yes. I was at a Christmas party there last year."

"Where were you a week ago Monday?"

"The night Bill Scanlon was murdered," Sonny added.

"I was probably in bed sleeping. And before you ask, I live alone, and no one was with me. Now, this interview is over. If you are accusing me of a crime, do it; otherwise, please leave me alone. Editing is waiting for me." Megan Findlay never looked back as she pulled the door open and left the station manager's office.

Nick said to his partner, "For a moment, I thought she was gonna lose it."

"Yeah, so did I. I stand corrected." Sonny grinned. "Maybe those anger management classes worked for her after all.

* * *

The drive back to the SIU was a short one and Sonny was unusually quiet. Nick broke the silence. "How come you're so quiet?"

"I'm just enjoying the view from this side. Hey, Gumby, I think you should hold the door for me when we get back."

Nick reached his hand down, grabbed his inner thigh, and said, "The only thing I'll hold is this."

Sonny grinned. "Drive on, Jeeves!"

CHAPTER 36

The List Grows

"So what do you think?" Sonny asked as he and Nick entered their office at the SIU.

"About what?"

"Megan Findlay. What do you think?"

"I doubt she did it," Nick responded as he sat down at his desk. "I watched her eyes the whole time. I don't think she was bluffing." He leaned back in his chair and shook his head. "You know, Sonny, sometimes it feels like we're chasing the horizon."

"Yeah, I know," Sonny said as he sat down at his desk and turned on his computer. He sat there for a few minutes before he got up and went over to Nick. "Okay, let's see what we got."

As Sonny sat down, Nick reached into his desk, pulled out a yellow pad, and said, "Okay, Lieutenant Madison, let's look at it." He wrote:

Megan Findlay
Harlan Jacoby
Katy MeKenna
Shannon Scanlon
Vincent Peruzzi

"Let's start with Findlay. She could've been jealous of Scanlon and Montgomery. What if she was in love with Montgomery and thought the rumors were true and decided to take them both out? Maybe the rumors were actually true. Scanlon was a good-looking guy. Maybe he was banging Montgomery and Katy McKenna, and Findlay found out about it."

"Sonny, I know you were on med leave for a while, but it sounds like you've been watching too many soap operas."

"Look, I'm just saying it's possible. I wouldn't rule her out. She's the right height and with loose clothing and her hair tucked up under a hat, she sort of fits the description the EMT gave."

"I'd think if she were jealous, maybe she'd take out her competition, but not her lover. Whoever is perpetrating these murders is on a mission. She doesn't seem savvy enough to me to concoct a plan like that," Nick commented. "But you never know. I guess it's possible, but there's one little thing."

"Yeah?" Sonny looked puzzled.

"I didn't notice a mustache on her, did you?"

"Bite me," Sonny remarked.

Nick laughed out loud. "What about Jacoby?"

"What about him?"

"He fits the description, and he has a mustache. Do you think he's telling the truth? Do you really think he didn't know his niece was gay?"

"He's either clueless or he doesn't want to admit it. I realize this is the twenty-first century, but I don't think he would want it to get out, at least not while her star was still rising. Besides, what would be the motive?"

Nick stroked his bushy mustache. "How about Katy McKenna?"

"Well, let's see, she was being replaced by Montgomery. If she thought her lover was banging the person who also threatened her career, well, we have jealousy times two equals big-time motive."

"Agreed. Now, what about Shannon Scanlon? What do you think about her?"

"She sure has a temper." Sonny grinned as he pointed to Nick's cheek. "You can hardly see it now."

While still holding onto the pen in his hand, Nick extended his middle finger to his friend, who grinned and said, "Just saying."

"How about Vincent Peruzzi?" Sonny asked.

"If he thought Scanlon was banging his wife, we have motive. But what about Montgomery? Why would he kill her? I realize she was replacing Katy, but I don't see how that would threaten her husband. I'm sure she made decent money, but that million-dollar home they have didn't come from her salary alone. I wouldn't think that to be enough motive for murder, but you never know. Besides, he doesn't have a mustache."

Sonny said, "No, he doesn't, but his brother does." There was silence for a moment. "Did you see the pictures in Katy's home?"

Nick shrugged. "Uh, I think so, huh?"

Sonny continued, "Didn't they teach you in master's degree school to be observant? There were pictures of Katy and her husband and some of the two brothers. In one of them, either she was smooching her brother-in-law or her hubby had a 'stache."

"Yeah, but he doesn't have one now, and he didn't have one when we first met him. The EMT said Shelley's attacker wore a mustache. There's no way he could have grown one that fast."

"Okay, so what about the brother?"

Nick took in a breath and let it out. "Motive? Where's the motive?" He thought for a moment and said, "Why don't you go ahead and see what you can find on him? See if you can figure out where he was at the times of all the murders?"

"I'll get on it. What else?"

Nick added a name to the list:

Victor Peruzzi

Nick thought for a moment. "I don't see a connection with the security guard, do you?"

"Nope," Sonny answered.

CHAPTER 37

Party Pooped

Charlie's Bar and Grill was more crowded than usual for a Monday night as Nick, Sonny, and a few of their friends gathered to celebrate Sonny's promotion to lieutenant.

Charlie's was a local neighborhood bar frequented by many of the Phoenix men and women in blue. Charlie was a retired Phoenix cop. The blood, and one might say the beer, ran blue when it came to patronizing cops and ex-cops businesses. The fact that Charlie served a great cheesesteak sandwich made it that much better.

Nick had just finished toasting "Lieutenant" Sonny Madison when both of their cell phones went off. He looked at his phone and shook his head as he read the text. "You gotta be fucking kidding me!"

"I don't believe it. Why tonight!" Sonny exclaimed. The text read: *Another one. State 48. Men's room. Sending help. You up to it?*

Deputy Chief Bruce Mannion had known about the celebration and wondered if either detective, or perhaps both, had had too much to drink to respond. Nick texted back: *I'm okay. Not Sonny.*

Sonny downed a shot and said, "Sorry to cut it short, guys, but duty calls."

Nick shook his head. "Stay here, buddy. It's okay. I'll handle it. This is your night to celebrate." He laid two twenty-dollar bills on the table and said, "The next round is on me. One of you guys see he gets home okay." He got up and headed for the parking lot. He jumped into his Taurus, fired it up, hit his chase lights, and was on the scene in less than fifteen minutes.

State 48 was a well-known bar and restaurant along Central Avenue. It had been named for Arizona being the forty-eighth state to be admitted to the union. After forty-plus years on this same site, it had become a Phoenix icon. Its rustic, western atmosphere drew a steady stream of tourists as well as local clientele. There was sawdust on the floor, and the waiters and waitresses wore western garb. The cowboy hats on their heads and the six-shooters on their hips made this a must-see for tourists. There was a sign on the door that read: Casual Attire Only. This place was famous for cutting off men's ties.

There were remnants of ties tacked to the walls throughout the entire establishment. Some of them had famous names attached to them. Bolo ties were permitted, of course.

There were several police cruisers in the parking lot when he arrived, and the area was already being cordoned off. He fished his badge and ID from his pocket, bent under the police tape and went into the establishment. About a half dozen people were parked at the bar and about the same amount were sitting at tables. A familiar face was questioning a man Nick assumed was the manager.

"Sergeant Thomas, we meet again."

"Lieutenant Greer. Welcome, I think."

"So what do we have here?"

Sergeant Thomas looked at the manager and ordered, "You stay right here. I'll be back."

He led Nick out of the main room and down a hallway until they came to a door. The sign read: Cowboys. The sergeant opened the door and led the lieutenant in. He pointed to the second stall and said, "There, see for yourself."

The tiled floor was red where blood had begun to coagulate around the white porcelain base. When the detective saw the slumped body sitting there with blood soaked into his white shirt, he knew the killer had struck again.

"Nemo?" Thomas asked.

Nick took in a breath and exhaled loudly. "Looks like it."

Another uniformed officer came in and said, "Excuse me, but the crime scene team is here."

Nick shrugged. "Tell them to come on in." He and Sergeant Thomas left and went back to speak with the manager.

Thomas said, "This is Ricardo Valenzuela. He manages this place." He looked at the manager and said, "This is Lieutenant Greer. He'll take it from here."

They shook hands, and Nick got right to the point. "Tell me, Mr. Valenzuela, exactly what happened?"

The manager was a little nervous as he sat down in a red-vinyl-covered booth. Nick slid into the seat across from him. "I don't really know."

"Who discovered the body?" Nick asked.

"I don't know who he was. Some guy came running out from the men's room yelling, 'There's a dead guy in there! There's a dead guy in there! There's blood everywhere!' Several of the women screamed and a lot of the patrons ran out." He pointed around the room. "Except for them."

Nick motioned to Sergeant Thomas who came over to them. "Chris, talk to everyone in here. See if any of them know anything. I doubt it'll help, but check anyway. Maybe somebody got a description. Maybe we'll catch a break."

"I already talked to some of them. No one saw his face. I had to stop—the news crews are here. You know how they are. There are three stations here already."

"Your point?"

"You know how pushy they can be. I can't shoot 'em, ya know."

Nick looked at the Glock on the sergeant's hip. "Who said?"

They both laughed. Nick turned to the manager and asked, "Where is the man who discovered the victim?"

He shrugged. "No clue. I think he took off. He sure looked scared."

"Do you know who he was?"

Valenzuela shook his head. "Nope."

Nick continued, "Did he eat anything or just drink?"

"I don't know. I think I saw him at the bar. My bartender is still here. I can check with her." He pointed to a lady standing behind the bar. "Her name is Sunnie."

"Bring her over here, please."

As the manager left, one of the police officers came to Nick and said, "Lieutenant, they want you in there."

Nick nodded and went back into the men's room. Immediately he recognized Tina Christopher, one of the crime scene investigators who had processed the Marti Montgomery murder scene. "Nick, I was just wondering if you recognized our victim?"

Nick shook his head. "Should I?"

"Does the name Jason Temple ring a bell?"

Nick thought for a moment. "Jason Temple, like in Channel Six TV? That Jason Temple?"

"Uh-huh!" Tina nodded. "That Jason Temple."

Jason Temple was a field reporter for KWEK-TV. In the last year, he had become a regular face on the evening and nightly news.

"It looks like somebody has it in for newscasters," Tina said. "Did you know when I started college I wanted to become a journalist?"

Nick shook his head. "I see you changed your mind."

"Yeah, I changed my major in my sophomore year."

Nick looked at the victim and back to Tina. "It's looking like you made the safer choice."

"Obviously."

"Uhh . . . any note?" Nick asked.

Tina shook her head. "We didn't find any."

He pulled his Android from his belt and typed a text to the deputy chief:

(Nick) *Vic is Jason Temple. KWEK reporter.*

(Mannion) *You sure?*

(Nick) *Yep.*

(Mannion) *Any witnesses?*

(Nick) *Still checking. Just thought I'd give you a heads up.*

(Mannion) *K.*

Nick put his Android back on his belt and went out into the restaurant and summoned Sergeant Thomas. "Did you get anything useful?"

"Nothing. Everybody said the same thing. Some guy came running out screaming. There were different versions of exactly what he said, of course, but it all adds up to the same thing. They all said he looked terrified."

"Do you see any reason to hold any of them?"

"Nope. We checked for any kind of weapons. They were all clean. I have their information. Mostly locals, but a couple of tourists. My partner ran them and nothing came up. I'll bet the perp had already left or was part of the exodus crowd."

"Yeah, we'll know more when we get the time of death." Nick's eyes scanned the room. "I don't see any cameras."

"There are none outside either," Thomas stated.

"Yeah, why make it easy," Nick said.

The bartender was sitting in the booth, and the manager was now standing behind the bar. Nick showed her his badge and sat across from her. "I'm Lieutenant Greer, Phoenix PD."

"Sunnie," she said as she extended her hand. She mirrored the typical cowgirl image. Her white cowboy hat sat on the back of her head, and long, straight brown hair fell from under it. She was an attractive woman in her early twenties. Her multi-colored shirt was unbuttoned just far enough to give a man a sample of what was hidden below, and her smile was inviting.

"Sunnie, that's a cute name. Is that your real name, or is it short for something? Which reminds me, I need to see your ID."

"My purse is behind the bar. I'll go get it." She looked nervous as she began to get up.

Sensing the change in her demeanor, Nick motioned for her to stay seated. "Don't bother." Nick motioned to Sergeant Thomas who came over to the table. "Chris, this young lady's purse is behind the bar. Would you get it, please?"

"I can get it myself," the bartender said as she began to get up again.

The detective nodded politely. "I'm sure you can."

She sat back down. Her hands were twitching, and nervousness consumed her body language. There was silence until Thomas returned with a small brown purse and said, "Is this it, ma'am?"

She nodded. The detective's instincts told him there was something in the purse she didn't want him to see. She reached into the purse, pulled out a wallet from which she produced an Arizona driver's license, and handed it to the detective. She quickly closed her purse and put it on the seat beside her.

"Dawn Rose Dailey," Nick stated as he looked at the name on the driver's license and saw the picture matched. "You go by Sunnie?"

"Yeah, with a name like Dawn Rose Dailey, and in the business I'm in, I get lots of shit. Dawn, you make my pecker rise daily, and stuff like that, so I just go by Sunnie."

Nick grinned. "I understand. I've been the victim of nicknames myself."

"Let me guess . . . Stretch?" She thought for a moment. "You know, I have an uncle who's tall like you. He goes by Shorty. My Dad calls him Gumby. He doesn't like it."

The detective didn't answer. "May I see your purse, please?"

Immediately she became defensive. "Uh, why?"

"Because I want to see what's in it."

"Don't you need a warrant?"

"Ma'am, this is a murder scene. We're checking everyone for weapons. I will need to see your purse, please."

She hesitated, looked down at the purse, and back to Nick, who said, "Now, Miss Dailey. The purse, now!"

She reached down and picked up her purse, set it on the table and slid it over to the detective.

"Please open it and dump it out."

She turned the purse upside down, and the contents fell out onto the table. Nick looked at the items strewn across the table—no razor knife.

Sunnie froze as Nick looked across the table at her. She knew the detective had seen the tiny, clear plastic bag lying among the items. She was certain he knew what was in it.

Seeing nothing resembling a murder weapon, he said, "You can put everything back in your purse, and thank you."

She seemed both surprised and relieved as she pulled all the items across the table into her purse, zipped it, and set it down on the seat. Surely he must have seen it, she thought.

"Now, do you have any idea what happened here tonight?" Nick asked.

She seemed calm now as she answered, "All I know is I was behind the bar, and one of our customers came running out yelling and screaming about a dead man in the men's room. He yelled, 'There's blood everywhere!' "

"Do you know who he was?"

"Uh, no. I don't frequent the men's room."

"I mean, do you know who the customer was? The one who was yelling?"

"Oh, yeah. That was Jerry. He's sort of a regular."

"Jerry who? Do you know his last name?"

She shrugged. "I don't know, just Jerry. He comes two or three times a week, has a couple of drafts and leaves. Sometimes he orders a sandwich. I think he works around here somewhere."

"How does he pay? Does he use cash or a card?"

"It depends. Cash if he only has a beer, but tonight he had a chicken sandwich. He paid for it with a debit card."

The detective called Sergeant Thomas over to the table. "Go with this officer," he said to Sunnie. "Pull all the credit and debit card receipts used within the past three hours. You should be able to match it up." He looked at the sergeant. "I want to know who found the body and why he booked so fast."

Nick turned to Sunnie. "Thank you for your help." He reached for his business card, wrote his cell number on the back and handed it to her. "If you think of anything else, please call me right away.

She nodded as she said, "Uh, thank you. I will."

"What is she thanking you for?" Thomas asked.

Nick shook his head. "Nothing." Nick had thought if he let her slide on the bag of cocaine, perhaps she'd be more cooperative. His instinct served him well.

CHAPTER 38

Deja Vu, All Over Again!

Nick Greer was sitting at his desk when Sonny Madison walked into the SIU. "So how was the celebration? You don't look like you got too wasted."

"You'd be surprised what a couple of Tylenol, a glass of Alka Seltzer, and a fried bologna and egg sandwich can do." Sonny grinned.

"A fried bologna and egg sandwich?"

"My father taught me that. I don't know why. Maybe it's the grease, but it seems to help the stomach the morning after it's been invaded with alcohol the night before." He grinned again. "What ya got from last night? Was it really Jason Temple? Has Nemo struck again?"

"Yes and yes. But it looks like our perp may be changing his MO a little."

"Go ahead. I'm listening." Anticipation emitted from Sonny's face.

"This time it wasn't just hit and run. This time he took the time to prop up the vic. He was sitting on the throne, but his pants were still up. I figure the perp must have put him there somehow."

"Maybe he put the vic in there to get him out of the way so no one would see him. That would give him plenty of time to get away," Sonny suggested.

Nick shook his head. "I don't think so. My gut tells me the perp propped him up after he killed him, but not to hide the body. If he wanted it hidden, don't you think he would've locked the stall from the inside and crawled out under the door?"

"So you think he was making some sort of statement?" Sonny offered.

"Maybe. It looks like he was killed inside the stall. There were splatters on the stall walls and the back wall, but nothing outside of it. There were no drag marks and no signs of blood outside of the stall, except for traces of blood transfer on the floor. It could've been from the perp, or it could've come from the guy who found the body. We'll see what the crime scene report tells us. See what you can find on a Jerry Freeman." He handed Sonny a plastic bag with a credit card receipt in it.

Sonny took the receipt and sat at his desk. He turned on his computer and interlocked his fingers. Nick picked up the sound of cracking knuckles as Sonny said, "Ahh, another day, another murder!"

About five minutes later the phone rang. "SIU, Lieutenant Greer."

He recognized Tricia's voice on the other end. "Chief Mannion would like to see you."

"Okay, we'll be there in a few." He hung up the phone and said to Sonny, "The boss wants us."

Sonny said, "Hang on a sec. I think I have something on your Jerry Freeman."

Nick heard the printer come to life. Sonny said, "Uh, you better get that. By the way, can I have your gun before you do?"

"Why?" Nick was puzzled.

"Uh, 'cause I don't wanna get shot?"

Nick looked at his partner like he was nuts as he went over to the printer, pulled the paper from the tray, and began to read the information. Suddenly he yelled, "NO! God fucking damn no!" He turned and looked at Sonny's desk. Lieutenant Sonny Madison was nowhere to be seen.

CHAPTER 39

Plow The Road

Deputy Chief Bruce Mannion was sitting behind his desk, and Sonny was seated in a chair as Nick entered the office.

Nick shook his head and collapsed into the chair next to his partner. Silence ruled the room as if everyone was waiting for one of the others to speak. Nick rubbed his forehead and finally looked at his partner. "Are you sure?"

Sonny reached over to the chair beside him and put his hand on Nick's gun and nodded. "Yeah, it looks like it." He waited a moment, then asked, "Hey, do you want me to go? With your history there and all."

Nick knew well what Sonny was referring to as he once again looked at the paper in his hand. It read: Reverend Gerald Freeman. His employment address was not far from the Phoenix police station. Four Hundred East Monroe Street—the Roman Catholic Diocese of Phoenix.

Lieutenant Nick Greer had made several trips to the diocesan headquarters in the past, but one case had caused quite a stir as he uncovered a web of corruption while investigating the murder of a local pastor. Several of the bishop's staff members had been involved in a fraudulent schemes ring, and some were arrested. Later, while on another case, another priest, along with a member of the diocesan staff, were both found to have committed a chain of murders. Both were shot and killed, and Sonny Madison was seriously wounded and almost died.

"No, Sonny. I'll go."

Chief Mannion looked at Nick and said, "Uh, do you want me to plow the road?"

"It wouldn't hurt," said Nick.

Mannion nodded and picked up the phone. The detectives left their boss's office.

On the way back to the SIU, Sonny said, "Don't forget your body armor."

"Why?"

"To protect you. I figure if they know you're coming—"

"Shut up, Sonny!"

Sonny grinned and shrugged. "Just a thought."

"What did the chief want, anyway?"

"Oh, just an update. I filled him in."

What Nick didn't know was Sonny had texted Bruce Mannion as soon as he discovered Freeman was a priest; before he told Nick:

(Sonny) *The guy who found the body last night is a priest.*

(Mannion) *No shit! Does Nick know?*

(Sonny) *Not yet.*

(Mannion) *You gonna tell him?*

(Sonny) *Call us into your office right away.*

Shortly after they returned to the SIU, Nick's cell phone rang. It was a text from Bruce Mannion: *The road is plowed. Good luck!*

He went to his desk and grabbed his keys. As he headed for the door, he heard Sonny say, "How long do you want me to wait?"

"Huh? Wait for what?"

"To notify your next of kin if you don't come back. What do you think? An hour, maybe two?"

Nick's long arm almost touched the ceiling as he stretched it as high as he could and made a fist. The single finger that popped out from the fist may actually have touched the ceiling.

CHAPTER 40

Sky Pilot

Once again Detective Lieutenant Nick Greer made his way along the sidewalk leading to the entrance of 400 West Monroe Street. The familiar letters on the door read: Roman Catholic Diocese of Phoenix, Arizona. He opened the door and walked across the lobby to the reception desk. He remembered the receptionist from his previous visits. "Welcome, Lieutenant Greer. It's good to see you again. You are here to see Father Freeman, I assume?"

Nick nodded. "Yes, ma'am, I am."

She pressed some numbers into the phone, waited a moment, looked up at her guest, and smiled. "Father Freeman is in his office. If you'll go through the door and turn right, it's the fourth office on the right. Have a blessed day."

He heard the buzz from the door. He opened it, turned right and followed the hallway to the fourth door. It was open, and he walked in. Standing behind the desk was a man dressed in black and wearing a clerical collar. He was short in stature, about five-feet-six with brown wavy hair. He looked to be about twenty-five.

"I'm Father Jerry Freeman," the priest said as he extended his hand.

Nick shook the cleric's hand. The grip was firm. "Lieutenant Nick Greer, Phoenix PD."

"Please, have a seat, Lieutenant. I understand you have some questions for me."

They sat and Nick's eyes scanned the small, but neat office. The walls were adorned with various certificates and pictures: one of the Pope, a couple of what appeared to be family, one of a small low-winged airplane, and one of an old yellow biplane. Nick asked, "I see you must like airplanes."

"Oh, yes. I'm a pilot."

"Really?"

The cleric saw the shocked look on his guest's face and said, "Lieutenant, don't be so surprised. We priests have lives, too. Most of us have a hobby of some sort; one of mine is flying. I've been doing it since I was fourteen."

Nick pointed to the pictures. "So, is one of them yours?"

"No, sir. I belong to a flying club. That's a Piper Archer on the left, the plane I prefer to fly. The other one belonged to my grandfather."

"What made you want to learn to fly?"

"Oh, it's sort of a family thing, I guess. My father and my grandfather were both pilots. My grandfather was a crop duster back in Georgia. My father just liked to fly. I guess it sort of runs in the family."

"How often do you fly?"

"Not as often as I would like, but I assume you didn't come here to talk about airplanes. I suppose you're here about the man at State 48."

Nick liked the man. He was young, but straight to the point. "Yes, I understand you discovered the body. Am I correct?"

"Yes, I did."

"Why did you take off? Why did you run?"

"I'm sorry about that. I discussed it with my supervisor this morning. I was just about to call the police about it when I got a call from the chancellor stating you were on your way here."

"Again, why did you take off? Why did you leave the scene?"

"You know, when I saw all that blood, I panicked, I guess. I've never seen anything like that before. I mean, he was all bloody, and, well, like I said, I panicked. I really am sorry, Lieutenant. I know I should've stayed there. Am I in trouble?"

"I don't know. Tell me, Father, how you came upon the body. Tell me exactly what you saw."

"Well, I had a couple beers; that runs in the family, too. Dad used to brew his own, and so did Grandpa. You might say that's another family tradition." He smiled, but his visitor was emotionless. "Well, anyway, I needed to relieve myself, so I went to the men's room."

"Did you see anyone coming out as you were going in?"

"Uh, not that I noticed."

"Was there anyone else in there?"

"No. I saw no one."

"Did you hear anything?"

"No, sir, nothing."

"Okay, please continue," Nick said. "How did you come across the victim?"

"Well, as I was washing my hands, I looked into the mirror, and I thought I saw something red on the floor underneath one of the stall doors. At first I didn't think anything of it. Then I thought it looked like blood, so I went over to the stall and knocked on it. 'Anybody in there?' I asked. The door opened when I knocked. That's when I saw it."

"Tell me exactly what you saw."

The priest squirmed a little. It was obvious he was uncomfortable, but he was able to retain most of his composure. "A man . . . a man was sitting on the toilet. The front of his shirt was . . ."—he took a breath and exhaled—"was covered with blood." He shook his head. "And his eyes . . . they were wide open. It was like I was in a horror movie. I don't like gory movies!"

"Then what did you do?" the detective asked.

"I panicked, I guess. I ran out of there as fast as I could. I got in my car and drove home." He looked at the detective. "I'm sorry, Lieutenant. I know I should have stayed, but the first thing I thought was what would happen if I were on the news? What would the bishop say?"

"You mean you were worried your bishop would find out you were at a bar?"

"Oh, heavens no. He wouldn't care about that. Like I said, we all have a life. He knows that. He tosses some down himself at times. I was worried about the publicity and how it would affect the church. You know how people are. They seem to think we priests should walk around with our hands constantly folded in prayer. Heaven forbid we should ever go near a bar or drink anything alcoholic except altar wine! Do you ever drink that stuff? Are you Catholic, Lieutenant?"

The detective ignored the questions. He rubbed his chin as he thought for a moment. He looked at the priest. He seemed sincere. "Thank you, Father. The next time something like that happens, stick around, okay?"

"The next time? I should hope there will not be a next time."

They shook hands. Nick left the building and headed back to the SIU.

CHAPTER 41

Discovery

Lieutenant Sonny Madison was on the phone when Detective Rick Yeager walked into the SIU. He motioned for his visitor to have a seat as he kept talking, "Uh-huh. Yeager just came in. Where are you? Okay, I'll tell him."

Sonny disconnected the phone and said, "Nick's on his way up. Go ahead and have a seat. How are you handling it?"

"Which 'it' are you talking about?"

"Jim. Jim Holder. You guys were tight, weren't you?"

"Yeah, I guess so. We were partners for a while, and we worked other cases together. You know the drill. Kinda like you and Nick."

Sonny nodded. "So, are you okay?"

"I'm still trying to work it out in my head."

"I understand," Sonny replied.

"If I can help you find this guy in any way . . ."

"We'll let you know," Sonny said.

"He was a good cop and a good man. He'll be missed."

"He wasn't married, was he?" Sonny asked.

"No. He had a live-in, but I never met her. He didn't talk much about his personal life."

Yeager looked toward the door. "I just stopped by to see Nick. I guess I owe him an apology. I wanted to let him know we got the perp who killed Jeffrey Winters."

"Who?"

"I'll wait until Nick gets here and tell you both at the same time."

Sonny pointed to the back of the room. "There's coffee if you want some."

Yeager poured a cup and stood staring out the window as he sipped the hot brew. He said to Sonny, "Remember how bad the coffee was in homicide?"

Sonny nodded. "Yeah, we thought it was the worst in the world."

"Second worst," Yeager said as he held up his cup. "This tastes like it's two days old."

"That's probably because it is. I reheated it from yesterday."

Yeager was about to comment when Nick Greer came into the SIU. "Hey, Rick, what's up?" Nick asked as he sat at his desk. Yeager sat next to the desk, and Sonny slid a chair over and joined them.

"I'm so sorry about Jim," Nick stated.

"Thanks. Just find the bastard who did it. If I can help—"

"I know. We'll handle it. We got a hold of it."

Yeager nodded. "Nick, I came to apologize to you. We found the person who murdered Jeffrey Winters."

"I'm not the one to apologize to. Just don't ever run into my ex-wife."

"Uh, I'll do my best not to, especially if she's anywhere near a lamp."

"It's not like we never charged the wrong persons. You know, glass houses–throw stones," Sonny said. Yeager nodded.

"So who did it?" asked Nick. "Was it because of the money he owed? He had a gambling problem. He probably owed the wrong people. I'd bet on it." Nick stopped for a moment and smiled. "Uhh, no pun intended."

"Actually, you were right. We found out he was a casino regular, and he also frequented some private high-stakes games, but we weren't able to connect any of them to the murder. You know how that is."

"Yeah, you're right. If you owe the bad guys, they may break something you need, but they don't usually kill you. They find it hard to collect from a corpse. Okay, so who did it? Who killed Jeff Winters?"

"Carmella Winters. The vic's wife."

"No shit!" Sonny exclaimed.

"You're sure?" Nick asked.

"Yeah. She confessed," the detective answered. "It appears they had been having problems for quite a while. You were right about his gambling. He lost a bunch of money, and she found out about it. Then she found out he was having an affair, so one day she kicked him out. Though it may look like he was the money in the family, a lot of it was hers. Don't get me wrong; he did all right, but he married Carmella Morales. Do you recognize the name?"

Nick and Sonny looked at each other. They both shook their heads. "Should we?" Sonny questioned.

"Do you remember the old pepper mill in Glendale?"

Both detectives nodded. Nick said, "Yeah, Morales Foods. That plant has been shut down for a long time."

"It was Grandpa's," Yeager said. "They sold out to some big national company about twenty years ago. I guess she's all that's left of the family and the money. Anyway, she said he wanted to come back to her. He told her he had quit gambling, and he had broken up with Cassie. He wanted to reconcile, so she took him back, but she didn't trust him. One day she found a receipt for seven thousand dollars from Jared Jewelry Store. It turned out to be for a diamond ring. It was dated a month after they had supposedly reconciled. She realized something was going on, so she hired a private investigator to follow him."

Sonny grinned. "Ahhh, . . . he went to Jared. She went to a PI."

"Exactly." Yeager laughed and continued, "She said the PI told her Winters was still seeing Cassie, so she decided to check it out herself. Winters told her he was going to Flagstaff on business, and he would be gone all night. She didn't believe him, so she followed him to the Valley Motel and waited outside. When she saw Cassie leave, she went into the room and bashed his head in with a tire iron. We found the murder weapon in her trunk with his blood and her prints on it."

"What about the ring?" Nick questioned.

"We found it in her jewelry box. You were right; it's a big sucker."

"Thanks, Rick. I appreciate the news. I'll let Cassie know. You'll tell Bruce?"

"He already knows. We played racquetball this morning. I told him about it." Yeager got up to leave, then turned around and said, "Nick, I'm really sorry about Cassie. I owe you one."

"Don't worry about it." They shook hands and Yeager left the SIU.

After Detective Yeager had gone, Sonny said to Nick, "So, should I ask how it went at the Diocese?" He looked up and down at his partner like he was inspecting him, then grinned. "I don't see any marks. Your clothes aren't torn, and you don't seem to be bleeding."

"The priest was okay. I don't think he knows anything." Nick described his visit with Father Jerry Freeman.

"So why the look on your face?" Sonny questioned.

"What look?"

He pointed to Nick's face. "That look. The look I know so well. The look that says those little wheels waaaay up there inside your brain cage are moving at warp drive. The look that says Nick knows something Sonny doesn't."

Nick shook his head. "Just thinking, that's all. Just thinking."

"Uh, yeah, well, that's what I'm afraid of."

CHAPTER 42

Who's Who?

"Holy shit! Hey, Nick, look at this!"

Nick got up from his desk and walked over to Sonny. "Whatcha got?"

"You know I was having a problem with the background for Leo Cardinale, right? Now I know why I couldn't find him." His face shone like a kid who just came down the stairs Christmas morning and saw a much-longed-for shiny new bicycle under the tree.

"Why?"

"He isn't."

"Huh? He isn't what?"

"Not what! Who! Cardinale isn't Cardinale; well, he is, but he wasn't."

Nick shook his head like he was shaking off some unwanted dust. "Sonny Madison, you're not making any sense."

Sonny looked at his friend and grinned. "Does the name James Leonard Mitchell make a ring-a-ding way up there in that bell tower of yours?"

Nick thought for a moment. He knew he had heard the name before, then he remembered the young girl who had been raped and murdered about four years ago. "The Hernandez girl? That James Leonard Mitchell?"

Sonny nodded. "Yep. That James Leonard Mitchell!"

"Yeah, I remember. Holder and Yeager caught the case. They arrested Mitchell and charged him with the girl's abduction."

"Right, but you'll remember later, when they dug up the body in the desert, they had to let Mitchell go because the DNA on her wasn't his."

"I remember it well. Boy, was Holder pissed! He came into the squad room and started throwing just about anything he could reach. We finally had to restrain him. I thought the captain was going to suspend him. Both he and Yeager were so sure Mitchell was good for it."

"Yeah, they found the real perp a couple of months later. He was a known sex offender who lived around the corner from the girl's house. The DNA was a right-on match. There'll be a needle in his future, for sure."

"Yeah, if he lives long enough." Nick looked at his partner. "Okay, so what does Mitchell have to do with Cardinale?"

"James Leonard Mitchell and Leo Cardinale are one and the same."

"He changed his name?"

"Yep, a couple of years ago."

"You know, I don't blame him. I'd probably do the same. Even though he was innocent, all that publicity would follow him around for ages."

"Yeah, me too, but I'd get my ass out of town. I'd move as far away as possible. I hear Maine is really nice." Sonny pointed to the computer screen and said slowly, "And . . . guess who the prosecuting attorney was?"

"Shelley?"

Sonny looked up and grinned. "Good answer, Mr. Master's Degree. I knew that fancy diploma wasn't completely wasted."

"Working for the security company sure gives him opportunity. Who has the case now?" He knew Shelley wouldn't be back for a while, and her cases would be assigned to other prosecutors.

Sonny answered, "Your buddy, Nero."

"Okay, let's go talk to ADA Cordova," Nick said.

As they left the SIU and headed for Cordova's office, Sonny said, "Oh, by the way, there's one more little thing."

"Uh, okay, what?"

"Cardinale, excuse me, Mitchell, was in the army—the first Iraq war."

"And?" Nick asked.

"Special Forces."

"So he knows how to kill."

"You betcha!"

* * *

Assistant District Attorney Clark Cordova was sitting at his desk when Lieutenants Nick Greer and Sonny Madison walked into his office. "Welcome, Detectives. What can I do for you today?"

As they sat down, Cordova looked at Sonny and said, "By the way, congratulations on your promotion, Lieutenant."

"Thanks," Sonny replied.

Cordova looked at Nick. "I'm glad to hear your ex is free. It looks like Yeager jumped on another one too soon."

"Sometimes we don't get it right," Nick said.

The ADA pointed to a manila file in front of him. "I've read over the case. Speaking of not getting it right, I see there have been two arrests, and both suspects have been let go. Are you guys and Yeager having some sort of contest?"

Sonny's face turned beet red, and he looked like he was going to stand up. Nick reached out and touched his arm and said, "We'll take that one, Clark, but I wouldn't push it too much further."

Cordova had seen Sonny's reaction. He leaned back in his chair and said, "Okay, Detective. I got it. What do you have for me?"

"Well, as you know, we got Scanlon's wife and Vincent Peruzzi as our best bets, but we know Peruzzi didn't go after Shelley, unless he can be in two places at once. We checked on Shannon Scanlon. She was called in to work early the night Shelley was attacked. Several employees substantiated that. We have a list of possibles, but we can't find a connection to Shelley with any of them."

Sonny added, "And there's no connection to her or to Judge Cavallo with Shannon Scanlon or her husband, or Marti Montgomery. As you know, there is a connection to everyone except Shelley with Peruzzi, but he was a guest at Fourth Avenue when she was attacked."

"It sounds like a game of connect the dots that just doesn't connect," Cordova stated.

"Anyone else we have talked to has no connection at all," Nick added. "We can't find a motive; however, do you remember the name James Leonard Mitchell?"

"Oh yes. How could I forget? We ended up with egg on our faces over that case. The detectives, uh, Holder and Yeager, I think, did a sloppy job." He stopped and, almost as an afterthought, said, "By the way, I'm sorry to hear about Detective Holder." Both detectives nodded.

"How well I remember," Nick commented. "We were all under pressure from the DA and the chief, and they were getting it from the mayor. The media was having a field day with us, remember? Inept was just one of the adjectives they used. We were even accused of not giving the case enough attention because the missing girl was Hispanic. The whole department was relieved when Mitchell was arrested."

"Yeah," Cordova responded. "He looked good for it. He knew the girl. She babysat his kids. He was supposedly seen in the vicinity the night she was abducted from her bedroom. He couldn't account for his whereabouts. He claimed he was in his office, alone, working late. Yeager checked with the alarm company. They said the alarm was never set that night. Mitchell claimed he forgot to set it. We had everything we needed, except the body. We figured it would show up somewhere and when those ATV riders found the foot sticking out of the ground, we all figured it was over. But the goddamn DNA didn't match! We sure looked stupid when we had to let him go!"

"Who was the judge who arraigned him?" Nick asked.

Cordova momentarily froze. Then he looked up at Nick. Both detectives could see the shock of discovery in his eyes as he said, "Uh, Richard Cavallo!"

Nick looked at Sonny. "Are you thinking what I'm thinking?"

"I'd bet on it," Sonny responded.

The two detectives got up simultaneously as if cued by the director of an important movie scene. "Where are you going? Hey, wait a—" Cordova's words were wasted; he could see their backs as they left. He knew the two detectives were on a mission.

CHAPTER 43

Secure-Max

"You should've let me smack the arrogant son of a bitch!" Sonny stated as they walked into the SIU.

"Uh, you would've had the shortest tenure as a lieutenant in department history."

"Yeah, well it might have been worth it."

"Yeah, I know. I considered it myself. But we need him on our side right now. Let's take a little ride to Tempe. I want to see what Secure-Max has to say." He smiled as he looked at Sonny. "Hey, I'll even drive."

"Shit! I can get used to this." Sonny grinned.

They pulled into the parking lot off of University Drive and Rural Road and walked into the Secure-Max office. It was a small company located in a strip mall. They were greeted by a lady who looked to be in her early thirties, wearing a blue polo shirt with a Secure-Max logo on it. Nick held up his badge. "Lieutenants Greer and Madison, Phoenix PD. Is your manager in?"

She smiled. "That would be me." She extended her hand and said, "Gloria Welker. How can I help you?"

Though she carried about thirty extra pounds, she was an attractive woman with long blonde hair hanging down to the middle of her back.

"Is Leo Cardinale working here today?"

"No, he's not here."

"Where can we find him?" Nick asked.

"I don't know. He didn't come in this morning. I had to split his calls up."

"Did he call or say why he wasn't coming in or where he was going?"

"No, sir."

"Isn't that a little unusual?" Sonny asked.

"Well, yes and no."

Both detectives could see she was beginning to feel uncomfortable. "Uh, what do you mean by yes and no?" Sonny questioned.

"Uhm, he . . . why do you want to know? Has he done something wrong?"

"We don't know, ma'am. That's what we're trying to figure out. Now, please tell us what you meant by yes and no."

"Uh, he has been known to drink a bit lately."

Nick took over. "Ma'am, how often does he do this? Not show up without calling, I mean?"

"Oh, not often. He's dealing with some problems, and sometimes drinking helps."

"What kind of problems?"

"You'll have to ask him."

"I assume you do background checks on all of your employees?" Sonny asked.

"Oh, sure, of course." The look in her eyes told Nick she was hiding something.

When Nick Greer was in college he obtained a lot of his spending money by playing poker. He had an uncanny ability to read a person's eyes and know if they were bluffing. He read hers. She was hiding something; he was sure of it. He decided to raise the ante. "How did Mr. Cardinale's background report check out?"

"Okay, I guess."

"You guess? Don't you know? Didn't you say you were the manager? What did you find on his background report? I'd like to see his file, if you don't mind."

"Yes, Detective, I do mind. That's confidential information. Why do you want to know?"

"It's a police matter, ma'am," Sonny said. "We'd like to see his employee file."

"Like I said, that's confidential information. I would need to see a warrant in order to show it to you." She looked into Nick's eyes. "Do you have a warrant, Lieutenant?"

Nick remained calm. "Ms. Welker, I don't think you're being straight with us. You seem like a nice lady, and I would hate to arrest you for obstructing a police investigation; that's a felony, by the way. I'm wondering if that would cost you your job."

"I own the company. My job is secure."

"That may be true, but what about your license?" Nick knew a small security firm like this would go under if their private investigator's license was suspended or revoked. She also knew these detectives had the power to have it done.

Her face flushed as she looked at Sonny, who had pulled a pair of handcuffs from his belt and was shaking them as he held them out in front of him. A trace of fear had begun to form in her eyes as she looked at the silvery circles of metal dangling from Sonny's finger.

"Now," Nick continued. "Please tell us if you knew he had changed his name from James Leonard Mitchell to Leo Cardinale."

Her face flushed, and she looked like she had just been caught with her fingers in the cookie jar. She sat down behind the desk, placed her elbows on the desk, and put her face in her hands. She emitted a sigh, then whispered something, but the detectives couldn't make it out.

"We didn't hear you," Nick said. "Please repeat what you said."

She looked up. Tears were running down her cheeks. "He's my brother. Jimmy is my brother."

Both Nick and Sonny's eyes widened as they looked at each other. Sonny put away the cuffs.

Welker said, "After he was arrested, he lost everything. He couldn't get a job. When their house was foreclosed on, Corrine left him and took their baby. That's when he started drinking. I tried to help him. It was I who suggested he change his name. As you know, being in the business I'm in, I know people, so I got him some help. Then I hired him to work here." The tears had disappeared, and her eyes exhibited resolve. "Look, my brother is a good man! What you cops did to him ruined his life! He was respected. He was somebody; then, all of a sudden, he became less than nothing. I owed him. Look around you." She motioned with her hands. "It was Jimmy who gave me the money for this company. I had to help him, don't you see?"

"I understand," Nick responded. "So tell us, where is he now? And I want the truth. You're in enough trouble already, Ms. Welker, so don't even think of lying to us."

She shook her head. "I guess he's at his place. I called there a couple of times, but he hasn't answered his phone. He's probably passed out."

Sonny had just hung up his cell phone and nodded to Nick who looked back to Welker and said, "You know you're in trouble."

"Are you going to arrest me?"

The two detectives knew time was not on their side, and it would only be worse if they took the time to arrest her. "Don't leave town, Ms. Welker," Nick stated. Both detectives turned and left.

They hurried to Nick's car. By the time they left the parking lot, Sonny was already on his cell phone calling for a warrant.

CHAPTER 44

The Search

Leo Cardinale's pickup was nowhere to be seen as the team took their positions. All twelve were in full body armor and armed with Remington 870P shotguns, except Nick and Sonny who just had their Glock 17s. Sergeant Thomas tested the side gate. He gave the signal to Nick that the gate was unlocked. Then he and his partner headed toward the back door with their guns at the ready in case the suspect decided to run through the back. There were homes behind and on both sides of the Cardinale house, with six-foot-high cement block walls around each of them. If he was home, he wasn't getting away, at least not through the back—not through Sergeant Thomas.

Nick knocked hard. "Phoenix Police! We have a warrant! Open the door." The steel security screen door would have been hard to break. Sonny saw a large rock, about eight by twelve inches and picked it up. Glass shattered as he threw it through the window next to the front door. One of the uniformed officers pulled his baton and cleared the glass from the window edges.

Sonny entered first and turned the deadbolt latches on both the inner and outer door, and the team rushed in. Two by two they moved through the house in different directions like a fine-tuned machine, calling out loudly "clear" as each room was checked and found to be void of human life. Suddenly they heard Sonny yell. "Nick, back here."

Sonny was standing in the middle of a bedroom-turned-office in the far corner of the house. In the room was a glass corner desk. On the desk were a computer and a printer. But it was what was on the wall, behind the desk, that had caught the detective's attention. It was a corkboard with an array of pictures pinned on it. Pictures of Marti Montgomery, Bill Scanlon, Richard Cavallo, Shelley Kisler, James Holder, and Jason Temple were all lined up beside each other. There was one more picture: Rick Yeager. Montgomery, Scanlon, Temple and Holder had a red X over their faces. Cavallo's face had only a slash over it and Yeager's was clean. Below each picture were photos relating to each of them. There were shots of the Scanlon, Holder, and Yeager houses, Shelley's apartment building, Cavallo's condo, and the State 48 bar and restaurant, along with photos of each of their vehicles.

Sergeant Thomas entered the room and said to Nick, "The place is secure." He froze when his eyes caught the collage on the wall. "Holy shit!"

Nick told Sonny, "Grab the computer." He looked at Sergeant Thomas. "Get this place sealed up. Park a black and white in front of it if you have to." Nick pulled his cell phone and took a picture of the corkboard.

Sonny donned a pair of gloves and disconnected the computer, and as he did, he stopped for a moment and pointed to the board. "Hey, Nick, what do you make of that? It looks like he might be heading south."

Nick looked at the bottom right-hand corner and saw a map of Mexico. Circled in red was Durango, a city in central Mexico. He took several more pictures, pulled on a pair of gloves, then reached out and pulled the bulletin board from the wall. "I'll take this with me."

Just then, Sergeant Thomas came back and said, "I just checked his bedroom closets and drawers. It looks like his clothes are gone."

Nick said to Sonny, "Get an APB out on his truck. If he's headed for the border, let's stop him. It's a fairly new white Ford F150 club cab with oversized tires. Get the plate number and call it in."

"Sergeant, did you check the garage?" Nick asked Thomas.

"Of course. It's empty."

"Empty? There's a car in there though, right?"

"No, sir."

"Are you telling me there are no cars in there?"

"No, sir. Except for some tools and a car cover, the garage is empty."

The lieutenant hurried to the garage. Sergeant Thomas followed. Nick opened the door and saw the garage was empty. The gray cover that once protected the shiny Mustang was lying on the floor, right where the car had been.

"It looks like he's in the wind," Thomas remarked.

Nick said, "Hmm, I wonder which direction the wind is blowing."

On their way back to the precinct, Sonny said, "Well, partner, I think we know who the perp is; now all we have to do is find him. There are a lot of places to hide between here and the border. I guess it depends on when he left. If he left last night, he may already be drinking tequila and sucking on a lemon."

"Sonny, change the APB. Extend it in all directions and include a 1967 Ford Mustang. It should be easy to spot. It has a shiny new paint job—candy-apple red!"

CHAPTER 45

Say Cheese

"I can't take it anymore. I've been waiting all morning. I'm going to the lab. They gotta have something by now," Nick said to Sonny as he got up from his desk and left the SIU.

Sue Kim was holding up a vial of clear liquid as Nick came into the lab. "What's happening, baby? What are you working on?"

She jerked when she heard him. "Don't sneak up on me like that. You almost made me drop this thing."

"Is that for our case?"

She shook her head. "Nope. You don't think I have other cases? I'm not your personal CSI, you know. Besides, doing double duty here and assisting in the morgue has put me way behind." She handed him the vial and said, "Here, hold this until I get back." She picked up a dropper, held it over the vial, and squeezed one drop into it. "Be careful not to spill it. I gotta go pee."

"What's in it?" he questioned as she took off her gloves.

"That's what I'm trying to figure out. It's either nothing or some pretty nasty stuff!"

"Uh, shouldn't I be wearing gloves?"

"Probably. It's too late now, anyway. Just be careful not to spill it, especially if it turns blue. That could mean it's the nasty stuff." His eyes followed her as she left the lab.

Nick had been holding the vial out in front of him, and he turned his head to look at it. It had turned blue. He looked at the gloves Sue Kim had thrown into the trash, and then he looked at the vial. Even if he could reach the gloves, the vial was full, all the way. He was afraid to move. He had no idea what was in it. Sue Kim said it was nasty stuff if it turned blue. He was afraid he would spill it, and he certainly didn't want it to spill onto his skin.

A few minutes later, Sue Kim came back into the lab. "Oh, no! It's blue! I gotta call HazMat right away. Don't move! Close your eyes! Don't breathe!" She saw the look of terror on his face, and she quickly grabbed her cell phone. But instead of dialing, she took his picture, then she broke out in a roaring laugh. She reached out and took the vial from his hand and dumped it into the sink.

Nick looked at her with a puzzled look on his face. She giggled. "It's only water and copper sulfate. It's harmless. You should have seen the look on your face. Wait 'til I post it on Facebook!"

"You wouldn't!"

She pressed her finger to her cell phone and said, "I just did. That'll teach you to go on a romantic picnic with your ex-wife."

"It wasn't romantic, and I told you, nothing happened. I wouldn't let it."

"You could have said no."

"The girls really wanted to go the lake. What did you want me to do? Pick up the picnic basket and tell Cassie we were going without her?"

"That would have been okay with me," she said. "So why are you here, Lieutenant? Why aren't you out arresting bad guys?"

"I actually came to check on Cardinale's computer. I thought I'd give you the privilege of my company, but I guess that ship has sailed."

"Reggie has it."

"Okay, I'll go see her." He looked into her eyes and said, "Okay, are we done now? Can we get back to life as usual?"

"You're taking me out for dinner Saturday. I'll pick the place. Then we'll see."

"Uh, I have the kids this weekend."

"Okay, let them pick."

"Kaitlin will want Burger King. I hate Burger King."

"Life's a bitch. Go, I'm busy." She motioned with her hand for him to shoo.

Nick walked into the computer lab. Regina Grayson was working on what Nick recognized as the computer they had removed from the Cardinale home. "Any luck yet, Reggie?"

"I just finished. The files were deleted, but I was able to recover them. There's nothing much here. He didn't seem to have much in the way of friends. He wasn't on Facebook, and he didn't have much in the way of emails. Mostly junk, a couple from his work. There were a lot of pictures and information on Mexico, though."

Nick nodded. "That makes sense. Thanks, Reggie."

A smile appeared on the technician's face, and she looked at Nick. "Uh, did you find something amusing?" he asked.

She lifted her cell phone and showed him the picture Sue Kim had posted. It was a close-up of Nick's face. His mouth was open, and his eyes were shut tight. He was holding a blue vial as far from him as his long arms could stretch. The caption read: Big bad brave cop! "Cute," she said.

Nick went back to the SIU. Just as he walked through the door, Sonny said, "I was just getting ready to text you. Cardinale's truck was found at the bus station. Sergeant Thomas is there now checking it out."

Nick sat at his desk without uttering a word. He placed his elbows on the desk, cupped his hand over his mouth, stroked his mustache, and stared at the corkboard they had put on an easel. After about ten minutes, he broke the silence. "Have they booked the sister yet?"

"I'll check." After a couple of minutes, he said, "She's in the matrix now."

Nick abruptly got up and left.

"Hey, Gumby! Where are you going?"

"Central booking."

"Why?"

"To see which way the wind is blowing."

* * *

Nick sat down with Gloria Welker and said, "Ma'am, I don't believe you've been truthful with us. I'm charging you with obstruction of justice and aiding and abetting a murderer. In case you don't know, you're looking at prison time. I'd say several years of it. And that little business you have? History!"

"Murderer? He said he was in some kind of trouble, but murder? Not my brother! You have the wrong guy again."

"I believe your brother has killed at least five people including a judge and a police officer, and he attempted to kill an assistant district attorney."

Shock seized her. "You're saying my brother is the Nemo killer they're talking about all over the news channels? I don't believe it, not Jimmy, no way. You're wrong!"

"I need to know where your brother is, or where he went, and I need to know now." Nick's voice tone was stern and direct.

"I don't know. He called last night and said he was leaving town for a while and not to worry. He said he'd call me when he could." She looked at the detective. He thought he saw sincerity in her eyes. "That's all I know, honest."

"You said his wife took their child and moved away. Do you know where they moved to?"

"No, I don't. She's from somewhere in Colorado though."

Nick's mind went straight to the corkboard and the map of Mexico. Durango, Mexico.

"It wouldn't be Durango, Colorado, would it?"

She shrugged and turned away from the detective. Now Lieutenant Nick Greer knew which way the wind was blowing.

* * *

It was about twenty minutes later when Sonny's cell phone rang. "Yeah, Nick. Where the hell are you?"

"What did you find out at the bus station? What did Thomas say?"

"Nothing. He even checked the video tapes. No one with that description even entered the building in the last twenty-four hours."

"I thought so. Change the search area. Concentrate it north. If he's really in the wind, I think it's blowing toward Colorado."

"How do you know? And what do you mean by if he's really in the wind?"

"I'll explain when I get there."

A couple of minutes later Sonny's phone rang again. "What did you forget?"

"Get a hold of Yeager. Tell him there's a twenty-four on him. Our guy may not be done yet. I already cleared it with Bruce."

"Okay," Sonny answered. "Oh, by the way, nice picture." The call was disconnected.

CHAPTER 46

The Wind

It was less than an hour later when Detective Rick Yeager walked into the SIU and went straight over to Nick. "Nick, what's going on? Why do you want me protected? And from whom?"

"His name is Leo Cardinale."

"Never heard of him."

"How about James Leonard Mitchell? Do you recognize that name?"

"How could I forget that name? What a cluster-fuck that was. I still think he's a murderer."

"So do we. But not the Hernandez girl." He continued, "Sit down, Rick." Nick motioned for Sonny to join them. "I'll bring you up to speed."

Nick began, "This is what we think. After Mitchell was arrested, his business went down the toilet. Do you remember what he did for a living?" He didn't give Yeager a chance to answer. "He was a big-time stockbroker. According to his sister, he lost everything including his family. I think this whole thing is about revenge. He's going after everybody he thinks contributed to his downfall."

Yeager said, "Okay, I understand. Holder and I were the arresting officers, but what about the others? What about those newscasters?"

"I don't know. Maybe he blamed the media for the bad publicity, we'll see. But Cavallo was the judge who denied bail, and Shelley caught the case as the prosecutor. He's gone after all of them, and I think you may be next."

Nick opened a file and removed copies of the pictures they had confiscated from the Cardinale home. Yeager's eyes widened as he saw his picture and those of his car and home. "That's why the protection," Nick said.

"I don't need protection. I can handle myself. I'm a trained police officer. I know the ropes. I don't need a goddamn babysitter!"

Sonny looked at Yeager and said, "Rob Holder was a trained police officer, too, and, no offense, more seasoned than you."

"Yeah, but he wasn't expecting it. I'll be looking for him. I can watch my own back."

Nick said, "Look, this perp has military training; ex-Special Forces. He knows what he's doing. He stalks his prey and strikes at the exact right time. None of the victims saw him coming."

"Hey, I did two tours. I can handle myself."

"Don't be so macho. You have a family to think about. So far none of the victims have had children around. If this guy goes after you, who knows what collateral damage could occur?"

"Let me think about it. I'll let you know."

"Rick, there's nothing to let me know about. The chief gave the order. If you have a problem, take it to him, for whatever good it'll do."

Just then Sonny heard a buzz coming from his desk. It was his cell phone vibrating. He went to his desk and picked it up. "Lieutenant Madison . . . Uh-huh . . . Okay. Thanks."

He turned to the two detectives. "Cardinale's debit card was just used at a convenience store in Winslow. It looks like you're right; he's heading north."

"Call the Winslow police. See if they can stop him."

"I already did," Sonny answered. "DPS is on the lookout, too."

"See, I don't need no goddamn guard," Yeager said. "Thanks for the offer, but I'll be fine." He turned and left the SIU.

It was about thirty minutes later when Sonny's phone rang again. "Lieutenant Madison."

"Lieutenant, this is Sergeant Coolidge, Winslow PD."

"Go ahead, Sergeant."

"Like you asked, we checked out the scene here in Winslow. We checked the videos, and this guy doesn't look like your perp."

"What do you mean? Why not?" Sonny motioned for Nick to come over as he pressed the phone's speaker button.

"Neither the suspect nor the vehicle match the information we have. The subject car was a red Ford all right, but a late model Focus, not a Mustang; and the driver didn't match your guy at all. He looks like he's about five-eight and two-hundred-fifty pounds and your guy is supposed to be five-eleven and one-seventy."

Nick spoke, "This is Lieutenant Greer. Did you get the plates?"

"Yeah, we're running them now."

"Read them off to me."

"Arizona, Mike Adam X-ray Zero Eight Zero."

"Thank you, Sergeant. You might want to be on the lookout for the car. I have the feeling he's heading south."

"Will do. What did he do, anyway?"

"Not sure, but it involves a murder case we've been working on."

"It's not that Nemo guy, is it?"

Nick shook his head and walked back to his desk. Sonny said to the officer, "You guys know about that up there?"

He laughed. "Yeah. We got TV, you know."

"I'll bet you do." Sonny disconnected the call.

"Get a hold of DPS. Have them be on the lookout for that Focus," Nick said. "Have them watch the northern border close, but I think the wind just shifted again. This guy is smarter than I thought. I have the feeling he sent us on a wild goose chase."

"What?"

"He's not done yet. He's on a mission, and it's not completed. Either he's coming back to Phoenix to finish it, or he never left in the first place. Run the plates. I wanna know who owns that car."

Sonny typed, waited a moment and said, "The twenty-eleven Ford Focus belongs to an Oscar Morales." He typed some more and said, "Holy fuckin' shit, Gumby. Look where he works." He turned the computer screen so Nick could get a better view.

Nick said, "No shit!" He looked back at Sonny and said, "Find out where they have Gloria Welker and text me." He picked up his keys and left the SIU.

The elevator doors opened. As Nick stepped out, his cell phone rang. It read: Sonny. "Yeah."

"She's still in holding, but they're getting ready to take her to Fourth Avenue."

"Tell them to hold her. Meet me there. Call Cordova."

"I'll call Bruce, too."

"No, Sonny—just Cordova. He's all we need for now."

* * *

Gloria Welker was sitting at a table in the interview room when Nick and Sonny came in. Sonny remained standing and Nick sat down and began, "Okay, Ms. Welker, the game is over."

"It's Mrs. Welker, and what game are you talking about?"

"We need to know where your brother is, and we need to know now."

"I told you, I don't know. He's gone." She looked at him, leaned back in her chair, and said in an arrogant tone with a slight smile, "He's in the wind, as you guys would say."

"A car registered to a Secure-Max employee named Oscar Morales was in Winslow about an hour ago. He purchased a tank of gas with your brother's debit card. Can you explain that?"

"Really? Maybe he is heading to Colorado. Maybe he borrowed Oscar's car to throw you guys off his trail. He's pretty smart, you know."

"Winslow may be a small town, but they do have surveillance cameras. It was Oscar Morales. They have video of him going into and out of the store."

Just then Sonny's cell phone rang. He removed it from his belt and walked over to the back corner.

Welker shrugged and said, "I don't know what to tell you, Detective. Maybe Oscar stole the card. Remind me to fire him when I get back."

Sonny returned to the table and said to Nick, "DPS just picked up Morales heading this way on I-40. He's singing like a robin on a spring morning. He said he was just following orders." He pointed to Welker and said, "Hers!"

Sonny looked at Welker and said, "It appears you sent Mr. Morales on a little trip. He told the officers you sent him on a secret training mission. He said he was ordered, by you, to take his car and drive to Winslow, get gas with your brother's debit card and come back home. He said he got paid a thousand bucks for the trip. What do you have to say about that? What is a secret training mission in a little piss ant company like Secure-Max?"

With insolence in her eyes, she said, "Morales is an idiot! He has the IQ of a toad."

Nick looked at Sonny, then to Welker. "Ma'am, we know your brother murdered five people, and he attempted to murder another one. I don't know if you realize the trouble you're in, but felony murder is biting you where you sit. If you cooperate, it might go easier on you."

"You said aiding and abetting. Where do you get this felony murder crap?" she asked.

Nick leaned toward her, looked her in the eyes and said, "Your brother killed Marti Montgomery, William Scanlon, Judge Richard Cavallo, Jason Temple, and a police officer and friend of ours, James Holder. You are an accomplice and that's a felony. You're going to prison, Gloria Welker!"

It was Sonny's turn to look into the eyes of the prisoner. "And as for your brother, what do you think his life will be like in prison as a cop killer, if he even makes it that far?"

"Jimmy didn't kill that cop. I did!" She paused as she realized what she had just confessed to. Evil consumed her eyes as she leaned back in her chair, crossed her arms, and said, "Now, I want a lawyer!"

Clark Cordova was waiting for the two detectives as they left Gloria Welker alone in the interview room. "Well, what do you think?" Nick asked. "She just confessed to murder. Do you want to offer her a deal? Maybe take away the death penalty if she turns on her brother?"

Sonny said, "I got a hundred bucks that says she won't turn on him."

Cordova thought for a moment and said, "Let's see how it plays out. If you guys are as good as I think you are, we may not have to. I'll amend the charges to murder. That way she won't be getting bail. That'll frost her lawyer's ass, whoever it may be. I'll freeze her assets, too."

"Freeze the assets of Secure-Max, too," Nick added. "They already read her her rights, so let's put her back in lockup. She can change that blue uniform for an orange jumpsuit."

CHAPTER 47

The Stake Out

The waiter had just filled their water glasses, and they were scanning the menu when Nick felt the vibration on his side. He pulled the Android from his belt and saw the blue letters: Sonny. "Yeah, Sonny. What's up?"

"A red mustang was just seen in the neighborhood, a couple of blocks from Yeager's house. The plates match."

Though Detective Rick Yeager didn't know it, the order was never really lifted, just adjusted. Deputy Chief Bruce Mannion had put Yeager's home under twenty-four-hour surveillance. There were two entrances to the subdivision where the Yeager family lived. The homes were about forty years old and in an active part of town. Across from each entrance was a strip mall that provided an easy place for a car to sit and watch.

Nick stood up. "I gotta go."

"What about me?"

"You can grab a cab."

"What's going on, Nick," Sue Kim asked.

"A red Mustang is in Yeager's neighborhood. I have to go."

"I'm coming with you."

"Bullshit you are!"

"Bullshit I'm not!"

He could see the resolve in her eyes as she stood up and looked at him defiantly and said, "We'd better get going!"

"No, you're not—" It was too late. Sue Kim was halfway across the restaurant floor. The waiter stood looking at them in wonder. "Goddamn women!" Nick said as he followed her out to the parking lot.

The waiter smiled and said, "Have a good evening, sir . . . I guess."

Sue Kim was already in the passenger seat when Nick opened the driver's door. He fired up the engine and headed straight for the Yeager home. He knew it was only a few blocks away. He said, "You WILL stay in the car. Do you understand me? Under no circumstances will you leave this car unless I say so. You got that?"

She saluted him. "Aye, aye, Lieutenant."

"I'm not joking, Sue. I don't know what we are going to find. It may be nothing, and it may turn into some serious shit. I don't want you hurt again."

He remembered back when they were first dating. His car had been blown up by a car bomb, and she had been seriously hurt and almost died. It was the first time either of them said, "I love you."

"Promise me you'll stay in the car."

"Okay, I promise."

Nick pulled into the parking lot next to a plain white car he knew was a surveillance vehicle. The officer said, "About ten minutes ago, a red Mustang turned in there." He pointed to the entrance to Sierra Dawn Estates.

"Did you see the driver?"

"No, sir, just the car, but the plates match our subject vehicle."

Just then, Nick's Android rang. It was Sonny. "Where are you?"

At the south entrance," Sonny answered.

"Let's do it!"

Nick instructed the two surveillance officers to start going through the neighborhood and to let him know if they found the red Mustang. He reminded them that the suspect was armed and had killed five other people.

There was no sign of the red Mustang as Nick drove past the Yeager home. Suddenly the phone buzzed. Nick hit "answer" and Sonny said, "There's a red Mustang in the access alley behind the Yeager house. I'm going there now; you take the front." The alley ran behind the homes and was used mostly for trash pickup. It was riddled with small pieces of trash, clippings from cut trees and bushes, and trash receptacles, some of them overflowing.

The Yeager home was on the corner of Sierra Verde and Thirty-Sixth Drive; it faced Sierra Verde. Nick stopped the car around the corner on Thirty-Sixth Drive. He got out of the car, pulled his Glock from his holster, looked at Sue Kim, and was about to speak when she said, "I know! I know! Stay in the car. You be careful, Nick." He opened the trunk of his car and quickly slipped a ballistic vest over his clothing.

Sonny was creeping along the alley looking for any sign of Leo Cardinale, when suddenly he was knocked to the ground. The subject had seen Sonny coming and had been crouched behind a black trash receptacle. Like a feline, Cardinale jumped the wall into the yard of the Yeager home. Sonny got up and saw an old wooden chair sitting against the block wall. He jumped on it, looked over the wall, and yelled, "Police! Stop or I'll shoot!" A second later, he fired, hitting the suspect in the leg. Cardinale staggered and fell to the ground. He almost rolled into the swimming pool, but he got back up, began to run and scaled the sidewall.

Sue Kim had heard the shot and was still sitting in the car when she saw the man running down the sidewalk. He was heading toward her. She ducked down, counted to three, pulled the door latch, and threw the door wide open as fast as she could.

The timing was perfect. She heard a thud as Leo Cardinale hit the car door and bounced off of it. His head hit the sidewalk hard as he landed on his back. He was out cold.

Sue Kim looked up and saw Nick standing over Leo Cardinale with his Glock pointed at his chest and Sonny running down the sidewalk toward them. As Sonny stopped and pointed his gun at the man lying motionless on the sidewalk, Nick looked at Sue Kim who giggled and said ever so innocently, "Hey, I did what you said. I stayed in the car."

Nick shook his head and smiled. Sonny laughed out loud. The two surveillance cars arrived on the scene. Cardinale was beginning to stir, so Sonny holstered his gun, turned the man over, pulled his hands behind his back and cuffed him. Nick told one of the other cops, "Take him in. Book him. Murder one—four counts!"

Just then a car rolled down Sierra Verde Drive. The white minivan pulled into the Yeager's driveway and into the garage. Rick Yeager emerged from the garage and went to the corner to see what was going on. A couple of his neighbors were watching from across the street. A police cruiser had arrived on the scene, and Leo Cardinale was being loaded into the back seat. Yeager recognized Nick and Sonny right away and asked, "What the hell is going on here?"

Sonny grinned. "Uh, we had a little party. Sorry you weren't invited."

"What are you talking about?"

Sonny pointed to the man in the back of the cruiser. "You had a visitor tonight. Leo Cardinale, aka James Leonard Mitchell."

A look of shock seized Yeager's face. He looked back at his house, and then to Sonny and Nick. "Was he in my house? Thank God, we all went out for dinner!"

Sonny shook his head. "No, we got here in time."

As the cruiser pulled away, Rick looked at Nick and said, "I'm sorry, but I never thought—"

"Don't worry about it, Rick. We got him now. It's over. Go be with your family."

Sonny pointed to a rip in the knee of his pants and said, "Don't worry about it, shit! I ruined a perfectly good pair of pants!"

Yeager smiled and said, "I'll buy you a new pair."

Sonny grinned. "Goddamn right!"

The three detectives laughed, and then they heard a small voice come from Nick's car. "Okay, can I get out of the car now?"

CHAPTER 48

The Offer

Leo Cardinale was handcuffed as he sat in the interview room with Lieutenants Nick Greer and Sonny Madison. Assistant District Attorney Clark Cordova was watching from outside, along with Deputy Chief Bruce Mannion.

Nick began, "Mr. Cardinale, or Mr. Mitchell, which do you prefer?"

With insolence in his eyes, the suspect looked at his accuser and answered, "I don't give a flying fuck!"

"Okay, Mr. I Don't Give A Flying—"

Sonny interrupted, "Should we add that to his aliases?"

Nick continued, "You're being charged with four counts of murder in the first degree and two counts of attempted murder. There will be a bunch of other shit to go along with them, but that's a start for now. The officers read you your rights. You understand them, do you not?"

"I understand I have the right to a life, and you bastards took it away."

Sonny said, "Oh, you're right. Your life will be taken away, but not by us, by some nice old doctor with a mixture of potassium chloride, something bromide and sodium, sodium . . ." He looked at Nick. "What's that sodium shit called?"

"Sodium thiopental."

"Yeah, that's it!" Sonny grinned as he went nose to nose with the suspect and glared into his eyes. "You add that all together, and it's lights out for Leo Cardinale or James Leonard Mitchell or Mr. I Don't Give A Flying Fuck, or whatever you might want to call yourself. Tell me, what are they going to call you in hell? Huh? 'Cause that's where you're going."

Cardinale was silent. The door opened and the detectives recognized the lady who entered. It was Peggy Crider, a well-known defense attorney. She was a partner in a downtown law firm that dealt mainly with criminal cases. They all knew she was a formidable opponent.

"Well, good evening, Counselor. To what do we owe the displeasure of your company today?" Sonny asked.

"You know damn well why I'm here." She looked at the suspect and said, "Don't say another word, Mr. Mitchell." She looked at Nick and said, "I'd like a moment to consult with my client, if you don't mind, and make sure all of your little recording devices are shut off!"

Nick and Sonny left the suspect alone with his attorney and went out into the hall. Cordova and Mannion were waiting.

"How the hell did he get Peggy Crider to represent him?" Sonny asked.

Cordova answered, "She represented him the first time, and she also represents his sister."

"She's pretty good," said Mannion.

"This one is a slam dunk. Clarence Darrow couldn't get him off," the ADA said.

They watched Peggy Crider walk around the table as she collaborated with her client. She was a petite woman, about five-foot-three, in her early forties, and fairly attractive. She was dressed in a light gray tight skirt and white chiffon blouse. Sonny commented, "She doesn't look at all like Clarence Darrow."

After about ten minutes, Crider motioned to the two-way mirror for the detectives to come in. Clark Cordova accompanied them. Sonny and Nick stood back as the attorney and her client sat beside each other, and Cordova took a seat across from them.

Confidence emitted from her as she looked at her opponent and stated, "You have nothing on my client except trespassing. You have no proof my client killed, or attempted to kill, anyone. You have no witnesses, no proof he was anywhere near any of the killings. In other words, you have nothing to prove my client is the so-called Nemo killer. This is the second time you have falsely arrested my client. I'm thinking a civil suit is in the future for you and the city of Phoenix."

Nick spoke, "Look at the evidence, Counselor. He had pictures of all the victims on his bulletin board and a red X over the dead ones, and a slash through Shelley's picture. Look, you'll see they're all right there in the file."

"Uh, don't forget the razor knife we found on him," Sonny added.

Nick looked at Cardinale. "Why was there only a slash on Shelley's picture? Was that because he had failed?" He walked over to the suspect, leaned down and took a whiff. "Hmm, do I detect Polo cologne? ADA Kisler said her attacker wore Polo cologne. And, the paramedic who caught you in the act said he could easily pick her attacker out of a lineup. I guess that's next. What do you think, Counselor?"

Nick knew the paramedic wasn't sure and most likely wouldn't be able to make a positive identification, but he also knew neither Cardinale nor his attorney was aware of that. His poker face prevailed.

She pulled the pictures from the file and said, "My client is a mystery fan. He's been following the story from the beginning."

"Yeah, I thought I'd write a book," Cardinale added. "I'm calling it *How The Cops Took My Life*!"

"I suppose the pictures of the victims' homes and cars and the one of Detective Yeager mean nothing to you?" Cordova asked the attorney.

She looked through the file at the pictures again. "I see no pictures of any homes or of your detective in here."

Nick pulled his cell phone, opened the gallery, pushed to enlarge the picture, and laid it on the table in front of the defense attorney. "This is a picture of the corkboard that was taken from your client's home. Look at the picture on the right. Do you see something interesting?"

She saw the unblemished picture of Rick Yeager, swallowed hard, and looked back to Nick. "Why aren't these in the file?"

"We're not finished yet, Counselor. But you should know the DNA on all of them is a right-on match with your client." He bent down and looked back and forth between Leo Cardinale and Peggy Crider. "And I must ask, if your client was collecting mementos for his fictional book, how did he know Detective Yeager was next on the list? Why was he at the Yeager home in the first place? Why did he have pictures of all the victims' homes? Why did he send us on a wild goose chase with the fake map, huh? What about the plan his sister concocted sending one of her lackeys up north? And if that isn't enough, what about little sis, huh?" He looked straight into the eyes of Leo Cardinale and continued, "Yeah, what about her confession? She killed a cop! But you don't have to worry about her getting the needle. Why? Because she won't last long enough in prison! Male or female, cop killers are cop killers!"

The attorney looked at the ADA and said, "I need a moment to consult with my client."

Cordova said, "Knock yourself out." The three men got up and left.

It was less than five minutes when Peggy Crider motioned for them to come back into the interview room. Again, Clark Cordova sat across from the attorney and the suspect, and the two detectives stood.

Crider began, "Okay, Clark, let's talk."

Cordova looked surprised and said, "Uh, what's there to talk about? You've read the file. He's done. If you're going to ask me to take death off the table, forget it. It ain't gonna happen."

"Clark, how would you like to not have to go through the expense of a long trial? How would you like to wrap this thing up quickly? I have something that might interest you."

"I don't know what you could possibly have that would interest me, but I'm listening."

"I'm also representing Gloria Welker."

"Your point?" Cordova wondered where she was going with this.

"My client may agree to plead guilty to all five killings if you'll drop all charges against his sister."

Sonny and Nick looked at each other in disbelief. Cordova looked across the table at the attorney and said, "And just why would I even consider something as ridiculous as that?"

"Gloria Welker says she was coerced into saying she killed the detective. She was angry, and she was glad the man who ruined her brother's life was dead. She now says she didn't kill him and if Mr. Mitch . . . , excuse me, Cardinale, says he did it, I'll have no problem selling that to a jury. I'm sure you know all about reasonable doubt."

She looked at the ADA, then at the detectives, and back to Cordova. She stood and began to walk around the small room. "Ladies and gentlemen of the jury. What we have here is a loving sister who would do anything to save her brother. Yes, she helped him plan his getaway, but she didn't murder anyone. Her brother has confessed to the killings, so why is the prosecution picking on another member of his family? Is she guilty of assisting a brother she loves? Yes, she is. Is she guilty of first-degree murder? Absolutely not."

Cordova said, "I'll get the judge to disallow his confession. You won't be able to introduce it."

Confidence spewed from her as she answered, "Even if you can get a judge to agree, and I doubt you can, I'll still get it in. You know I can." She paused for a moment, smiled, and said with a confident resolve, "And then, when I talk about reasonable doubt, well, what do you think the verdict will be?"

She sat back down next to her client, picked up the file, closed it, and dropped it on the table. She leaned back in her chair, folded her arms, and looked across the table at ADA Cordova. "Think about my offer, Clark. You have twenty-four hours."

Cordova was silent as she got up and left the room.

CHAPTER 49

The Deal

You're really considering this?" Nick asked.

Clark Cordova took in a deep breath and exhaled as he leaned back in his chair. He was silent as he fiddled with the pencil in his hand. Finally he dropped the pencil on the table and shook his head. "Look, I was awake all night thinking about this. Peggy Crider is right. If Cardinale confesses to Holder's murder, no jury will convict Gloria Welker. Whether or not she killed Jim Holder, I can't convict her. I can't win!"

Sonny almost yelled, "What? Is this all about winning? Is it all about your conviction record? We have a good detective who is dead. His parents are in mourning, and you want to let the killer off because you can't fucking win?"

"Look, Sonny. I understand what you're saying, but Peggy Crider is right. No jury is going to convict her if Cardinale takes credit. I really have no choice."

They heard a voice behind them. "I'm sorry, Sonny, but I have to agree." The two detectives turned and saw Bruce Mannion. He had been standing at the door and heard it all.

Sonny's eyes read help as he looked at his partner. Nick just shook his head ever so slightly. The look on his face told Sonny it was over, and he realized there was nothing more they could do.

Sonny let out a breath and said, "I guess you're right. But it sucks! The whole goddamn thing sucks!"

An unusual sense of compassion seemed to come over Clark Cordova's face as he said gently, "That it does, Lieutenant. That it does. But look on the bright side."

"Uh, there's a bright side?" Sonny asked.

"Yeah, with all the other charges we have on her, she'll still be in prison when her brother gets the needle." He smiled, took a breath, and said as he picked up the telephone, "I guess I'll call Peggy Crider."

"Crider and Hobbs," came the answer on the other end.

"This is Assistant District Attorney Clark Cordova. I'd like to speak with Peggy Crider, please."

"One moment, please."

"Well, hello, Clark. I've been expecting your call. I assume you're ready to deal."

"We talked it over and we'll accept your offer, providing your client admits to all of the other charges."

"Thank you, Clark, but it appears there's been a slight change."

"A change? What change?" The word change grabbed the attention of the three policemen, and Cordova put the phone on speaker.

"First of all, I'm no longer representing Gloria Welker. My partner and I have discussed it, and we feel there may be a conflict of interest."

Cordova squinted and pursed his lips. "Go on."

"My client says he didn't kill the judge."

"You gotta be shi . . . , uh, messing with me, Peggy."

"No, sir. I'm not messing with you, nor am I shitting you. He swears he didn't kill Judge Cavallo. He says he doesn't know who did."

"Meet me at Fourth Avenue."

"I'm on my way."

* * *

Leo Cardinale and Peggy Crider were already seated at a metal table in the visitors' section of the Fourth Avenue jail. The prisoner was shackled, handcuffed, and wore an orange jumpsuit. A uniformed corrections officer stood stately behind him with his arms folded. He was about six and a half feet tall and weighed well over three hundred pounds with shoulders that looked like tree stumps.

As Lieutenants Greer and Madison came into the room accompanied by Assistant District Attorney Clark Cordova, Sonny caught sight of the huge guard and said to Nick, "Uh, does Gibraltar know their rock is missing?"

As the group approached, the guard stepped back. Once again, the detectives stood as ADA Cordova sat and began the conversation. "Mr. Cardinale, I understand you want to change our agreement."

"There was no agreement finalized," said Crider. "My client has agreed to our previous terms, except he wants the charges dismissed as far as Judge Cavallo is concerned. He didn't kill him."

"Come on, Counselor," retorted Cordova. "What's going on? He's gonna get the needle anyway. Why is he reneging on the judge?"

"I didn't kill the fucking judge," Cardinale shouted. The guard was about to come over, but Cordova shook his head and held up his hand, advising the guard it was okay. "I wanted to, but somebody else beat me to it," Cardinale continued.

"Your sister, I'll bet."

"Nope. Not Gloria. It must have been someone else who beat me to it."

"And you expect us to believe that?" Cordova asked.

"Hey, why would I lie?" He nodded toward his defense counsel. "Like you said, I'm going to get the needle anyway. I didn't kill the judge and neither did my sister. Someone else did!"

Nick interrupted, "It's okay, Clark. Go with what you have." Sonny was puzzled when he heard his partner's words, but he did not question them.

"Okay," Cordova said. He pulled out a tape recorder and pushed the record button. "Let's hear it. All of it."

Cardinale began, "First of all, do you know who I am? Or, shall I say who I was? I am Mitch Mitchell." He looked up and stuck his chest out like a proud peacock. "Remember the radio show *Get Rich With Mitch*? That was me. I was important. When I spoke, people listened. I was somebody! I was living the good life, and I taught other people how to do the same. They all took it away."

"Who are they?" Cordova asked.

"Your goddamn cops! And that little bitch from the television stations."

"I assume you mean Marti Montgomery?"

"Yeah!"

"What did she do?" Cordova questioned.

"She took her fucking news crew to my house looking for a story. She went to my neighbors and knocked on their doors. Then she went to my business. Yeah, and do you know what she did? She took a close-up picture of my sign, James Mitchell and Associates, and plastered it all over the fucking newscasts for three days! She and that other reporter, they ruined me! They ruined my life! My clients left in droves. Even after I was freed, they still left. I lost everything! Did you know I had a house in Paradise Valley worth over two million dollars?

Huh? Do you know what happened to it? Huh? The bank took it. I had a beautiful wife and a daughter. Do you know what happened? Huh? Do you?" He didn't wait for an answer. "She left me. She took my daughter! I don't know where they are."

"So is that why you killed her?" asked the ADA.

He stared into the eyes of his accuser. "Goddamn right!"

There was silence for a moment. Cordova said, "Tell us how."

"I worked security there sometimes, enough to know the ropes. I shorted out the motherboard on the video surveillance system. I knew it would take a few days to get another one." He took in a breath, let it out, and continued, "I watched Munder. That stupid ass didn't even know I was there. He's about as vigilant as shit. I saw him answer his radio. I knew she was coming. I busted the window of a car so the alarm would go off. It was on the top floor, so I knew it would take Munder a while to get his dumb ass up there and back. I met her as she came through the elevator door. She saw the uniform, and she had no clue. She thought I was going to walk her to her car."

"So that's when you killed her?" Cordova asked.

"Goddamn straight! I cut the little bitch's throat! She never saw it coming!"

Cordova looked at the two detectives. Nick's face showed no emotion. Sonny shook his head in disgust. The ADA said, "What about William Scanlon? Why did you kill him?"

"He was the cameraman. He took the picture. He zoomed in on my sign. He was just as guilty as the little bitch!"

"Now, what about Judge Richard Cavallo?" Cordova asked.

"I told you, I didn't kill him."

"Okay, but why was he on your list? Why was his picture on your corkboard?"

"He could have let me out on bail. My attorney argued that there was no proof I was anywhere around when the girl was abducted and that there wasn't even a body. She told the judge the girl might have run away. She told me the judge should have at least had some compassion, but no! He listened to that bitch prosecutor."

Rage seized Sonny. Nick stepped in front of him and held him back.

Hate and anger spewed from Cardinale as he continued, "Do you know what happened to me in jail? Huh? Do you have any idea what they did to me there? Huh? Well, let me tell you. I was beaten! And I was sodomized! They all got what they deserved, except the bitch DA. She got lucky!"

Sonny couldn't take it anymore. He pushed Nick aside and lunged at the suspect. He knocked Clark Cordova out of his seat as he flew across the table and landed his fist perfectly in the center of the Cardinale's face. Peggy Crider jumped up out of the way as blood squirted onto her clothes. The alert guard caught the shackled prisoner before he fell to the cement. Nick pulled Sonny off of Cardinale and ordered, "Out! Now!" Sonny looked at Nick and left the room.

ADA Cordova got up from the floor, sat down, and began to collect the papers that had been strewn all over the place. Peggy Crider straightened her hair and sat back down next to her client. She pulled a handkerchief from her purse and tried unsuccessfully to wipe the bloodstains from her blouse.

Blood was streaming from the suspect's nose. "You broke my nose! You broke my fuckin' nose! Police brutality! Arrest him!"

The guard had let go of the prisoner, and Nick leaned over the table and looked into his eyes. "You're lucky he didn't bust your fucking head!" He reached into his rear pocket, retrieved a handkerchief and threw it at Cardinale, who lifted his handcuffed wrists, caught it, and held it to his nose.

Crider spoke, "Was all that necessary?"

"Uh . . ." Nick stroked his mustache like he was thinking and answered, "Let's see. . . . Necessary? Uh, let's see now; that would mean, was it a required action, so I'd say probably not." He stared at the attorney and added, "Now ask me if I think it was appropriate."

Cardinale said, "Aren't you going to do something? He should be punished!"

Cordova looked at the defense counsel and back to the prisoner and grinned. "I'll send him to bed without his dinner." He looked back to Crider and asked, "Ms. Crider, do you think you can control your client's mouth, or do you want to take a break?"

"Do you think you can you control your officers?" she retorted.

The ADA looked at Nick, who just shrugged. "It's up to your client," Cordova responded. "Shall we continue, or not?"

She looked at Cardinale who was still blotting his nose. "Leo, you need to calm down a bit. You aren't helping things by being abusive.

Do you understand?" He nodded, then he looked at Nick and extended his middle finger, but he was silent.

Cordova checked the recorder. It was still taping so he continued, "Okay, so far you have admitted to killing Marti Montgomery and William Scanlon. You deny killing Judge Richard Cavallo. You admit attempting to kill Assistant District Attorney Shelley Kisler. Is that correct?"

Cardinale looked at his counsel. She nodded. He looked at Cordova and said, "Yeah!"

Cordova continued, "Now, what about Detective James Holder? Do you know who killed him?"

"I did!"

"Are you sure?"

"I said I did it!"

"Tell me how you did it."

"I watched him. I knew he went hiking at the peak Sunday mornings. I was at the top of Summit Trail when he got there. I followed him down. When the time was right and no one was in sight, I slit his throat, and I just kept going on down the trail."

"You said you came up from behind, is that correct?"

"Yes."

"The autopsy report says he was attacked from the front. How do you explain that?"

Crider interrupted, "We have a deal, Clark, remember?" She looked at her client and said, "Do not answer that question, Leo."

Cardinale looked at the ADA and said, "Maybe your medical examiner fucked up."

"What about Jason Temple? Do you admit killing him?"

"Yeah, I killed the little fag."

"Why?"

"He did it, too! He did a report and put my company name and my picture all over the fucking television, just like the bitch did." Hate and disdain gushed from the suspect like water from a broken dam as he leaned forward and looked the ADA in the eyes and said, "It's too bad I couldn't find out who was holding that camera or you'd have another corpse in your morgue."

Peggy Crider interrupted, "Leo, please, just answer the questions. These comments aren't helping you one bit!"

Cardinale leaned back in his chair. His nose had stopped bleeding, but he was still holding the handkerchief in his cuffed hands.

Cordova continued, "So tell me, how did you kill Jason Temple?"

"I watched him. I knew he was a little fag. I followed him into State 48, and I sat next to him at the bar. I kept saying how horny I was. I waited until he went into the restroom and I followed him. I talked to him for a minute or so and told him I was really horny. He went into the stall and left the door cracked. I went in. He was sitting down, and when I walked up to him, he began to reach for my zipper. That's as far as he got. He never saw it coming. I propped him up so he wouldn't fall off the seat. Then I closed the stall door and left."

The detective and the ADA both could see the look of disgust on the face of the defense attorney as she shook her head.

Cordova said, "And how about Detective Yeager?"

Cardinale leaned back. A look of insolence mixed with challenge was in his voice. "You guys got there too soon."

"We like to think we got there right on time," Nick commented.

"Tomayto–tomahto," he answered.

"Okay," said ADA Cordova. He pulled a sheet of paper out of a manila folder and handed it to the defense attorney. She read it over and nodded. He handed the paper, along with a pen, to Leo Cardinale, and said, "Sign."

Cardinale reached his cuffed hands out, picked up the pen, and signed the confession. Cordova took the paper and put it into the folder.

Nick asked the prisoner, "Tell me, Mr. Cardinale. Why did you send the note telling us that Shannon Scanlon was innocent?"

"I didn't want her to go to jail for something she didn't do. Look what happened to me!" His eyes widened as he rolled his head and looked around the room. "Look where I'm at. I didn't want it to happen to someone else. I have a conscience, you know."

Cordova looked at the detective. The look in his eyes said "conscience?" The ADA got up and began to leave, but turned and asked the prisoner, "Why Nemo? What's the Nemo bit all about?"

"You ever read Homer's *Odyssey*?"

Cordova nodded. "Nemo. Yes, I remember."

"Before all this happened, I was important. I was somebody. Now I'm nobody, just like Ulysses!"

Nick whispered out loud, "Sonny was right."

"What did you say?" Cordova asked.

"Nothing. Nothing at all."

Sonny was waiting outside as Nick came through the door. "Well, what happened? Did he sign the confession?"

"Oh, yeah." Nick smiled. "Uh, by the way, you're not getting any dinner tonight."

"Huh?" Sonny was puzzled.

"Never mind," Nick answered.

CHAPTER 50

Covert Ops

Rene's Restaurant was unusually quiet for a Friday as Detective Rick Yeager walked in. Only one person was at the counter, and a couple of booths were occupied. Lieutenant Nick Greer was sitting in a booth in the back corner. Rick sat down across from him and said, "Hey, Nick, what's so important that you couldn't talk at the station?"

The waitress came over and asked, "Would you like to see a menu, Officer?"

"No, thank you," Yeager responded. "Just coffee. Cream, please."

The lieutenant began, "Rick, you said you owed me one, remember?"

"Yeah. After the other day, I owe you a hatful. Thanks, by the way. You know Tina and I had the kids with us and the house was empty. Who knows what would've happened if he had gotten in. We have an alarm, though."

"Cardinale is an alarm technician. Don't you think he could've disabled it?"

Just then the waitress poured hot coffee into a cup for Yeager and asked Nick if he wanted a warm-up. He shook his head.

"Uh, maybe," Yeager said as he poured cream into his coffee and stirred it. "But I'm—we're glad—you and Sonny were there." He took a sip of coffee and asked, "So, what's so important and secretive that you wanted to meet me here?"

"Rick, I need your help. I have a special situation I must keep on the DL."

Yeager knew if Nick wanted this kept on the down-low, it must be important. "This ain't anything illegal, I assume."

Nick shook his head. "Not illegal, but it's very touchy. I guess covert would best describe it. I really need your help, and most of all, I need your silence. I don't even want you to say anything to Sonny, and especially not to the brass."

The intense look on Yeager's face told Nick he understood. "This sounds serious."

"It is."

"Okay, I guess. What do you want me to do?"

Nick explained his plan to Detective Yeager.

That night Nick Greer sat down with his fiancée and said, "I may need your help with a certain project. We have to keep it between us for now. Are you up to it?"

"Ohhh, sounds serious," Sue Kim said.

"It is. It could cost me my shield."

CHAPTER 51

Monday Morning

Deputy Chief Bruce Mannion was sitting behind his desk as Lieutenant Nick Greer walked in with a large paper bag.

"Good job, Nick. You and Sonny finally got our killer. There will probably be an accommodation in the works for both of you, though I should suspend Madison for punching out the suspect."

"I don't blame him. I wanted to bust him up myself. You're not really going to suspend him, are you?"

"Naw! I'd have done the same thing. I read the report. Even his attorney admitted the attack, as she called it, was aggravated, but deserving. It's a good thing the recorder kept going. I played a copy for the chief. He laughed and said to tell Lieutenant Madison he deserves an accommodation just for that. Where is he, by the way? You two are usually joined at the hip."

"He's in the SIU. He doesn't know I'm here. There's something I wanted to discuss with you. I didn't want him involved."

"Okay, Lieutenant. What's on your mind?" Mannion's eyes caught the bag in his detective's hand. "What's in the bag?"

Nick was still standing as he turned the bag upside down and spilled its contents onto his boss's desk. It was a clear plastic bag with an evidence tag on it. "I believe this is yours, Bruce."

Suddenly Mannion's eyes became like golf balls as he stared at the garment lying on his desk. Though faded, the white letters—PPD—still stood prominently against the dark blue cloth. He knew what it was and that it had belonged to him. "Where the hell did you get that?"

Nick sat down and looked at his former mentor. "From your locker at the club."

The deputy chief was silent for what seemed like minutes before he leaned forward and asked, "What the hell do you think you're doing, Lieutenant?"

Nick answered, "My job, Bruce. Unfortunately for both of us, I'm doing my job."

"You're doing your job? You're doing your fucking job?" Mannion leaned forward and continued, "If it weren't for me, you'd still be under the command of Spencer Lovett, and your buddy Madison would be in a squad car busting hookers and pimps!"

The lieutenant ignored his boss's comments. "Bruce, this is your PPD hoodie. It has blood spattered on it. I had it checked out. The blood matches Richard Cavallo."

Bruce Mannion leaned back in his chair, folded his arms, and was silent. Nick finally broke the silence. "Why did you do it, Bruce? Why did you kill your best friend? Was she worth it, Bruce? Was Helen Cavallo worth it?"

Again, Bruce Mannion was silent for a moment, then he lightly nodded his head.

"Do you know the worst part?" Nick said. "Richard Cavallo was on Cardinale's hit list. If you had only waited, he would've probably taken him out and Helen Cavallo would have been all yours. You know, that happily ever after stuff."

Nick sighed and slowly shook his head. He hated what he knew was going to happen next as he said, "There are two detectives from internal affairs outside in the lobby. They'll take it from here."

Nick got up, and, as he left, two detectives walked into Mannion's office. As he walked away, Nick heard one of them say, "Bruce Mannion, you have the right to remain silent."

AFTERWORD

Bruce Mannion was consumed by Helen Cavallo from the moment he met her. She was a beautiful ex-beauty queen and fifteen years younger than the judge. Her flame for sex burned brightly, and even before Mannion's wife died, Helen and Bruce had had several flings. She thought about divorcing the judge, but she liked the lifestyle she was accustomed to and the ironclad prenup would have left her penniless.

Shortly after the death of his wife, Mannion moved into the condo complex in order to be closer to Helen. The appearance of a serial killer, and his knowledge of the case and the system, gave Mannion the perfect ruse for his sinister plot; one he was sure he would get away with. What he hadn't planned on was the killer to continue as he did and the efforts of his two detectives.

It was the Nemo note that caused Nick to begin to believe there may be two killers. The only time it appeared at a scene was at the Cavallo murder. He knew it could have easily blown away at Piestewa Peak, but what about at State 48?

This haunted him as he continued the investigation. There was one thing Nick was sure of about Nemo—he was smart and disciplined. He wouldn't make any stupid mistakes.

When Detective Yeager mentioned that he played racquetball with Mannion, Nick remembered playing with Bruce in the past, and that Bruce Mannion had a locker at the Phoenix Racquet Club. So he got Yeager to look at it the next time they played racquetball and see if there was any evidence of a dark hoodie. Upon Yeager's confirmation, Nick acquired a search warrant and confiscated the hoodie. He bagged it, and he had Sue Kim covertly perform the DNA and blood check.

* * *

Gloria Welker did kill Jim Holder, but it was not premeditated. She was hiking the Summit Trail and recognized him. She carried a hunting knife with her, and as she passed him on the trail, she reached out, cut his throat and shoved him off of the trail.

She signed a plea agreement and was sentenced to ten years in the state prison for each count of accessory to murder. The judge denied her attorney's motion for concurrent sentences, so Gloria Welker will be a guest of the State of Arizona for a long time.

* * *

Leo Cardinale will no doubt die in prison, one way or another.

ACKNOWLEDGMENTS

A special thank you to:

Amy Kijewski, R.N., Phoenix, AZ

Dr. Kathleen Nichols, Peoria, AZ

John D. Shackelton, Asheville, NC

Officer Christopher Thomas of the Surprise, AZ police force.

CPSIA information can be obtained at www.ICGtesting.com
Printed in the USA
BVOW07s0453280115

385310BV00002B/104/P

9 781939 870179